RAVE REVIEWS FOR P. D. CACEK
AND *THE WIND CALLER*!

SAY GOODBYE

Josh leveled himself up over the side of the truck until his face was inches from the old man's. Sheltered from the wind, it was quieter in the flat bed, although, without the wind, the smell coming off the old man was enough to make Josh's eyes water.

"What?"

"Ah said, yah best say g'bye to yer friend."

Josh could feel his lips trying to form a smile as he strong-armed himself back to the ground. *The old man was delirious, just like he thought. . . . Will wasn't going anywhere.* But there'd been something in the old man's voice that made Josh turn and cup his hands around his mouth to make sure he was heard.

"WILL! GET YOUR ASS OVER HERE. WE'RE LEAVING RIGHT—NO!"

Will had turned around when he heard Josh . . . and then the wind hit him, sucking air and blood out through his mouth and nose . . . sucking the face right along with it.

Josh felt his own guts threaten mutiny when a debris-filled whirlwind settled down over the closest thing he had to a friend, and began to rip him apart . . . piece by piece by piece.

By piece.

One minute, Will had been a man, the next he was a rag doll with the stuffing pulled out of it. The only trouble was that Will didn't know he'd been reduced to a toy . . . he kept screaming as if he were still alive. . . .

P. D. CACEK

THE WIND CALLER

LEISURE BOOKS NEW YORK CITY

To Don D'Auria, for keeping the dark dream alive.

LEISURE BOOKS ®

July 2004

Published by

Dorchester Publishing Co., Inc.
200 Madison Avenue
New York, NY 10016

ISBN 0-8439-5383-7

The name "Leisure Books" and the stylized "L" with design are trademarks of Dorchester Publishing Co., Inc.

Printed in the United States of America.

Visit us on the web at www.dorchesterpub.com.

THE WIND
CALLER

PRELUDE

The hot summer day was gone, conscripted against its will into the army of rolling black clouds that had been marching in from the west since midafternoon. And it wasn't happy about going, either. He could still hear the day complaining about its forced enlistment, rumbling and gnashing its teeth from somewhere deep within the boiling mass of clouds.

Gideon Berlander leaned against the front porch railing and licked his lips, smiling up at the random lightning flashes and nodding. To a casual observer, he might appear to be nothing more than just another dry-land farmer, silently beseeching the heavens to open up and save his crop from ruin.

But looks can be deceiving.

Gideon Berlander was no farmer, and no one, casual or known, observed him without his permission. And permission was something he didn't give often.

1

The wind was the only thing he allowed to have free rein on his land.

If it behaved itself.

Gideon watched a tiny dust devil dance across the parched front yard, inscribing unknown words into the dirt with its tail, and wondered if the message was a curse or a blessing, not that it mattered. The rust scent of water was stronger now, and whatever had been scratched into the ground would soon be obliterated by rain.

"And it's about time, ya greedy ol' devil," he muttered at the whirlwind as it spun itself out. "Ya think Ah don't know what yer doin'?"

The wind suddenly shifted, gathering in strength as if swept in from the ridge above the cabin. Gideon watched it come, flattening a path through the dry grass like a herd of invisible buffalo, and shook his head when the wall of air coiled over on itself and slammed into the widow maker next to the cabin. The twisted oak, which had been struck by lightning thirty-odd winters ago, disintegrated into a mound of kindling.

Gideon yawned. "Was that supposed to impress me?"

And when a smaller gust, littered with aspen leaves and pine needles, swarmed at his face, he lifted one hand and brushed it away. The heavier needles beat the leaves to the ground.

"Gettin' a mite playful in yer ol' age, ain't ya?"

A rumble of thunder answered him.

"Quiet down now," he yelled up at the densest part of the clouds. "It's gettin' on to mah suppertime, and Ah don't want to have to listen to yer bellyachin' all night. Likely to ruin mah digestion."

The wind softened to a gentle breeze.

"That's better. Now stop playin' nice and start the waterworks. Mah ridge's been lookin' poorly for long enough."

The growling in the sky dissolved into the sizzle of rain as the wind gently wound itself around his legs like a pet cat.

"That's better," Gideon said, and leaned out into the warm rain so he could watch the thirsty ground take a good long drink. And that's when he saw it, the thing that didn't belong on his land.

He smiled, but felt the muscles tighten across his shoulders as he watched it pick its way through the dense brush that surrounded his front yard. It whimpered when it saw him. *Poor little thing.* Too small to be a coyote and nowhere near the right color.

"Hand Jesus another nail, Mary."

He hadn't meant to scare it, at least not yet, but his sudden laughter sent it belly-flat into the newly formed mud. It was a dog, or at least its ancestors had been dogs. From where Gideon stood, dripping sweet rain, it was hard to see any connection between the half-wild, rawboned hounds of his boyhood and the lump of nothing cowering in the muck at the edge of his yard.

The miserable thing was no more dog than an old biddy's canary was an eagle.

If that.

"Hell, yer hide wouldn't even make a decent pot-holder."

At the sound of his voice, the creature—Gideon still couldn't think of it as a real dog—cocked its head and whined with the sound of a rusty gate opening. A bedraggled pink bow, the same color as the sparkly collar it wore around its scrawny neck, flopped down over one bulging brown eye when it lifted its head.

"Yer one of them ugly son-of-a-bitch Frenchy dogs, aren't 'cha?" Gideon kept the tone of his voice gentle, even though he had to shout above the constant hiss of falling rain. "Ah seen pictures in books, but damned if Ah ain't never seen one of yer kind in the flesh. Homely as it is. So ya get yerself lost, did'cha?"

Gideon smiled when the dog sat right up on its haunches and pawed the air with both front legs. Damned if the thing's nails weren't painted the same color as its bow and collar. Someone had gone to an awful lot of trouble fussing with it.

"Well, Ah suppose yah'd like to get in outta the rain, huh, little fella?"

The animal brought its tiny paws down into the mud with a slash and barked. Gideon could see its sodden tail whipping the mud into a froth. Sometimes it was just as easy to fool an animal as it was a man— not often, but enough times to keep life interesting.

"Well, what'cha waitin' for?" he said. "C'mere."

Sopping ears twitching at the familiar word/command, up on all fours, the little animal took one tentative step forward.

"That's right," Gideon coaxed, "c'mere, you mangy runaway from a freak show. C'mere, little fella."

It began to move forward, picking its way between the larger puddles, tail wagging a mile a minute.

"Poor little mite," Gideon crooned at the animal's

simpering advance, "bet yer folks are goin' crazy lookin' for ya, ain't they?"

It was less than six feet away, snapping its jaws together and whining like it was trying to talk. Like it was trying to thank him for his kindness.

Stupid thing.

Gideon backed up to the center of the porch, putting a little more distance between them.

"Well, what'cha waitin' for? Git it."

The animal stopped, not understanding that the command was not directed at it, and cocked its head. It managed to get out one thick, earsplitting yelp just before the funnel of rain-jeweled wind sucked it up like candy.

Gideon leaned down and watched the speck of muddied fur spin inside the swirling void—three feet . . . then five . . . then ten feet off the ground . . . tumbling in midair, tail over head, legs over spine, while the wind stripped the flesh off its bones. Thin ribbons of rain-diluted blood danced around the outer edge of the cyclone like a devil's halo.

It was a beautiful thing to behold.

Smiling, he let the wind play with the denuded carcass and ruptured gut sack for a few more seconds, before nodding that playtime was over. On its final rotation, the wind shot the frayed body toward a clump of old-growth pine. The remains joined those of other "Missing/Beloved Pet *(Reward/Please Call/Owner Worried)*" animals that had wandered up from the new development butted up against the foot of his property.

Damn people and their damned animals.

He kept hoping that one day one of those worried

owners wouldn't stop at his posted NO TRESPASS-ING/VIOLATORS WILL BE EATEN sign and join their beloved pets. Now, that was something he'd love to see.

The rain lightened into a mist as the wind funnel died.

"What do yah think yer doin'?" he asked, glowering through the drizzle at the twisted thing that lay in the middle of the yard. "Yah ain't finished yet."

The wind brushed against him, tugging at his beard.

"Ah thought Ah taught yah to pick up after yerself."

Gideon pointed and watched a mist funnel instantly appear above the sparkly collar and pull it from the mud. A few of the glittery stones were missing by the time it reached Gideon's outstretched palm, and there was a small patch of fur-covered skin wedged under the metal buckle, but once it was washed off it would make a fine addition to his collection.

"This'll make 'bout twenty-seven, Ah think," he said, flicking the skin away. "Just don't appreciate uninvited guests, man nor beast . . .

". . . and that goes double for Indians.

"Ah woulda thought yah'd know that last part by now, Joseph."

Gideon waited until the soft sounds of boots in mud stopped before looking up. And when he did, he couldn't help but smile.

The old Hopi was soaking wet.

Water trickled down the gullies and arroyos of wrinkles that covered his sun-leathered face and dripped from the twin braids he had worn since they were boys. Keeping the traditional ways even after the once raven's-wing black had turned the color of tin. There were some traditions worth keeping, and Gideon had fought hard all his life and would continue to fight to keep those . . . but things that made a man look like a dime-store dummy went far beyond ceremony and duty.

Even to the gods.

"Don't remember invitin' yah up for a visit, Joseph," Gideon said, and felt a small chill race up along his spine when he noticed the man was standing in exactly the same spot that the animal had occupied a moment before. "And yah know Ah don't like unexpected guests."

"Was that necessary?" the old man asked, pointing to the collar in Gideon's hand.

"My land, my laws," Gideon answered, forcing himself to keep the wry smile in place. Joseph had always made him feel like he wasn't good enough, that whatever he did was tainted by being white. One day he was going to pay for that condescending attitude. One day. But not today. "And mah first law is 'no tresspassin' . . . thought yah'd see that sign—Ah made it big enough."

The collar almost slipped from his fingers when Joseph shook his head.

My land . . . my laws. His own words mocking him. *You still understand nothing, little brother.*

Little brother. The buckle bit into Gideon's palm as he tightened his hand.

"Yah dare to come onto mah land and say somethin' like that? What's the matter? Gone brave in yer old age? Ain't like yah, Joseph . . . yer were always so

7

scared. Goddamn coward who couldn't even face the greatest gift a man might get without hiding. Hell, Joseph, yah wanna have it out now, go for it. Yah can even have the first—"

A cold gust of wind—heavy with wet leaves and smelling of blood—hit him full in the face.

Sputtering a curse as old as the tradition that had kept Joseph in pigtails, Gideon wiped the debris from his lips and threw the collar. It hit the muddy ground exactly where Joseph had been standing. *Had* been.

"God damn yer black soul, Joseph!" he shouted at the empty yard. "Yah try that again in person and see what happens."

The wind trembled in the tall weeds that had overrun the abandoned tomato patch. His daughter had loved tomatoes, couldn't get enough of them . . . ate them at every meal. He should have burned it off right after she died and sown it with salt. He should have done a lot of things.

A distant rumble of thunder in the eastern sky brought him back. He glared at the shivering grass.

"Yah think that was funny, Joseph?" He spoke into the wind, letting it caress his face in atonement. "Ah swear by the gods that if Ah see yer face again, real or not, Ah will take it as a challenge. Yah hear me, ol' man?"

The wind whispered against his ear, tugged at the thin hairs at the back of his neck.

"Yah take him that message."

Gideon followed the wind out across the front yard, watching the shallow puddles ripple as it passed. When he bent down to retrieve the collar, he could hear it singing down through the cottonwoods of the lower canyon. A minute or two and it would reach the new development's cookie-cutter homes. A half-minute later it would reach town, and then it was a straight shot across the desert.

"Yah tell that ol' man and make him understand. This is mah land, and Ah will defend it. Even against you, brother."

The wind delivered the message hidden in a puff of sand.

Joseph Longwalker brushed the sand-colored grit from the front of his shirt and shivered, even though the wool was dry and warm. His other self could still feel the clinging dampness against his skin and smell the bittersweet stench of the poor animal's blood.

He hadn't even been thinking about the man who had become his brother so long ago. He'd gotten up to go into the kitchen to make a cup of tea, and then, suddenly, he found himself standing, drenched and shivering. . . .

Joseph shook the image away from him and focused on the voice of the wind. He had always pictured her as a child—a thing of whim and little direction, full of mischief and pranks, who needed a firm hand to hold when she was frightened and to guide her and keep her from harm. Gideon, his brother, saw none of this. To him, the wind was a slave to do his bidding and nothing else.

His bedroom window rattled softly.

"I know, Little One," Joseph whispered as he placed his hand over the narrow crack in the pane. His daughter-in-law was only a few yards away, preparing dinner in the kitchen. "You've done well.

Don't worry, I understand."

The wind brushed against his palm, tickling his skin. He smiled and watched it dart away, dancing itself into a tiny funnel as the first raindrops began to fall.

Shivering again, Joseph lowered his hand and watched patterns form on the dry earth.

There was another message there, one that would change things forever unless he was very lucky.

Yaponcha, he mouthed without speaking, *help me*.

CHAPTER 1

Richland, Arizona, had been built on a whore's philosophy: "Screw 'em now and die rich." And that ideology still held true a century-plus later.

The town was conceived one bone-dry day in the last month of the last year of the nineteenth century when a scrubland farmer's mule, pawing at the water along the edge of the area's only constant stream as it drank, accidentally kicked up a duck egg–sized nugget of gold. The stream was immediately christened "Jackass Luck," and the second coming of gold fever descended on the arid land like a biblical plague.

Jackass Luck Stream gave up its last fleck of gold five years later, around the time copper was discovered not more than twenty miles from the stalwart assortment of brothels and saloons that lined the waterway. Since copper mining involved open pit mines that didn't lend themselves to the boomtown pattern, Richland was still the only town within driving or riding distance where a man could squander his hard-earned cash.

The jackass's luck was still holding.

Families from the east were called for and laid claim to the semifertile crescent. The Homestead Act of 1862, until this point completely ignored by the founding fathers, was deployed by a cavalry detachment to move three hundred and fifty Hopi Indians from their own reservation—in what was deemed to be prime farming land—onto the already well-established Navaho reservation. The fact that the Navaho and Hopi had for generations been at war was not the concern of the Richlanders. Indians were Indians. The whore was becoming respectable, and nothing would stop her from obtaining that goal.

In 1917, the Chamber of Commerce commissioned a brochure to be created that described the therapeutic benefits of the "high desert's naturally clean and healthy environment in a community devoted to spiritual and cultural civility."

The brochure worked better than even the founding fathers had hoped. The Army, eagerly looking for a "clean and healthy environment" for its more injured children fresh from the trenches of World War I, took Richland up on its offer. The conjoined Navaho-Hopi reservation was moved another twenty-five miles, into a less clean and heathy environment, and a military convalescence hospital was built. Two years later, the complex grew to include a firing range, an ammunition-storage facility, and a ten-acre cemetery.

The whore took off her corset and relaxed.

At the last national census, Richland had a registered population of 31,843.

White, Hispanic, African American, and "Other."

The Navahoes and Hopi, all 5,043 of them, were listed in the "Other" category.

The old whore still knew how to carry a joke too far.

Sky Berlander made sure her second-graders at the reservation school knew the history of the town they visited only on weekends to pick up supplies not readily available at the trading post or, if the school raised enough money from bake sales and recycling aluminum can, on field trips. Of course, she did clean up the history a bit. But only a bit: These were only seven-year-olds. She'd never been one to back away from the truth or sugarcoat it—much to dismay of the government-run school board.

"Ms. Berlander, I do understand your point"—the man speaking was Dave Kershner, a man born and educated in the frozen wastes of upstate New York and the school's current principal—"but you have to understand my position here."

Sitting down on your fat ass in your comfortable chair in your toasty-warm office, Sky wanted to point out, but instead leaned forward in her own, uncomfortable chair and pointed to the offending pale blue "educational poster" she had found on her desk that morning. There had been a bright pink Post-it note attached to the front of the poster: "Display for Hygiene Week *dk*."

He didn't even have the nerve to sign it, just scribbled his initials. Signed, sealed, and delivered. As if she were going to tack it up on her bulletin board without question.

"I understand, Mr. Kershner," Sky said, tapping the *Are Our Hands Clean?* poster just above the silhouette of a child's hand made out of red construction paper. Black smudges and scribbles had been added to the tips of each finger and across the palm. The hand next to it, unscribbled and titled "Clean," had been cut out of white paper. "But you don't honestly think that any teacher in this school will put these posters up, do you?"

She watched the man's narrow eyes dart back and forth and the wrinkles in his overly high forehead deepen as he stared at the Bureau of Indian Affairs-approved placard without seeing any problem.

And that was the problem.

"What color is this hand?" she asked, tapping the "Clean" side.

The man's forehead didn't unwrinkle when he looked up. Sky could already tell he wouldn't last long and that she might not even have all that much to do with his decision to leave.

"I beg your pardon?"

"This hand," Sky repeated, tapping the white cutout. "What color is the paper?"

"White?"

She gave him a blinding smile, the same kind she usually gave students who remembered to raise their hands to ask permission to go potty.

"And this one?" she asked, pointing to the other cutout.

"Red. Ms. Berlander, is there some point to all this?"

"Just that no kid in this school will be able to wash their hands hard enough to turn them white."

The man's face remained poised on the edge of utter bafflement as he squinted down at the poster. He had no idea what she was talking about. *Christ*, Sky thought, biting the inside of her cheek to keep from voicing the sentiment out loud, *you probably won't last out the semester.* She could only hope.

"I'm afraid I still don't . . . Oh." He looked up, the faintest hint of a blush blooming in his cheeks. "The red hands are the dirty ones."

"That's right, dirty little red hands, Mr. Kershner," Sky added just in case he still didn't have a full grasp of the situation, "just the thing for dirty little Indians to see."

The blush swept across his face like a prairie fire. "Ms. Berlander, I'm shocked at that statement."

"Well, you should be, Mr. Kershner, because that's exactly what the kids in my class are going to think when they see that poster."

The expatriated Upper New York Stater raised his hands, fish-belly-white palms toward her.

"Now, let's not blow this out of perspective, Ms. Berlander. These posters were created solely for the purpose of promoting cleanliness in children whose reading skills are still developing. I seriously don't think the staff of educators who created this were implying any sort of ethnic criticism. Besides, I don't think the children in your class will even notice it. They're very young and—"

"Impressionable, Mr. Kershner . . . and you'd be surprised what they notice. Let me ask you a question," she continued, staring at the pink lines that criss-crossed his palms. "Would you put up the same sort of poster in a central-city classroom if the illustration representing the 'dirty' hand were black?"

Sky watched the man's hands clench into fists, fingers closing over the pink lines like the legs of a dying albino spider.

"Of course not."

"Why? The color black is most often used to show dirt or mud."

The red tint in the man's cheeks had deepened to the same shade as the tiny construction-paper hand on the poster.

"Because it would be inappropriate, Ms. Berlander."

"Because the children in those schools are black, Mr. Kershner," she said, lowering her hands, her red hands, into her lap. "And that's why I won't hang that racist piece of propaganda in my classroom. But what I will do is have the children trace their own hands and scribble on one to show the difference between clean and dirty, because hygiene is a very important concept to learn. Will that do?"

The man picked the poster up off his desk and glared at her over the top of it. The vein in his right temple, the color of blue corn, throbbed.

"I think that's an excellent idea, Ms. Berlander."

"I'm so happy you agree, Mr. Kershner."

Flashing him another *you've done well* smile, Sky stood up and walked to the door she had closed behind her after storming into his office twenty minutes before. She could feel his eyes on her, but his stare had a much different feel to it than the looks she got from other men—white and Indian. The only thing

Mr. Kershner wanted from her was for her to get out of his office and take her radical ideas with her.

Halfway through the door, Sky stopped and turned around.

"I'm afraid I will need to requisition a new box of red crayons for this project," she said.

"Make out an order slip and leave it with Mrs. Willowstick."

"I'll do that, thank you, Mr. Kershner."

"Anytime . . . Ms. Berlander." His chair creaked when he leaned back. "I do hope your class hasn't missed you too much."

Sky looked out the window behind the man's right shoulder, shaking her head. Her class was sitting in a semicircle on the hard-rubber tetherball court, hands folded neatly in their laps, mouths (surprisingly) still, attention focused on the old man hunkered down on a child-size chair in front of them.

"I don't think they even know I'm gone," she said. "It's their story time."

CHAPTER 2

Joseph stopped only long enough to tuck a stray wisp of hair back under his headband. The hair hadn't bothered him at all, but he'd wanted to check his audience to make sure the children were still caught fast in the story's web. Even his own two grandsons, who had heard the story since they were infants and knew it almost as well as he did, had wandered away from their recess time and sat down to listen. And they weren't the only ones: The original class of eleven had almost tripled in size, starting with the ring of Sky's second-graders and moving back, like ripples in a quiet pool, to the line of adult playground supervisors.

Smiling, he leaned forward over his knees and continued, keeping his voice low so his audience would have to be quiet in order to hear.

He hadn't been a storyteller for almost seventy years without learning a few tricks.

"And the Old One said, 'I will be master over You, as a man is master over his own dwelling.' But the Wind spoke back and asked, 'How can You be master over Me? For I am like the Earth beneath your feet and the Sky above your head. I am alone unto Myself . . . and no man shall call himself master over Me.' And then the Wind hurled herself at the Old One and carried Him up into the great blackness beyond the rim sky's blue bowl. She had hoped to kill Him and so silence His boasting, and if He had been just a man, She would have hurled him back onto the earth like a stone."

Straightening suddenly in the tiny, uncomfortable chair, Joseph clapped his hands together and smiled at the startled gasps. A few of the adults giggled behind cupped hands, embarrassed at having fallen victim to so simple a trick, but none of them walked away.

"But the Old One held on to the Wind as if She were a wild pony and sang to Her the words He had heard in His dream that was not a dream. He had hoped to calm Her with this song, and yet still the Wind would not listen. 'I am the Wind,' She told Him again, 'I will not be mastered by man or a song.' But still the Old One sang.

"For thirteen moons the Wind carried Him above the Earth . . . sometimes so high the stars twinkled below Him, sometimes so low that the grass of the great plains whipped against His skin . . . and still He sang, holding Her gently as a father would his child.

19

For thirteen moons it was so, and then, in the Moon of the Whispering Wind, She began to tire."

Elbows on knees, Joseph leaned forward and let his eyes scan the silent, eager faces before him.

"And what do we call that moon?" he asked.

"Osomuyaw," his youngest grandson, Andrew, answered without hesitation.

Joseph smiled, nodding. "Osomuyaw, yes. She began tiring then, and Her voice grew harsh until She could only whisper. Finally, like a wild pony that realizes it can't escape the rope around its neck, the Wind lowered Him softly onto the tender shoots of new grass that dotted the land. And still the Old One sang His song . . . stopping only to blow into the spirit whistle He had made from a willow stalk. At the sound, the Wind became as a stallion . . . rising up as a giant tornado that blocked the sun and brought darkness down over the Old One."

Joseph lifted his face toward the clear sky and closed his eyes.

"But even in Her rage, the Wind was powerless to harm Him because He had used His magic bravely and continued to play the binding song. And when She knew She would never be free again, the Wind accepted Her fate and slowly settled back to the earth.

" 'What do you want of Me?' She asked. And the Old One lowered the whistle from His lips and sprinkled an offering of blue corn to Her, for He respected Her power and strength. 'I will master You only to help Our People,' He said. 'I will not break Your spirit or bend You to My will, for You are a holy thing. Together We shall bring the rains from the high mountains to water the fields. Together We shall keep the deep snow away from the village. And Together We will destroy all those who wish Our People harm. And Man will worship You and give You blue corn and the first spring lamb to eat and sweet water to drink, and You will be one with Our People.'

"And the Wind listened and considered and found it to Her liking . . . for She had always been alone and never before had belonged to a tribe. 'I shall come with you, Old One,' She said, 'and from this day onward, Our People will call You Yaponcha, the Wind Caller, and We shall be together always.'

"With this said, the Wind Caller broke the spirit whistle and the Wind stayed and did His bidding from that day to this."

The adults moved away first, drifting back to their playground duties, followed by the older children, Joseph's twelve-year-old grandson and namesake leading the pack toward the basketball court for a quick game before the bell rang. The rest of the children stayed where they were, wondering, perhaps, what it would feel like to ride the wind through the sky.

"Grandfather?"

Joseph looked over the faces until his eyes settled on a thin-faced boy, one of Andrew's friends. All the children and most of the adults in the reservation addressed him as "Grandfather." It was an archaic term of respect and status, and Joseph was proud of it.

"Yes, Billy?"

"Is the Wind Caller still alive, Grandfather?"

"Of course he's still alive," Andrew said, nudg-

ing his friend in the ribs. "Don't be such an iggy—
igney-amous—igner . . . dope, Billy."

A few of the children giggled, and it was hard for
Joseph not to join them. Andrew, he knew, would
carry on after he was gone as the new Storyteller.
Clearing his throat, Joseph raised a finger to his lips
and waited until the gigglers quieted down.

"Yaponcha lives, Billy, but not like you or I live.
He is a spirit who dwells high in the mountains."
Joseph pointed to the misty purple shapes on the
northern horizon. "Alone in a cave until He is
needed to control the wind."

"And he never comes out until then?" Andrew
asked, caught up in the legend.

"Well, sometimes, on nights when there is no
moon and the wind creeps low to the ground, He
comes out of the cave to sing His ancient songs."

He could almost feel the shiver of excitement that
raced through the children. Joseph knew there would
be no moon that night—he'd checked it in the
weather section of the morning paper—and also
knew that at least half the children would lie awake
in their beds, listening.

"What does he look like, Grandfather?" a girl near
the back asked. "Yaponcha, I mean. I've never seen
his Kachina or mask at any of the dances."

Joseph felt the wind against the back of his neck
and pulled his coat tighter over his chest. Winter was
not yet ready to give up its hold on the land.

"Yaponcha has no mask or Kachina. He is the God
of the Whirlwind, and no man may impersonate
Him. To do so would call down His anger."

The girl whispered something to her friend, who nodded gravely.

"But if he's a god, Grandfather," Andrew asked, even though he knew the answer, "how can he control the wind?"

"He can't," Joseph said, and heard the sudden intake of breath, "so once in a generation a Chosen One is selected from the people and learns the ancient secrets. And if that living man has listened and learned well enough, the Old One allows him to become the living image of the Wind Caller."

"Can a girl become the Wind Caller?"

The children exploded into laughter and openly jostled the questioner—a girl of ten or eleven with eyes the color of polished obsidian. She shoved back, smiling.

"The Wind Caller," Joseph began, then waited until the children were once again paying attention, "can be whoever Yaponcha feels is worthy, man or woman . . . or child."

The wind circled around him, swallowing the soft murmurs.

"Has Yaponcha ever spoken to you, Grandfather?"

Joseph met his grandson's eyes. It was the one question he had never answered.

And this time he was literally saved by the bell.

As the combined sounds of buzzer, voices, and pounding feet became just an echo across the quickly abandoned school yard, Joseph stood up and tried to push the stiffness out of his lower back.

"If you'd let me know you were coming," a sweet voice said, "I would have brought out a bigger chair."

Joseph felt his smile falter as she came toward him.

"You're too thin, Cielo," he said as she kissed his cheek, "and there is fire in your eyes. Come eat with us tonight and tell me what happened. Did you argue with your principal again?"

The sound of her laughter, though forced, brought the smile back to his lips.

"I only fight *for* my principles, Grandfather. You should know that by now."

He nodded, knowing all too well. "But you should still come to eat."

Sky was shaking her head as she stepped back. "You're worse than a Jewish mother, you know that? I'm fine, really. So, what story did you tell them this time?"

"About the Wind Caller."

"Yaponcha." She spoke in a whisper, with reverence. "You know that's all they'll be talking about for weeks now, don't you? And we just finished our unit on the Kachinas last week."

"A week to study their heritage?" Joseph sighed as he touched her cheek. "Cielo, that's not right."

Sky pulled the thick sweater she wore tighter across her chest.

"Maybe not, Grandfather, but they have to learn other things besides Hopi legends. When they grow up, they'll have to know how to live outside the reservation."

"Like you, Cielo?"

She pressed her lips together in what might have been a grin or a grimace. "It'll be easier for them. They'll be Indians living in a white world, not some half-breed pretending to belong to both."

"Is that how you truly feel, Cielo? You know you're accepted here."

"I know, Grandfather, it's just that I'm . . ." She shook her head and brushed the hair away from her eyes. The wind had picked up and was swirling around them. "Forget it. I guess I am still a little upset with the idiocy of the educational system. But it's nothing I can't handle, really. And speaking of education . . . my kids have probably torn the classroom apart by now. I have to get back to them. And next time give me some notice that you're coming, okay?"

"I'll try to remember." Joseph walked next to her until they came to the door leading into the building. He'd been sent away to an Indian school when he was twelve and still could not bring himself to willingly enter such a place again. "Will you come to eat with us tonight, Cielo?"

"I can't, sorry." She kissed his cheek. "I'll probably be up all night correcting papers, but thank you for the offer, Grandfather."

Without another word, Sky turned and walked away into the world of overhead fluorescent lights and learning history from books. Joseph watched her disappear around a corner, then walked to one of the wooden lunch benches that bordered the playground to the west. School would be over in less than an hour; he'd wait for his grandsons.

The wind caught up with him halfway across the playground, kicking up dirt and debris around his feet before speeding off toward town.

Joseph stopped and watched a small dust devil play with the tattered remains of a white plastic shopping bag. The bag moved like the ghost of a dead warrior, twisting and turning north across the barren land without pause.

And gathering speed.

Joseph stuffed his right hand deep into the pocket of his coat and absently fingered the small willow whistle that rested there. Tonight, if any of the children did stay awake, they'd hear more than imaginary songs.

Sky stood at her classroom window, alternating between waving to those children who had were already outside and heading home, and trying to hurry the usual slowpokes. Normally, she would have let them take as long as they liked—the current record was held by Timmy Cainimptewa at fifteen minutes, ten seconds—but she had plans tonight that had very little to do with grading papers, as she had told Joseph.

She hated lying to him, even so small a lie, but telling the truth would have embarrassed them both.

Or maybe it would have just embarrassed her.

"Come on, you guys," Sky said, clapping her hands at Timmy and the two other children. All three of them jumped as if they'd just been woken up. "You don't want Mr. Wiharu to lock you in when he comes to clean up, do you?"

The three children looked up at her in horror, and Sky turned quickly back toward the window to keep them from seeing her smile. Tom Willis had been the janitor at the school for almost as long as anyone on the reservation could remember, and had danced as Wiharu, the White Ogre Kachina, for even longer. Tom Willis, the man, loved children, but Tom Wiharu, the White Ogre, was duty-bound by his Kachina to frighten children into behaving. Being accidentally locked into the school by this man was not an option most children ever wanted to face.

Sky could hear renewed scuffling behind her— books being tossed into backpacks, coats *finally* being pulled on—as she watched Joseph and his grandsons walk out of the schoolyard. He was bent forward, listening intently to something Andrew, the youngest, was saying. The older boy, Joey, lagged a few yards behind—close enough to still hear what was being said, but not so close that any of his friends would think he was actually walking home with his grandfather and kid brother. God, the humiliation.

She remembered being the same way, wanting to be so independent before she was ready.

God, what she wouldn't do to be that naive again.

"Bye, Ms. Berlander! See ya tomorrow, Ms. Berlander! Bye!"

There was only the faint scent of Vicks VapoRub hanging in the air, and the fading sounds of sneakers against linoleum from the hallway when she turned around.

"Bye," she said to the empty classroom, and listened to the muffled echo of her shoes as she snagged her shoulder bag off the desk and headed for the door. If she was lucky, she'd still miss most of the early rush-hour traffic.

But, just in case, she began planning alternative routes. When she reached the doorway, she jumped as Tom Willis suddenly appeared, push broom in hand.

"Sorry," he said in a voice as soft as spring rain, "I didn't mean to frighten you."

27

Without his mask and whips, it was hard to picture the old man being able to frighten anything more stalwart than a butterfly.

"You didn't," Sky tried to assure him. "I was just thinking. . . . My mind was a million miles away."

The old man nodded.

"It's been a long day," Sky added, unsubtle in her attempts to look over his shoulder toward the exit door down the hall. "And I'm just a little tired."

The old man nodded again but didn't take the hint.

"Um, do you need something, Mr. Willis?"

The old man nodded a third time and stepped back, tipping the handle of his push broom to the left.

"Mr. Kershner would like to see you in the conference room."

"Oh. Do you know why?"

The old man shook his head and stepped aside, waiting for her to pass. "I'll lock up here when I'm finished. Have a good night."

Sky licked her lips and, after realizing that no further explanation would be coming, hurried down the hall toward the combination conference room/teachers' lounge. *If the impromptu meeting is Kershner's idea of getting back at me for my reaction to the hygiene poster,* she thought as she hurried past dark classrooms, *he's about to see just how much of a temper I have.*

"You wanted to see me, Mr. Kershner," she said, slamming open the door. "Oh."

The entire teaching staff, including the two part-time PE coaches, glared up at her from their places around the banquet-sized table. Each had a full-color xeroxed copy of the damned hygiene poster in front of them.

28

"Ah, 'and the last shall be the first,'" Dave Kershner said his fingers tented over the original poster. "Good of you to finally join us, Ms. Berlander, considering you're sort of the guest of honor. Please sit down and we'll get started."

Sky slipped in as quickly and quietly as she could between Blanche Many-Horses, the "Cafeteria Lady," and Al Makya, who taught the sixth grade and computer science. Neither of them smiled at her.

"Now," their BIA-appointed principal continued, "the reason I've called this emergency meeting—"

Emergency meeting? Sky didn't like the sound of that.

"—is to discuss the potential racial ramifications concerning posters like this one and what we, as the staff of this school, can do to see that it doesn't happen in the future. Ms. Berlander, since you were the one who initially brought this concern to my attention, perhaps you'd like to start."

Sky could feel every tired, overworked, and wanting only to "get home and relax" eye turn toward her with hate and malcontent as she stood up. Save one. Dave Kershner was beaming.

Bastard.

"Well," she said around a throbbing lump in her throat, "I just thought it was a . . . bad thing?"

The rest of the meeting went downhill from that point.

CHAPTER 3

Gideon waited until dusk was settling comfortably along the ridge before walking down to the spring-house for his evening rations. He didn't mind the city's slow encroachment as long as he couldn't see it, and except for the occasional sweep of headlights of some fool off-roader and twinkle of light from the development at the end of his private road, the thick layers of pine, oak, and scrub were pretty effective for preserving the self-deception that he was still iso-lated from a society he never felt a part of.

The trees, however, couldn't do much to block out the pink-orange urban glow that had been bleeding into the night sky for the past two decades. If things continued the way they were going, it wouldn't be long before he'd stop being able to tell where his world ended and the other began.

Not that he'd ever let that happen without a fight.

And for the past six months, while the cookie-cutter houses spread over the valley like a fungus and the "land speculators" had come sniffing around his ridge like a dog after a bitch, Gideon had been spoiling for a good fight—one-sided though it would be.

If that damned old Indian would stay out of it.

A sharp pain just above the belly button stopped Gideon a yard short of the springhouse. He should have known better than to think about Joseph on an empty stomach.

"Goddamned ol' man," he said, kneading the pain with a knuckle joint and not sure which goddamned old man he was talking about, him or Joseph. "Both of us gettin' older'n dirt and yer still playin' games like yah were nothin' more'n a green sprout. Sneakin' up here and then—"

Disappearin' like yer were some kinda damned snake-oil magician.

"—callin' me little brother. Ah ain't yer brother, Joseph, we're equals. Right down the line, and yah know it. Equals!"

Gideon shoved the knuckle into the center of the pain, driving it down . . . deeper and deeper, until it exploded from his mouth as a piercing howl that shot into the darkening sky and caught hold of the wind. He could hear the sound echoing from cloud to cloud as it raced toward the reservation.

"Did'ya hear *that*, brother?"

Not even the wind answered, and that was fine with him.

Hawking up a mouthful of copper-flavored bile,

31

Gideon spit it into the shadows as he returned his attention to the matter at hand. The one-sided confrontation had more than renewed his appetite.

"Mah land, brother, mah rules," he shouted to the deep silence around him, "and the next time yah come sneakin' up here—in flesh or spirit—Ah'm gonna show yah exactly what Ah mean by that. Yah got no right up here, and yah know it. Yer place is down there, crawlin' on the sand like a scorpion. Yah had no right comin' up here . . . spyin' on me like that."

When he got to the heavy plank door, Gideon turned and raised the burlap gathering bag toward the still-bright patch of sky over the western mountains.

"YAH HAD NO RIGHT! THIS IS MAH LAND!"

Panting as he shouldered the door open, Gideon began snatching items from the handmade bins without waiting for his eyes to adjust to the storehouse's perpetual darkness. Not that he had to see. He knew every inch of the cramped building by heart, just like he knew every damned inch of his land.

"Man's got a right t'protect what's his. Goddammit!"

Stumbling back a step, Gideon rubbed his forehead and squinted at the pale, oblong shape that was slowly swinging back and forth at head height. Without taking his eyes off the object, he pulled the buck knife from its sheath on his belt and leaned in slow. He could hear the spring running beneath his feet as he poked the thing.

And felt mighty stupid a moment later.

He knew every inch of what was his, but he'd forgotten about the block of ewe's-milk cheese he'd bartered off a Navaho woman and hung from an exposed cottonwood root in the ceiling. It was a reward to himself for having survived another winter.

"Goddamned ol' fool," he chided himself as he sliced off a good chunk and licked the knife blade clean. "Next thing yah know, Ah'll be talkin' to mahself."

Gideon added two potatoes, the size and shape of river stones, and a carrot to the wedge of cheese in the bottom of the burlap sack and slowly made his way back to the meat chamber. A haunch of cottonwood-smoked venison hung from rafters constructed from wood he routinely stole from building sites. It was good wood made better by the larceny involved. Same thing went for nails and whatever hand tools found their way into his possession.

It was only right, all things considered.

Gideon wiped the buck's blade clean against one sleeve of his flannel shirt and sliced off just enough meat for his supper. He'd have to go hunting again soon, and the thought lightened his mood as he walked back to the cabin. There was enough meat wandering his land that it almost took the sport out of hunting. Although there were times that the hunt still got interesting.

Only a dozen or so times in as many years, but he could recall every one of those times.

Poachers. Trespassers. Every one of them sporting orange vests and caps bright enough to ruin a man's eyesight for life, and each with a license and an area map issued by the Arizona Department of Fish and Game that they were more than eager to flap in his face. They had a legal right to be there, they told him, and they weren't going to leave until they got a deer.

They left, and not one of them with a deer.

The deer, like the land, were his. Period.

Tossing the sack onto the kitchen/dining table, Gideon watched the night suffocate the last rays of sunlight. There'd be no moon that night—it'd be perfect for a hunt. . . . And Lord knows he needed something to aim his thoughts on.

"So, what'cha think?" he asked out loud while his hands began to get busy with the business of fixing dinner. "Feel like doin' a little meat-gatherin'?"

The wind moaned softly in the eaves.

"Yeah," Gideon said, "me, too."

Sky didn't scream when her supposedly locked apartment door began to swing open. She didn't even think about screaming, although she knew the sound would almost definitely entice one of her neighbors in the complex away from the six-o'clock news. Maybe. But she didn't scream.

The only thing she could think of, as the door opened enough for her to see the large, man-shaped silhouette standing in her apartment entranceway, was that she should have asked for plastic instead of paper at the market. Plastic bags, when hanging from the wrists, made decent flails. Paper bags, filled with the ingredients for an intimate though not fancy dinner, probably wouldn't have made decent shields.

I knew I should have just ordered Chinese, Sky thought, but she didn't scream—even when a muscular arm reached out and snatched a bag from her.

She did, however, yell.

"How the hell did you get into my apartment?"

Sam Reynolds, the man she'd met two months earlier while jogging one morning, and had been dating ever since, winked as she stormed past.

He'd winked the same way the first time they met.

She'd just gotten dumped, for the hundredth time or so, and was burning up the track at a local recreation center. He'd started pacing her the third time around. Sky hadn't really notice until he pulled in front of her and slowed down—and then she noticed, all right: 6 feet 3, 195, no fat, brown hair, brown eyes, a walrus mustache dusted with gray set on a face as craggy as a dried riverbed . . . broad shoulders and tight buns that clenched and unclenched in perfect rhythm beneath a pair of blood-red nylon shorts. A dead woman would have noticed.

And when he was sure he had her full attention, he fell back next to her and winked.

It was the wink that did it.

If he had said anything or done anything else, she would have completed the last lap and chalked the experience up on her mental blackboard under "Stupid Male Tricks." Instead, they finished the lap together and split a double order of chili fries afterward.

He was funny and kind and a generous lover—but, of course, that was before she caught him in her apartment.

"Well?"

"Well what?" he asked, an East Texas accent rolling off his tongue like honey as he closed the door.

"You, here?" She sniffed the air. "Making dinner? I was supposed to make dinner."

"Yes, you were . . . and if you'd just stumble into the twentieth century and go out and get yourself a cell phone, you would have been able to call the adored man in your life and tell him you'd be"—he looked at his watch, large and gold and expensive—"almost three hours late getting home and would simply *love* for said adored man to come over and prepare dinner for you."

Sky shoved her hands into the coat's pockets. "I hate cell phones."

"And answering machines. On which, had you had one, you would have found ten calls, all from that adored man, telling you not to worry because he was coming over to make dinner." He winked and, grabbing the grocery bags, one in each arm, gave her a quick peck on the cheek and headed back to the kitchen. "Take off your coat and get comfortable."

"You didn't answer my question."

Pots and pans rattled, cabinet doors opened and shut, but he was quiet.

"Sam!"

He poked his head out from her microkitchenette. Her blue-paisley bib apron hung around his neck. "I asked the landlord to let me in. When I didn't hear from you by six, I figured you must have gotten stuck in traffic, so I took it upon myself to make dinner. Hope you like marinated steak and grilled mushrooms. Also got a batch of early asparagus that I'm fixing to smother in Hollandaise sauce, so if you want to continue the interrogation, you best come in here."

He disappeared back into the kitchen. Sky slipped

out of her coat and tossed it, unceremoniously, over the back of the couch.

"No dessert?" she asked.

He reappeared briefly. "Chocolate-dipped strawberries."

"Oh," she said when he disappeared the second time. "And he cooks, too."

"What?"

"Nothing. Shall I open up some wine?"

"Already on the table," he said. "Pour yourself a glass and relax. Dinner'll be ready in ten minutes."

"I can do that," Sky said, and was halfway through her second glass when he placed the first course— wilted spinach salad and crusty bread—down on the coffee table in front of her.

"Hey, go easy on that wine," he said, taking the glass out of her hand and replacing it with a fork. "I want you to be able to taste things."

Sky speared a crouton and giggled. "Oh, don't worry about me, this Injin knows how to handle her firewater. Sorry . . . something happened at school today that . . ."

She pushed the fork down until it shattered the hard bread cube.

"Was that the reason you were late?"

"That and the fact that my principal is a racist asshole."

He reached out and moved the wine bottle to his side of the coffee table.

"Hey!"

"Hey, nothing. Now tell me what happened."

"Then can I have another glass?"

"We'll see, lady. Now, talk."

Sky told him, leaving nothing out and probably adding more "color" to her commentary than was needed.

He poured her half a glass when she finished. "Want me to talk to him?"

"What?" Giggling, she took the glass and nudged him. "Sam, no . . . but thanks anyway. Besides, I thought your job keeps you pretty busy."

More than busy, Sky wanted to add, but finished the wine instead of the thought. Sam worked as a "closer" for one of Richland's biggest ad agencies and was, by his own admission, a dyed-in-the-gray-flannel-suit workaholic. He told her that right from the beginning and she understood, having spent most of her evenings—until they met—grading papers or cutting out patterns for the next day.

Until they met.

"You're still mad at me for having to cancel last Friday, aren't you?"

Sky licked a drop of wine from her top lip. "Last Friday? Oh, you mean the concert. No, I'm not still mad."

"Liar."

"No, really. You had to fly to L.A. for a last-minute meeting. Believe me, I understand."

He leaned over and kissed the tip of her nose. "Thank you, liar. Now, finish that salad so I can bring in the steaks."

Sky leaned forward over the coffee table and forked a mound of dripping spinach into her mouth.

"You know," he said when she looked up, "you

might want to consider moving into a bigger apartment. Say, one with a dining room?"

Sky swallowed so quickly she almost choked. *Was
that a proposition or a proposal?* They hadn't known
each other long, but maybe that didn't matter. It
didn't for her.

"Oh?" she asked.

"Yeah." Sam popped a crouton into his mouth and
crushed it between his teeth. "I know of a new development about to break ground, and if you like, I could
get your name on the waiting list. It'll be spectacular,
from the concept drawings I've seen. The town
homes are going to start in the low two hundreds, but
I think I can negotiate it down a bit for you."

The wine in Sky's belly turned sour when he
winked at her, closing the deal.

"Oh."

There was something stirring in the air. Something
she could not smell or taste or hear, but something
that pricked the short hairs along the arch of her
neck and made her pause for a moment in the shadows. She could smell the water and life she carried
twist lazily inside her womb, but still the doe remained hidden. Waiting to see if the *something* would
show itself.

When nothing did, she let her thirst pull her toward the stream.

More cautious now as she entered the clearing, the
doe tensed as her hooves sank into the spongy moss
at the water's edge. Whatever she had sensed was
close; if the need for water hadn't been so strong, she

would have turned and run back to the safety of the trees.

Slowly, the doe dipped her muzzle into the cold water and drank.

Something moved in the underbrush directly behind her.

The weight of her unborn fawn threw her off balance and she stumbled through the stream instead of bounding over it. Once on the opposite side, she stopped and craned her head back over her shoulder; trembling until her pricked ears recognized the sound of tiny claws scampering over dried grass.

The something was small. Harmless.

The fear forgotten, the doe lowered her head back to the water and drank her fill. Within her womb, the fawn twitched in its sleep and stretched. The doe swung her head to one side and nudged the unborn fawn into a more comfortable position. She was in her final week of gestation and was growing restless waiting for the impending birth. Instinct told her it would be soon, but until then she would have to endure the nightly urge to wander far from the harem and its antlered guardian.

The wind shifted, rippling the water around her legs.

Lifting her head, the doe sniffed the moving air and trembled. There was something else, not small or harmless, moving in the darkness toward her. Something large and fast, still far off but moving quickly down the butte toward her. The doe backed out of the water, muscles tightening against the moment she would use them, then froze, a living statue, when a young sapling directly opposite her crashed to the ground. The thing was here. She could feel its presence, but still there was no scent or sound on the wind of cat or man or bear.

There was just the wind.

Only the wind.

The doe bleated in fear, and the wind answered, sharp and clear with a voice that pinned her ears flat against her head.

It was the last sound she heard before the wind funnel engulfed her.

Blood and fluid from the ruptured amniotic sac gushed from the birth canal and were sucked into the swirling wind as shards of chert and jasper in the funnel's tail opened up her belly with the precision of a doctor's blade. The dead fawn slipped from its mother's body on a tide of entrails.

It was a sight he never got tired of watching.

Untying the empty burlap sack from his belt, Gideon stepped out from behind the dense curtain of brush and watched the wind roll the torn bladder out of the gut pile as gently as if it were full. That was the one thing he just couldn't teach it—how to kill an animal easily.

With a sigh, he placed the willow whistle to his lips and blew a low, quavering note.

"Okay," he said, "that'll do."

The wind settled to the ground, barely stirring, when Gideon walked over to the dismembered animal and shook his head.

"Can't use this," he said, nudging the heart. It was torn in two, split right down the center and filled with dirt. "And the liver's all but ruined. Those intestines coulda done for sausage casin', but yah twisted 'em all in knots. Damn me for ever teachin' yah t'enjoy this."

The blood was black under the faint starlight. It was a good color for blood, he thought. Red was just too flashy.

"Now this," he said, tucking the whistle back into his shirt pocket as he squatted down next to the unborn fawn, "this here's a real treasure. Yah done a'right—Ah ain't had unborn venison in a long time."

The wind circled him, accepting the praise, while he wrestled the fawn's body into the sack. Just the thought of the tender white meat roasting whole on a spit made his mouth water.

"What about you, brother?" Gideon asked as he added a severed haunch and liver to the sack, being careful not to bruise the fawn any more than it had been already. The rest of the meat he'd leave for the scavengers to clean up. It wasn't as if he couldn't go hunting again when the mood struck him.

"How long's it been since yah ate like yer ancestors, Joseph?"

Gideon was almost surprised when he looked up and didn't see the old Hopi standing there, looking disapproving and disappointed. It would have been the perfect ending to a perfect night.

"What's the matter, brother," he asked as he tied the bag shut with a length of rope, "no guts? Well, here's some for yah."

Standing, Gideon poked the intestines with the toe of his boot.

"Yah know what they say, don't yah, brother? No guts, no glory. . . . No Glory." *Damn, what made me think of that?* "Yah think yer the only one who suffered that day, don't yah? Hell, old man, yah don't even know what sufferin's like."

Gideon could feel the old ache starting up again, like rheumatism in the bones, and shook his head. *Not now, not tonight . . . but soon*, he promised it, *soon*.

It took longer than he expected to toss the blood-soaked bag up onto his shoulder, and when he did the weight, despite having left so much behind, staggered him a bit. *Joseph isn't the only one gettin' old.*

"But we'll see which one of us'll last the longest, won't we, brother?"

The ache in his heart didn't leave even when he closed his eyes and sang the ancient chant he'd learned so long ago.

"Grandfather?"

Joseph woke with a start, gripping the blanket over his heart as he blinked the sleep out of his eyes.

"Grandfather?"

"What . . . what is it, Andrew? Are you all right? Do you feel sick?"

Pushing himself up on one arm, Joseph could feel his eyes still stinging when they finally focused on his grandson. He was standing at the foot of Joseph's bed, the large stuffed dog he had slept with since infancy clutched to his chest.

"You had a bad dream."

The boy shook his head. "No."

"No?" he asked, but he was already tossing the blankets aside and muttering an apology as he moved to the side of the mattress on which the spirit of his dead wife slept. He didn't think she'd mind for one night. "But since you're already here, would you like to stay?"

Andrew accepted the offer and clambered in next to Joseph without a word. His little body was ice cold. Too cold for having only walked from the room he shared with his brother to the enclosed porch where Joseph slept.

"Have you been outside?"

"Only for a minute," the boy confessed. "Really."

"That was very foolish, especially without a robe and slippers. Do you know how sick you can get?" Joseph scolded. "Why did you go outside?"

The old box spring squealed when the boy curled into the crook of Joseph's arm.

"I wanted to hear him better."

"Who? A coyote? Did you hear something around the chickens? Is it still there?"

"No, Grandfather . . . *him*."

"Who . . . oh, the story I told today." Smiling, he pulled the covers over the child's shoulders and ruffled the thick hair. "You went outside to listen for the Old One, well . . . you should have still put on a robe. I hope you're not too disappointed, but it's hard to hear the Old One's songs sometimes."

The boy yawned. "But I did hear him, Grandfather."

Joseph looked down at the child. He was almost asleep, his breath soft and slow.

"What? Andrew, what do you mean?"

"I heard him."

"You couldn't have," Joseph whispered, afraid to say it louder. "It was only a story."

"Nuh-uh. Listen, Grandfather. Can't you hear him?"

Joseph would have continued trying to explain the difference between reality and make-believe if the little boy had still been awake and if he hadn't heard the ancient song on the wind.

In the morning, he'd tell the boy it was only a dream, and he hoped that story would be as easily accepted.

Unlike his spirit brother, Joseph had never been good at lying.

"NO!"

The sound was tearing her apart, slicing through the flesh and bone of her skull like a scalpel.

"Grandfather! Stop it, please!"

But he wouldn't. She had done something wrong, and he had to punish her.

"Please, I didn't mean to. Please don't."

She saw his eyes as he filled his lungs. He enjoyed watching her suffer, and now he wanted to watch her die. He even smiled at her from around the small whistle an instant before the piercing sound ripped her face in two. She couldn't stop it, couldn't catch her face before it fell. . . . Someone was holding her down. . . .

"NO!"

Sky lashed out at the hands holding her and woke up when Sam hit the floor next to the bed, followed by the clock radio that had been on the table next to the bed. God, she'd have to remember to apologize to her downstairs neighbors in the morning.

"Sam?"

When he didn't answer, Sky turned on the reading lamp attached to the headboard and leaned over until she could see over the edge of the mattress. He was flat on his back, a tangle of blankets wrapped around one leg.

"Are you all right? Oh, God, I'm sorry."

"Apology accepted . . . and I'm fine, don't worry about it. But I do think you're going to need to replace this." He sat up and handed her the clock radio. There was a crack in the clear plastic faceplate. "Have a nightmare?"

Sky scooted back against the headboard, hugging a pillow against her naked breasts while he untangled himself from the bedding and fanned it over her and the mattress.

"No, thanks," she said when he crawled in next to her, "already had one."

"You're a riot. Of course, I guess it might have been something you ate." He pouted up at her. "I may have overdone it with the beer in the Hollandaise sauce."

"Beer?"

"No? Oh, that's right. Beer goes in Welsh rarebit. . . . Darn, I always get those two confused."

She snuggled against him, loving the sound of his laughter and the feel of his flesh against hers. It made her feel safe.

"Remind me to get you an audition for *The Iron Chef*."

"My dream come true," he whispered, kissing the top of her head. "And speaking of dreams . . . yours must have been a doozie. Are you sure you don't remember any of it?"

Sky ran her fingers through his thick pelt of chest hair and shook her head.

"Nothing?"

She was kneeling in front of her mother's grave, planting flower seeds—marigolds and morning glories—but each time she pressed her finger into the warm soil, it would immediately fill with blood that dribbled down, like rain, from—

"No, not really. Why, did I . . . say anything?"

—the ragged stump of his right arm. "Oh, God, what did you do?" He stood there looking at her while his blood dripped onto her mother's grave and shook his head. "Ah didn't do this . . . it was yer fault. Yah did this t'me." "No, Grandfather. I didn't. How could I?" "Same way yah killed mah daughter, by bein' born."

And then he pulled a small willow whistle to his lips and blew her world apart. Poor Sam—he suffered the brunt of her nightmare.

"You mumbled something, but I really couldn't make out what you were saying. Especially with a fist aimed at my eye. Believe me, if I knew you were going to turn into Jackie Chan and tossed me out of bed, I would have left you alone." He reached down and brushed his fingertips against the side of her breast. Goose bumps sprang in their wake. "You know, if you want me to leave, that's—"

Sky reached up and covered his mouth.

"That's not okay, or all right, or whatever it is you were going to say. Understand?"

His licked her palm.

"Goof," she said, and retaliated with a quick mustache tug.

"Hey, watch the cookie duster." Slapping her hand

away, he stroked the wiry hair on his upper lip as if it were a cherished pet. "There are women in ten states who would throw themselves in front of trains if anything happened to it."

"Oh, really? That many, huh?"

"Depends. Are you talking about the U.S. or worldwide?"

"Hah, hah."

Sky knew he was only joking. They'd been together long enough for her to know that, but that was the only thing she was sure of. The joke that might not have been one at all. He talked less about his past than he did his present, and even then he'd turn the subject back to her and her life. . . . Did you have a good day? Is the Hernandez boy still having problems understanding subtraction? How's your grandfather doing? Aren't you worried about him being up on that mountain all alone? Have you ever talked to him about "assisted living" facilities?

He was everything she'd wanted in a man. The kind of man who put her first in their relationship, who never—with the exception of this evening— stopped by without calling, who sent her flowers for no reason, and who always brought her a "touristy trinket" from his frequent business trips.

But what was the old saying—be careful of what you wish for, because you might just get it? Well, she could have done worse.

Sky glanced at the newest piece in her collection, the Buddy Holly glow-in-the-dark snow globe on her dresser. He'd brought it back from a five-day conference in Cleveland.

48

Sam's weight shifted against her as he yawned. Behind the broken faceplate, the time was 2:43 A.M.

"Penny for your thoughts," he said.

"Only that it's way too early in the morning to be up."

"Well, I wouldn't say that exactly."

He took her hand and placed it on his erect penis. That had been another thing on her "Always Wanted in a Boyfriend" list. She shook her head but didn't move her hand away.

"You're kidding, right?"

He grabbed her around the waist and inched both of them down onto the mattress. "Do I look like I'm kidding?"

Sky began a slow and steady caress of the turgid flesh beneath her fingers.

"No, but sometimes the flesh is willing where the soul realizes it has to get up and on a plane bound for Hawaii at eight."

That had been her reason for inviting him to dinner, even though her planned menu had not included anything that required Hollandaise sauce. She had wanted to impress him with her meager skills before he left for the week-long seminar on what he described as "the basic fundamentals of ass-kissing among the palm trees," and suffered through five days of eating coffee-shop food, or, more than likely, skipping food in favor of vending-machine snacks and happy-hour peanuts.

She felt guilty about not having done anything except eat, but the best-laid plans of mice and thirty-seven-year-old half-breed women. . . .

"I can sleep on the plane," he said, kissing her neck, "but what about you? You think you'll be able to handle a class full of overenergized kids?"

A new pang of guilt wiggled its way under the covers. Tomorrow . . . or, more precisely, later today, was the monthly "Teacher In-Service" day. She didn't have to be at the school until ten, which meant she didn't even have to wake up until nine.

"I'll be fine."

"Well, I don't know," he said between kisses, "just thinking of you sleep-deprived makes me feel bad. Although I suppose if some lady finds my mustache just too hard to resist and keeps me awake . . . AH."

Sky had moved out of range at the same time she reached down and got a firm grip on his balls. "Pardon me?"

His mustache bristled around the grimace. "Only kidding."

"I hope so. Will you at least bring me back a puka shell necklace?"

"Consider it done," he said once he'd removed her hand from his balls and placed it back where he thought it belonged, "but wouldn't you rather have a nice Hawaiian lei?"

It was an old joke, but Sky forced herself to laugh because that's what a woman did to keep her man happy.

Among other things.

"Turn off the light," she whispered.

Sam winked at her and switched off the lamp.

She knew he'd rather make love with the lights on—most men did, according to her friends and certain *Cosmo* articles—but it was something Sky had never felt comfortable with. A lover could see her, he could judge her . . . and she'd already been judged enough already.

"My God, you're beautiful," he said, pulling one of her nipples into his mouth.

Safe now in the dark, Sky arched her back and moaned long and low. If the lights had been on, she wouldn't have been able to do that . . . or to push him onto his back and tease his already swollen hard-on with the tip of her tongue.

If she had seen her reflection in his eyes, she wouldn't have been able to act like the whore her white grandfather thought she was.

Sam groaned and laced his fingers into her hair, gently pulling her toward his chest.

"God, easy, baby, easy."

"Why," she teased, letting the ends of her shoulder-length hair brush against the hollow of his throat, "didn't you like it?"

"I loved it. Hell, if I'd had a teacher like you, I would have studied a lot harder."

Stretching out over him, she lowered her head and bit him on the shoulder. "If you'd had a teacher like me, she would have been in jail for statutory rape. You pervert."

"You know it, sugar."

Sky didn't even have time to gasp when he looped his leg over hers and threw her, like a sack of groceries, onto the mattress.

"Sam!"

"Shh."

Gently, shushing her when she tried to speak, he slowly spread her legs apart and began to slowly massage his way up her calves.

Sky yelped when he reached the sensitive spots on the inside of her knees.

"Don't! It tickles!"

"Hush, little baby."

His hands slid past her knees to her thighs, fingertips inscribing tiny circles across her flesh as they continued moving higher and higher and . . . stopped just short of her pubic mound. It was his turn to tease her now, and she could tell he was going to make her suffer.

"Uncle?" she whined.

"Don't say a word."

"God, come on, Sam."

"Shh. Quiet now, or papa won't give you a mockingbird."

She was about to sit up and tell him exactly what he could do with that damned mockingbird, when she felt two of his fingers slip in between the lips of her vagina. There were no more words spoken as he continued to stroke and prod with the expertise of a sexual sadist.

And she loved every shivering, sweat-soaked moment of it.

She loved *him*, God help her.

When he finally entered her, it was with a single thrust that sent her friction-raw nerve endings into sensual overdrive. Thrashing, raking his back with her nails, Sky wrapped her legs around his waist as the first orgasmic wave swept through her body.

The scream would have awakened more of her neighbors besides the Gutierrez family downstairs . . . if he hadn't covered her mouth with his own.

He knew her so well.

He tied a second knot in the condom and tossed it into the swirling water, absently scratching the small circular bruise just below his collarbone. He'd told her he got it moving his CD tower—a typical "dumb-guy" sort of thing to do. . . . *"I thought I could move it without taking out the CDs and . . . well, a whole batch of them started to fall, and when I tried to push them back with my hip the tower slipped out of my hands and a corner caught me. Dumb, huh?"*

It was actually brilliant, but she'd agreed that it was dumb and even kissed his "boo-boo" to make it all better.

Sometimes it was just too easy.

Turning off the light as he left the bathroom, Reynolds paused next to the bedroom door long enough to confirm that she was still deep in postcoital dreamland before walking into the living room.

Their clothes were scattered around the combination living/dining area—evidence that the chocolate-dipped strawberries hadn't been the only dessert item on the menu. He smiled at the memory as he picked up his jeans and pulled out the small clamshell phone. She might not like cell phones, but damn, he'd be lost without his.

He'd also be pretty far up shit creek without the company's twenty-four-service line.

"You have reached the automated systems of SC Industries," the electronic secretary purred. "Please enter your security code followed by the pound sign now, or press star-one if you wish to speak to an assistant."

Reynolds glanced at the luminous face of his watch and punched in his nine-digit code, followed by the pound sign as requested. Daybreak was still an hour away, and he knew from experience that leaving a message with any of the high-school dropouts hired to work the graveyard watch was a waste of effort.

And he wasn't getting paid to waste anything.

"Welcome, Mr. Reynolds," the voice said. "You may begin recording your request . . . now."

"I'll need a puka shell necklace, smallest diameter possible, in either white or white-gray combination, and a Hawaiian lei, Plumeria, color nonspecific. Five working days from today."

He thought if there was anything else the company could supply that he couldn't—and smiled.

"Add one Hawaiian shirt, silk. Extra large and . . . with a pineapple motif."

That should cause a little hustle down in Shipping and Receiving.

He smiled and punched the star sign to signal he was finished.

"Your request of"—he heard the playback of his own voice—"and time of delivery has been entered. You will be notified when items arrive for pickup. Thank you for using the automated services of SC Industries."

The line went efficiently dead before he flicked the tiny phone closed.

Renyolds felt a burning sting across his shoulders when he bent down to gather up his boxers and undershirt, and he flinched when the salt on his fingers came in contact with the scratches she'd left on him. Of all the women he'd known over the years, this one was the most active in bed.

There was blood on his fingers when he looked at them.

Damn, the things I do for stock options.

CHAPTER 4

With a curse that would have delighted the kids in her class and shocked their parents, Sky rolled over and slapped the clock radio's oversized snooze bar.

"Five more minutes," she told it, and collapsed, facedown, onto the crumpled bedding.

Five minutes later, she hit the bar again and cut her palm on the broken faceplate. The pain woke her up to a couple of things: that she'd have to buy a new clock radio and that she was alone.

"Sam?"

Sky pressed a corner of the night-soiled sheets against the cut and frowned at the time displayed behind the shattered plastic. It was only ten after six, her usual time to get up when both showering and the morning commute had to be taken into consideration. Today she had planned on sleeping in until at least seven, which would give her . . . *them* time for a

56

little more fun and games before he had to leave for the airport. She'd made the standard offer to take him to the airport, but he declined, telling her he'd already booked a shuttle pickup.

That was standard, too. She offered, he refused.

She didn't even know exactly where he lived. They always got together at her place, never his.

He's married . . . that's probably one of the things you don't know about him, stupid.

Sky pulled the sheet off the bed and wrapped it around herself, toga-style, as she headed for the hall-way. The blood from the cut had left a stain on the pale blue cotton.

"Sam?"

It was too early, and he wouldn't just leave without waking her up. *Would he?*

"Knock it off," she hissed at her reflection in the bathroom mirror. There was no fog on the glass, and the toilet-seat lid was down. He hadn't gotten up to take a shower. *Maybe he's in the kitchen, making a surprise preflight breakfast for both of us.*

"Sam, you really shouldn't—"

And he didn't.

The kitchen was empty, the grocery bags she'd brought in still on the kitchen counter where he'd put them—minus the perishables, of course. He had left a note, scribbled in red ink on a sheet of notebook paper and Scotch-taped to the coffee-maker:

You looked so peaceful I didn't have the heart to wake you.
Call you when I get back into town. Luv ya—S.

Sky folded the note in half, being careful not to smudge the ink or get blood on the paper, and put it with the others he'd left her. The new one made eighteen.

She was contemplating whether to go back to bed or take a shower when the apartment's forced-air heating rattled to life and she realized she'd been standing on the cold vinyl floor in her bare feet, shivering. Going back to bed would first mean remaking it, but that would require more manual labor than she was ready to face at the moment. Taking a shower would only wake her up completely and leave her to squander the few extra hours of freedom she still had with correcting papers or doing housework.

Or . . .

Sky pulled the sheet up over her shoulders and looked at the half-empty bags of groceries. *Or I could drive out to replenish the old man's supplies and collect my weekly dose of abuse.*

"And we have a winner," she whispered to herself.

Sam Reynolds filled his lungs with the sweet mountain air and nodded. This was going to be the view from his bedroom window. He'd decided that the moment he stepped out of the car. Since subcontracting out his services to the man and his company, Reynolds had seen some pretty remarkable scenery, but nothing compared to this. Mackay had told him he could name his price if—when he closed the deal on the property, and this view, wrapped around what was going to become his "snowbird" winter retreat, was it.

And considering what he usually charged, the company was getting off easy.

One house—hell, that was chicken feed.

Picking up a handful of small stones as he walked to the crest of the hill, Reynolds pegged each of the trees he planned to have the company cut down. Trees were nice, but there was nothing like being able to look out and have an unobstructed view of sparkling city lights and urban sprawl.

With it, a man could feel like a king.

Without it, he was just another ant looking up.

Turning, Reynolds lobbed the last rock at the old man's cabin. He understood the old coot's animosity, more so now that he was standing on the property, but that didn't matter. SC Industries wanted the property and the promise of a 25 percent commission on top of his flat fee—and, by God, they were going to get it.

Even if he had to stay up there all day, mentally sketching out the floor plan of the house the company would build for him. Besides, SC Industries owed him that much, if not more. Since signing on as the "Executive Senior Manager of Advertisement and Acquisitions," a fancy title and fancier paycheck for what amounted to driving around town and the outlying areas and bullying people into giving up their land for far less than it was worth, he'd been responsible for seven of the ten most recent Sun Country Homes "Family Oriented Communities—Starting in the low $300s."

Reynolds tossed the last stone from one hand to the other as he backed away from the edge. A crested jay squawked at him from the branches of a scrub pine.

"You're right," he told the bird, "it does need a wraparound porch with a little dining alcove in that corner. What do you think?"

The jay cocked its head to one side.

"No? Well, how about a Jacuzzi?"

The bird ruffled its feathers and pooped.

So much for asking a bird's opinion, he thought as the electronic version of "The Entrance of the Toreadors," from Bizet's *Carmen*, began playing from the inside breast pocket of his Sun Country Homes bright blue blazer.

"Excuse me a moment." He nodded to the bird and flipped open the phone to check the caller ID. Instead he found a message waiting for him. The caller was much too busy a man to spend any of his precious time talking to an employee—regardless of how much profit that employee generated.

IMPERATIVE PROPERTY #3-475/SE/B ACQUIRED ASAP. PROPOSED TECHNO CENTER CONFIRMED, BUILDING ON SITE MUST COMMENCE BEGINNING OF NEXT MONTH. INCREASE OFFER TO $1100 PER ACRE. TAKE WHATEVER STEPS NECESSARY AFTER THAT. —J. MACKAY

$1,100 per acre . . . that was about twice as much as he'd ever been permitted to offer. The Great and

Powerful Mackay, Wizard of SC Industries, must be planning on building mansions for the upper-upwardly-mobile technology geeks who'd soon be pouring into town.

"A wraparound porch with a Jacuzzi *and* dining alcove," Reynolds said with a bit of regret as he flipped the cell phone shut and tucked it back into the blazer's pocket. Time was suddenly money again, and that was what he regretted.

His mother had always tried to teach him that patience was a virtue, and God knows he'd had more than enough practice in the art of waiting. It seemed he'd been waiting for one thing or another for most of his forty-three years on the planet.

He could wait, no sweat, but the Company couldn't.

Running a thumb over the rock, Reynolds studied the cabin that looked like something left over from a low-budget remake of *Deliverance*. There was evidence of the bowed roof having been recently patched with mismatched materials ranging from tar paper to plastic sheeting to the occasional wooden split. The heavily creosoted walls were lopsided and weathered to the shade of a month-old corpse. The porch looked well cared for, but the three steps leading up to it had been worn smooth.

All it needed was a mental defective sitting in a hand-made willow rocker, strumming a banjo.

The two-car garage Reynolds was already envisioning on that same spot would look much better.

"Yes, indeed," he said, more to himself than the eavesdropping jay, and threw the last rock.

A gust of wind came up at the last moment and ruined his shot. The rock hit the side of the cabin with a dull thud, shaking off only a small cloud of dust that the wind swept away.

He'd hope to hit the window, but his disappointment was short-lived when he saw a flicker of movement that solidified into a shape behind the wavy glass. The shape stared out at him, and he waved back.

"Morning," Reynolds shouted, dusting off his hands as he walked toward the Company car, a metallic-blue Mercedes SUV. The wind changed directions again, swirling the dust up into his face.

Damn! He hadn't noticed the wind the couple of times he'd been up on the ridge—quietly and on foot, and wholly unauthorized—but he was sure as hell noticing it now. Reynolds stopped when he got to the four-by and watched a tiny dust devil raise havoc through a patch of weeds. There went his plans for an exposed-to-the-elements Jacuzzi, especially after he cut down the natural windbreak. He'd have to rethink the floor plans a bit more.

But he kept the smile on his face and an easy slope to his shoulder while he opened the driver's-side door and reached inside. The Sun Country Homes briefcase was a modern, imitation-alligator equivalent of a Bedouin's tent, filled with everything that he might possibly need in order to fulfill his mission: contracts, in triplicate, a block of cashier's checks issued from Richland First National, a receipt book, a dozen logo pens and calendars, a half-dozen airline-size bottles of Johnny Walker Red Label to be used as either a means to an end or to celebrate the success of that end, and a chrome-platted .22 automatic. Unregistered and untraceable.

Just in case.

He'd never had occasion to use it, hadn't even bothered taking it out of the case, but his gut was telling him it might be wise to have it handy this time.

Just in case.

The little gun felt cold in his hand and surreal when he slipped it into the side pocket of his blazer. Better safe than sorry.

The wind changed directions again, buffeting the vehicle from the passenger side. The gusts were stronger, shaking the high profile four-by-four like it was a leaf. *Shit, if the wind gets this bad I'll have to go with a ranch style—single story and double-pane glass all around.* Reynolds didn't like the idea, he'd wanted a two-story mediterranean or ski-lodge alpine, but if the wind was this bad, he had no choice but to be practical. And that probably extended to the view, as well. *Have to leave more trees standing, dammit . . . can't take the chance of a whole tract of asphalt singles getting ripped o—*

The sharp tap of a rifle barrel—large bore, .30-.30, clean, well cared for, not a speck of dust—against the windshield instantly directed his attention, and body, toward the open door. *Move, get out, run . . .* all good ideas if he'd heard the man sneaking up on him and had the time to plan his escape.

It was the damned wind. If it hadn't changed direction, he would have heard the footsteps sneaking up on him.

Sch-lock!

The wind shifted again, and this time there was no mistaking the sound of a bolt action sliding home.

Reynolds's funny bone collided with the edge of the steering wheel when the instinct for self-preservation jerked him backward out of the car.

"Jesus! Shit!"

"Ah'm sure he did," a ragged voice answered, and Reynolds followed the sound back to its source. If the numbing-aching-throbbing pain in his arm hadn't hurt so much, he might have laughed. Instead, he rubbed his elbow and looked through the driver's-side window at the gnarly wisp of a man standing there, holding a bolt-action rifle that was almost bigger than he was.

It was the rifle that held Reynolds's attention.

"But," the old man continued, a big smile working its way across the white stubble field on his cheeks, "yah can bet it didn't stink."

It took Reynolds a moment to put the two comments together, but that didn't stop him from laughing first.

"Right," he said, stepping around the door to offer his hand. The old man didn't move anything but the direction the rifle was aiming—straight at the embroidered SUN COUNTRY HOMES logo on his blazer. "Mr. Berlander, I presume?"

The grin on the old man's face didn't move an inch. And neither did the rifle.

Reynolds kept his hand outstretched for another second, out of professional courtesy, before lowering it slowly toward his pocket. Playing stop and go, inch by inch, until his fingers reached the business-card holder . . . next to the little gun. He was suddenly very glad he'd listened to his gut after all. The old man might look as insubstantial as cottonwood fluff, like all it would take was one good gust of wind to knock him on his ass, but that rifle . . .

Reynolds felt his well-practiced grin wobble just a bit.

The wind had stopped as suddenly as it sprang up. *Strange weather up here.*

"Sumthing the matter, boy?" the old man asked. His smile hadn't faded a degree. "Yah suddenly looked a bit peaky. Might be the altitude, yah know . . . some lowlanders don't take t'it. 'Specially if they got puny innards."

Reynolds laughed with the man at his own expense—*patience, Sammy . . . that's Mama's good boy*—and held out one of his business cards. It, like the offered handshake, was ignored.

"I'm Sam Reynolds, Mr. Berlander, from Sun Country Homes. And I'm here to make you an offer on your property."

The old man cradled the rifle up to his chest like a beloved child and leaned back against the Mercedes. The handle of the sheath knife hanging from his belt left what Reynolds hoped was just a smudge in the paint.

"Ah, well . . . as you may or may not already know," Reynolds continued when the old man, though not enthusiastic, hadn't walked away, "Sun Country Homes is one of the largest growing residential construction firms in Richland, offering top-quality homes at affordable prices. In fact," he stepped away from the car and out into the open—a perfect target, "the Prairie View development directly below us is a fine example of the types of communities Sun Country Homes is committed to create. Which is the reason behind my visit today, Mr. Berlander. My company is looking to expand this particular community, and since we can't very well build out onto the highway, that would really create problems at rush hour"—*hah, hah, what a knee-slapper*—"I'm here to offer you a very lucrative amount for your land, Mr. Berlander."

The pitch was so second nature that Reynolds never bothered to listen to himself anymore. This point, for instance, was where he raised his hands to prevent any comment from the client-to-be.

"I know," he said, raising his hands, "you're asking yourself what the hell. Why did this man come all the way up here to talk about buying my land? I don't want to sell my land. I never even thought about selling my land. Well, let me just suggest that you think about it right now, Mr. Berlander . . . because, my company has authorized me to offer you nine hundred dollars per acre."

Reynolds folded his arms over his chest, saving the real offer for if and when it was needed. His mama had taught him patience, but his daddy taught him never to lay down his cards until he was sure the other man wasn't bluffing.

The old man nodded, which was a good sign.

"Nine hundred an acre," he said, tilting the rifle so he could sand the muzzle with his chin. "What would Ah do with all that money?"

"Travel," Reynolds suggested, because that was what the board of business psychologists hired by the company had decided most people would do if they suddenly became wealthy. "See the world . . . then find the place where you've always wanted to live and settle down."

The muzzle tapped against his chin. "That'd be right here. Lived here all my adult life and wouldn't want t'live nowhere else."

Reynolds huffed the air out of his lungs slowly, but it was an act, pure and simple. He'd heard the same thing before, dozens of times. It was the patterned response of the old and unimaginative.

"Yah know how much land Ah got?"

Reynolds knew exactly, but shook his head, playing his cards as he shrugged and nonchalantly slid his hand into the pocket of his coat. The little gun was warmer against his skin now.

"I can't recall offhand," he said, nodding his head at the briefcase on the passenger's seat, "but I know it's written down on the contract, if you'd like me to check."

"No need." The old man tilted the rifle barrel and sanded the muzzle with his chin. "Ah know . . . all of it. All this ridge 'n' the next, right up into the high country. That's almost three hundred acres. Yah think yer company'll pay out that much?"

Reynolds started to laugh, closing his hand over the gun to keep it from jiggling.

"Say sumthing funny, did Ah?"

The wind came up again, fluttering the old man's clothes around his thin frame like he was nothing but a scarecrow standing out in some long-forgotten field. Reynolds laughed harder.

Until the muzzle swung in on him.

"Sorry," he said, wiping the tears and windblown grit from his eyes. "No offense, Mr. Berlander, it's just that . . . well, your name appears on a deed for about two hundred and twenty-two acres, one hundred and twelve of which were appropriated by the United States Bureau back in . . . '88 or '89, I'm not sure. Excuse me a moment, will you?"

This time Reynolds didn't bother with formalities—real or staged—as he reached into the Mercedes and snapped open the case. The Berlander file was right in front, exactly where he had put it that morning before leaving the office.

"Let's see . . ." Stopping at the edge of the open door, just in case he had to suddenly duck behind it for cover, Reynolds opened the file to the first page and pretended to search for the information already underlined in yellow highlighter. "Yeah, okay, here's the problem. The Land Appropriations Act notified you about annexing the aforementioned acres for a firebreak and access road back in '88, but didn't actually put a lien on it until '89, and then acquired it by default in '90."

He looked at the old man as he turned the page.

"That left you one hundred and ten acres, Mr. Berlander, which you never paid taxes on. Sun Country Homes acquired eighty-seven of those for back taxes and built the Prairie View development." He closed the folder. "That leaves you only twenty-three acres, Mr. Berlander, and only three do you have any claim to at all."

The old man ran the tip of his tongue back and forth over his lips as he listened. The wind was picking up again; Reynolds could feel it rush past his legs.

"And, um . . . and that's only because you have buildings on them. It's called squatters' rights, but I doubt that any court in Richland would uphold them against my company's claim. However, Sun Country Homes doesn't want to see anyone thrown out into the cold, so the offer is still good: nine hundred dollars for the entire twenty-three acres. That's over twenty-thousand dollars, Mr. Berlander. You can get yourself a nice little apartment in one of those retirement communities and still have some left over to enjoy your remaining years."

The rifle shifted in the old man's hands, and Reynolds felt the muscles in his groin twitch.

"Ah heard this before, son," he said, "but it sure as hell sounds like it's all new t'yah."

"Pardon?"

The wind was stronger, kicking up a layer of dust that crawled across the hardpack yard like a snake.

"Last time yer company's offer was a thousand an acre. Looks like somebody's been playin' yah for a fool, boy. But Ah ain't no fool, so why don't yah just crawl on back into that fancy company car and haul yer ass off mah land before something bad happens t'yah."

Reynolds closed the file and leaned back against the door frame. "Was that a threat, Mr. Berlander?"

"Nope," the old man said, "a promise."

And before Reynolds could move or return the threat, the wind hit the door and slammed it back into him. The gun left a dimple in the side molding, and his spine left a much bigger crease when the wind wrenched the folder out of his hands and scattered the loose pages out over the valley.

Reynolds could feel the air being sucked out of his lungs as he tried to shield his face as best he could from the swirling, stinging debris, but it didn't do any good. A fragment of stone sliced open his forehead from the middle of his left eyebrow straight up into his hairline.

"Shit!"

Another stone, this one the size of a hen's egg, smashed into his forearm.

"FUCK!"

Okay—forget the Jacuzzi, forget the dining alcove . . . forget the whole damn house! I'm not going to live in a fucking wind tunnel!

A hail of gravel rained down over him.

"YOU STILL THINK THIS AIN'T MAH LAND, BOY? THIS IS"—the wind stopped, just stopped, and Reynolds felt his ears pop from the change in pressure—"mah land, and it always will be. Ah told yah once t'get off, and yah saw what happened. Now, Ah'm tellin' yah for the last time, get off mah land before Ah—"

The sound of a car engine struggling up the steep access road filled the suddenly still air.

"Aw, hell," the old man said as he shouldered the rifle and started walking back toward the cabin, "just when we were about t'have more fun."

Reynolds recognized the green Geo Tracker a split second before he saw the look on the driver's face.

"Shit."

CHAPTER 5

"Sam?"

Sky's first thought when she saw the man standing next to her grandfather was that he *looked* enough like Sam to be his twin. She knew, of course, it couldn't be Sam, because he was in Hawaii. Even the car was wrong: Sam drove a year-old fire-engine-red Toyota truck, not a Mercedes.

She knew it wasn't him, couldn't be him, until he looked up and she noticed, in rapid succession—

"Sam, what are you doing here?"

—the blood on his face—

"Oh, my God, what happened?"

—and the gun in the old man's hands—

"Grandfather, what have you done?"

—and heard his voice—

"Grandfather?"

—and finally noticed that the emblem on his

bright blue coat, the one she'd never seen him wear before, was identical to the logo on the Mercedes's door. The same logo she'd seen on billboards and banners springing up like jimsonweed all over town.

SC Industries—Your Hometown Developers.

If you were white and upper middle class.

Sam had never told her whom he worked for, and she, goddamned idiot that she was, didn't ask. Why would she? He was kind and gentle and had just made dinner for her the night before . . . just left her bed and left a note and that's all—she never even bothered to ask him where he worked.

Or for whom.

"Sky, I can explain."

"How can you?" she asked. "You're in Hawaii."

"Sky."

Sky didn't look at him again, but could feel his— and her grandfather's—eyes on her as he walked around to the back of the Tracker. The metal pull was already hot against her fingers as she unzipped the back plastic window, and she could feel the heat radiating off the canned goods she'd brought. Or maybe it was just her, maybe she'd come down with some rare tropical (*Hawaiian*) disease. God knows, she could feel her cheeks burning as she pulled the box toward her.

"Here, let me get that."

The words were moving so quickly in her head that they never made it to her lips. She didn't say a thing when he bent down to take the box from her.

"Look, honey, I can explain."

Honey? Sky felt the muscles tighten across her shoulders.

"Didn't know yah two knew each other."

Sky looked over at the old man and saw him smiling at her like she was a prize lamb about to be led off to the slaughter pen. He'd tossed the rifle up over one shoulder and was scratching his chin against the back of one hand as he walked toward the cabin.

"And Ah can't say much about yer taste . . . company man. That breed'll do yah more'n some mischief, yah mark mah words. As for yer kind offer . . . like Ah said, land ain't for sale. None of it."

Sky could almost hear the bones in Sam's neck grind against one another as he looked from her to the old man, back to her—

"I'll . . . I'll explain everything."

—before finally settling on the old man. The cans clunked hollowly against one another as Sam hurried across the yard, his long strides eating up the distance that separated him from his prospective client. Sky closed the tailgate and did her best to ignore him . . . ignore both of them.

"Look, Mr. Berlander, we got off to a bad start and I apologize for anything I may have said to upset you. So what do you say we go inside and just sit down and talk about—"

Sky gasped, hands closing over her belly, when the old man suddenly spun around. The rifle was still on his shoulder, but the knuckles of the hand holding it had gone white. *God, Sam*, she prayed, *don't push him.*

"Ain't nothing more t'talk about, boy," her grandfather said, still smiling, still outwardly calm, "and Ah don't go around invitin' vermin into mah home on purpose."

Sky watched Sam's back straighten even as he was

chuckling over the stupid box of canned chili and beans and condensed milk.

"I'm not that easy to get rid of, Mr. Berlander," Sam said, and Sky felt all the heat drain out of her body. It was the same thing he'd said to her the first time they'd me.

"I'm not that easy to get rid of, Sky . . . especially when I see something I want."

"Especially when I see something I want," Sam continued. "And what I want is to make you the best deal on this land that I can. What do you say?"

The old man took a deep breath and looked right at her.

"What do Ah say? Well, how 'bout . . . yah stop tryin' to screw me and do that t'mah granddaughter. Don't suspect it'll be the first time. Now, if yah'll both excuse me, ah need t'take a walk."

Sky watched Sam watch her grandfather amble off toward the narrow path leading to the woods north of the cabin. He stopped just inside the first layer of shadows.

"Oh, and yah can just set that box on the porch, if yah will. She won't take 'em back, even though ah keep tellin' her ah don't need or want any of that stuff." He started laughing as he turned and disappeared behind the thick screen of pine and scrub. "'Course, yah may just want t'talk t'her . . . likely enough one of those cans'll poison me one of these days and then she'll own this land . . . *all* this land . . . all of it. . . ."

His voice got fainter and fainter until it was finally swallowed by the trees and shadows. The wind shifted after Sam set the box down on the porch, and carried the sound of his steps to her long before his shadow slithered across the ground in front of her.

Sky climbed back into the car before it could touch her.

"Sky, wait." His hands settled over the door frame, holding it open. "We have to talk."

She shook her head and started the engine, willing herself to shift into reverse and drive off. But she only clutched the steering wheel instead. *Coward.*

"Okay, how about we start off with you answering a question," she said. "Were you fucking me to get to my grandfather's land, or were you hoping I'd offer to help your company steal it? Oh, sorry . . ." Sky met his eyes. "That was two questions, wasn't it?"

"Sky, you have to believe me, but I didn't make the connection when I saw his name on the file." Tiny wrinkles appeared in the narrow gulf between his brows. "I swear to you, honey, I wouldn't have taken this assignment if I'd known he was your grandfather. . . . You have to admit you don't look anything like him."

The joke fell dead.

"But seriously, there's not any mention of any living relatives in his . . ." He'd gone too far and finally realized it. "I'm sorry, Sky, I didn't know."

Half of her wanted to accept his apology . . . doubtless the white half.

"You're hurt," she said without moving her hands from the wheel. "Did he do that?"

Sam's smile bristled up his mustache as he gingerly touched the caked blood on his temple.

"No," he chuckled, making light of it even though she saw him twitch in pain, "got nailed by a flying rock."

"What?"

"A sudden dust storm blew in." Sam lowered his hand toward her cheek, brushed it gently with fingers that smelled like brand-new copper pennies. "You get some pretty strong winds up here, don't you?"

Sky moved away from his touch. "You got lucky, Sam," she said. "He was only playing with you this time, but if you come up here again . . ."

"*When* I come up here again, it will be with the sheriff and maybe a couple of lawyers and tax accountants to explain a little reality to your grandfather. Sky, the only land he has any claim to is what that puny cabin is sitting on . . . and maybe—just maybe the access road, which is the only reason I'm here at all. Although I didn't tell him that and . . . and I'd rather you not mention that part to him either."

She leaned her head back against the seat and closed her eyes. "Why would I?"

His soft laugh, the one she loved—past tense—to hear sounded so different out in the bright morning sunlight, up on her grandfather's ridge.

"That's my girl. You know you can help me."

"How?"

"By helping me convince your grandfather to sell what little land he has. Sun Country Homes is offering him a small mint for what doesn't really belong to him."

Sky opened her eyes slowly.

"The truth is, Sky, that my company already owns everything from this ridge to the valley floor, with the exception of the twenty-odd acres your grandfather may, or may *not*, hold squatters' rights to. We're talking twenty lousy acres of what is mostly steep grades and scree patches—that can, with time and money, be made into usable building sites. Help me convince your grandfather, Sky, and you'll have enough money to move out of that low-rent apartment and—"

He'd gone too far again, but this time he hadn't caught himself in time.

"Aw, shit, Sam." Sky dropped one hand to the gearshift. "I have to go. . . . I—I'm going to be late."

"Sky, listen to me." His hand settled on her shoulder. "Look, I'm sorry . . . I shouldn't have said that, but I'm a little off balance. I'm not used to having someone pull a gun on me when all I'm trying to do is my job."

"Funny," she said, "I thought you said your job was in advertising. Is this a promotion or demotion?"

"I'm sorry for that, too, but I know how your people feel about realtors."

"My people. Which people is that, Sam? If you're talking about my white side, you just found out how my white grandfather feels about the whole real-estate game . . . and as far as my *other* people, they've had generations of experience dealing with land developers. *For as long as the grass grows and the water flows* . . . and the wind blows."

He moved his hand before she had a chance to shake it off.

"I keep putting my foot in it, don't I?" He didn't try to laugh, and Sky silently thanked him for that small mercy. "I can be a real asshole sometimes, Sky, which I'm more than sure you've noticed in the last few moments. But you know I didn't mean it. If you can, would you forget everything I've said up to this point, including that idiotic request for you to help me? I mean that. I know this might come off sounding a bit hard, but from the little I saw of your grandfather today, I'm not convinced he wouldn't hurt you—and hurt you very badly if you tried to get involved in this.

"I'm serious, Sky."

"I know."

The wind teased a strand of hair into her eyes as she shifted the Tracker into reverse. She could have ignored it all the way back to town if she had to, but Sam reached up and gently tucked the stray hairs behind her ear.

"Can I call you later?" he asked.

No. Yes. Maybe. I don't know. "No, I don't think so. Not tonight, maybe . . . No, not tonight."

Sky let out the clutch and felt the Tracker shimmy into a reverse spin that ended on a relatively level spot less than a yard from her mother's grave. If her grandfather had seen that there would have been hell to pay, but Sky didn't plan on staying on the sacred patch of ground any longer than she had to.

Sam walked directly in front of the Tracker as Sky power-shifted into drive.

"Get out of the way, Sam," she said, feeling the vehicle shudder. The wind was blowing in from the north.

He moved, but toward her window instead of away.

"Sky, please, we have to talk. I need to explain

about all this." His hands brushed the front of the bright blue blazer.

"*Blue as the bright Arizona sky—You can trust the men and women in blue to bring you home . . . Sun Country Homes.*" She must have heard that advertisement at least a couple dozen times a day—more on weekends when she and Sam would go out on long drives through the desert—but she'd never noticed just how *blue* those damned blazers were.

"Did you write it," she asked, "the 'blue as the bright Arizona sky' ad? Or are you even involved in advertising at all?"

His face looked paler than she remembered it, or maybe it was just the drying blood that made the contrast more noticeable. He pulled a pair of sunglasses out of his pocket before he answered, and Sky wondered if he knew the old legend about being able to see the truth in a man's eyes.

If he didn't, he got lucky. The only thing she saw was her own frightened reflection.

"I have a degree in communications and marketing," he said, which may or may nor have been the truth, she suddenly didn't care, "but so do a lot of people. But a lot of people can't close deals like I do, and that's all I'm doing up here. There's nothing wrong with that, is there?"

"No, there isn't," Sky agreed, "so why didn't you tell me in the first place?"

When he didn't answer, she eased her foot off the clutch and let the Tracker ease forward.

"He'll stay away as long as you're here, so you might as well leave." Sky desperately wanted to snatch her own sunglasses off the passenger seat and put them on, but she wanted him to see her eyes and know she was telling the truth. "Don't come back, Sam. He's never going to sell this land."

He smiled, and the dried blood cracked around the laugh lines. "Well, you'd be surprised how many people have told me the exact same thing and are now living the good life in Florida thanks to my company."

My company. Sun Country Homes. She'd have to remember that.

The wind crawled in through the open back window. Sky could hear it behind her, rustling softly through her class folders. She pulled her sweater tighter over her chest.

"I'm serious, Sam—if you come back here, he'll kill you."

His smile widened into a laugh. "Sky, I appreciate your concern, but the next time I come up here, I won't be alone. My company doesn't want to take this land—we've offered him a fair amount." He leaned down, elbows against the window edge. Sky could see the frown above the rim of the sunglasses when she angled away. "Nine hundred dollars an acre for twenty-three acres, but my company's willing to do eleven hundred an acre if we have to . . . and it looks like we're going to have to. But that's it, Sky, and you can tell him that. He'll take it or he'll lose it all.

"Tell me, you think you'll be able to support the two of you on a teacher's salary?"

He tapped the side of the door as he stood up and backed away. "Tell him, Sky. Try to convince him this is the twenty-first century and man cannot live on the charity of his granddaughter alone. I'll call you tonight."

Sky glanced over his shoulder as she eased the car down onto the road. Twilight-colored clouds were gathering along the northern edge of the ridgeline.

"You'd better leave," she called through the open window. "There's a storm coming, and you don't want to be up here when it breaks."

He waved to show he'd heard, then turned and started back toward the Mercedes. Sky alternated between watching the road and casting glances in the rearview mirror. She was halfway through the first bend, looking in the mirror instead of the road, when the wind gored the Tracker's side like an invisible bull.

The car slid sideways into a patch of buckthorn, the bare branches scraping paint and leaving a scratch in the vinyl side window. Sky cranked the car hard to the right and found herself aiming at a thirty-foot drop. She hit the brakes just as the wind changed direction.

Standing on the brake, hand clutching the wheel, Sky felt the wind nudge the car closer to the edge.

"Stop it."

Sky shifted into reverse and eased up on the brake, and the wind continued to push the car forward as easily as if it were a toy.

"I SAID STOP IT!"

The wind died.

For a moment, Sky was afraid to move or even breathe.

"That wasn't funny, old man. I didn't have anything to do with him being here. I didn't even know he worked for them."

A twig hit the hood.

Taking a deep breath, Sky slowly maneuvered the Tracker back into the middle of the road and stopped. Nothing moved—not the trees, not a blade of rabbit grass . . . nothing. It was as if the world were holding its breath. Waiting.

Or the old man had found someone else to play with.

"Get out of here, Sam," she whispered, but didn't stay around to find out if he'd taken her advice.

A storm was coming, and the last place she wanted to be when it hit was up on the ridge.

Sam walked over to the Mercedes and kicked the side panel hard enough to leave a size-13½ impression. Screw it. If the merry band of anal-retentive company auditors questioned the dent, he'd tell them the truth—that he got it on the job.

His mama had always told him to tell the truth, *whenever possible*, and given what he'd just learned, the truth would be a new concept in the hallowed, pressboard halls of SC Industries.

Sam thought about adding a cracked windshield to the bill and blame it on the freak windstorm, but decided against it as he reached into his pocket for his cell phone. There was such a thing as *too* much honesty. Especially on an expense account.

When the company's electronic receptionist asked if he'd like to speak to a real person, Sam punched in one code followed by a second. The second code was for Jennet Mackay's private office line.

"What?"

Sam felt the cut on his forehead begin to throb. Mackay had risen to the top of his pile of dog shit too quickly to grasp the concept of consideration for others. Except when there was money and/or contracts visible.

"It's Reynolds."

"Yeah. Did you have to give him the whole eleven hundred per, or were you able to Jew him down? Give me the number."

Sam could picture the man—dressed in the height of Arizona Chic: western-cut business suit and dress Wellington boots and hundred-dollar-an-hour "Executive" tan—plucking one of the Sun Country Homes promotional pens from its cut-glass pencil cup to hold, expectantly, above a neon-blue Sun Country Homes memo pad.

God, he hated blue. "Zero," he said.

"What?"

"Nil. Nothing. Goose egg." Sam reached up and slowly began picking the dried blood away from the scab. "Let me know if I'm going too fast for you."

"Have you been drinking?"

"No, but that's an excellent suggestion."

He pulled off a flake almost a half-inch long while he listened to the brief silence on the other end of the phone.

"Look, Reynolds, I hired you because you came highly recommended as a head-buster. If I'd wanted a comedian, I would have hired Jerry Seinfeld."

"At least he would have had a script to work from," Sam said, crushing the strip of dried blood—*his fucking blood*—between thumb and forefinger.

"The old man's not buying it . . . excuse me, he's not selling it."

"I see." Mackay took a deep breath and exhaled. When the rushing air passed, Sam could hear a faint *ping, ping, ping* competing with the background static—the sound of cheap No. 2 (bright blue) wooden pencils striking cut glass. "And he's still breathing?"

"His granddaughter showed up unexpectedly."

"Well, I suppose that ruined your best-laid plan, didn't it?"

Sam walked around to the front of the Mercedes and took a deep breath as he looked down at the wind-dusted hood. He'd been so goddamned careful . . . learning everything he could about her and the old man before "accidentally" running into her at that damned convenience store. Thank God she was a bit on the clumsy side, or he would have had to resort to the old "I'm sorry, did we meet before?" pickup line.

And that would have been all she wrote.

Sky might be a little naive, but she wasn't stupid. He could still see the look in her eyes when she saw that damned blue blazer. And where the hell did he come up with "*I know how your people feel about realtors*" shit.

All of that was going to make getting back in her good graces difficult, if not impossible.

She'd been his backup plan from the start—his ace in the hole, in more ways than just the "any port in a storm" sense, even though he hadn't originally planned on her becoming his exclusive lover.

The "best-laid plan" was to keep her in reserve

when—not if—the old man turned down this final offer.

Taking the land for back taxes had never really been an option. "Pioneer Ridge," as the newest development of "Personalized Executive Mansions" was already being called, was scheduled to begin ground preparation in six weeks; with the first happy, wealthy, techno-geek families moving in three months later.

A court case now would draw unwelcome notice from the media and shine a very bright light on the fact that Jennet Mackay didn't quite own the land he already had half sold.

Including the lot Sam had picked out for himself.

The wind slapped against his back. Sky was right—a storm was coming.

Dammit, why didn't she just sleep in? She should have been tired out from the workout I gave her.

Best-laid plans. Sky was supposed to stay on the sidelines until she got the call from the sheriff that her granddaddy had died of natural causes. Natural causes never involved police investigations and were surprisingly easy to re-create if one was careful, and, up until just a few minutes ago, Sam had considered himself one of the most careful men on the planet. Best-laid plans notwithstanding.

He knew he'd be the first person she'd call after getting the news—who else would she call but her lover?—and he'd drive right over to hold and comfort her while she cried, and give her his expert advice on what she should do now.

"Listen, baby, I know what you're feeling—I lost my mother and father a while back and it's never easy . . .

even when you know there was nothing you could have done to prevent it. Your grandfather was an old man, and I'm sure he died peacefully—you have to try to remember that. Now, I know you're a big girl and completely capable of handling all this on your own, but if you'd let me I'd like to help you put his affairs in order—you know, sell his house, whatever property he had, that sort of thing—so you won't have to deal with it. Then, who knows, maybe we'll take a trip to get our minds off the past and onto the future. What do you say?"

It was such a good speech, and he was sorry he'd never get a chance to use it.

"Did you hear what I just told you?"

Sam blinked hard behind the dark glasses and felt a twinge of pain up near his scalp. Damn cut would probably need stitches.

"Sorry, no," he said.

Mackay sounded a little less congenial after that, if that was possible.

"I said to get your ass back here a-sap. I think you've sabotaged the project enough for one morning, don't you?"

He hung up before Sam had a chance to argue the point.

The wind pinged a pebble off the Mercedes's left headlight as he pocketed the cell phone. The pebble didn't leave so much as a dirty speck on the halogen, so Sam helped it out with a side kick.

Acceptable damage, considering the terrain.

Gideon stepped out of the trees and watched the big car's taillights flash once before disappearing behind the cluster of raspberry vines he'd let go wild after

Sky ran away. There didn't seem much point in keeping the vines up on trellises after that, since she was the only one who ever ate the damned berries. He'd never developed a taste for the tart, seedy fruit, although he had loved watching her pick them when she was little—three in her mouth and two down the front for every one that reached the bucket.

But that little girl was gone, and the woman she'd become had sided with his enemy.

"Pretendin' like yah didn't know him ain't gonna save yah, gal. Yah fight me and yer gonna wish yah'd never been born.

"Same as me."

Lifting the small whistle to his lips once more, Gideon filled his lungs and let the wind carry the message down into the valley.

CHAPTER 6

The first seizure was nothing more than a mild flutter just above his belly button.

The second and third seizures came one on top of the other and were stronger, the flutter becoming a pain that radiated outward like an explosion and shook the spoonful of pinto beans from his hand.

The clatter of his spoon hitting his plate brought a momentary silence to the table.

"Dad?"

Joseph looked at his son as he dabbed splattered beans off the front of his shirt. "I'm fine. It was just a cramp in my hand. Sometimes when it's cold, old muscles don't work as well as they did."

"Are you cold, Father?"

"I got a cramp in my leg when Joey was chasing me the other day, and he wouldn't stop even after I told him."

"Tattletale," his older brother hissed.

"Well, you didn't."

"Baby."

"Am not!"

"Stop it, you two."

Joseph smiled at the sounds of fraternal bickering and their mother's attempt to quench it—they were the sounds of normal life and helped take his mind off the pain that was devouring his insides.

"Are too!"

"I said *hush*, both of you," their mother said over a single clap of her hands, making certain they'd heard her before turning her attention on him. "Are you cold, Father? Can I get you a sweater?"

Six months pregnant with her third child—a girl this time, she was sure of it—Joseph's daughter-in-law was already half out of her chair. Seated next to her, at the head of the table, his son Daniel tore off a wedge of white-corn tortilla and shook his head.

"Can you remember if she was this bad the last two times, Dad? Seems to me she's much more active this time around."

Estralita's eyes narrowed, making her look more Apache than Hopi. "I was talking to your father, not you."

"And she's much more belligerent this time," Daniel said, dredging up beans on the wedge of tortilla. "That must be the proof that this one's going to be a girl, huh? I wonder if the *National Enquirer* would be interested in the first-ever recorded case of infantile PMS."

Daniel wasn't fast enough to avoid his wife's small fist, much to the delight of their sons.

Joseph barely noticed. The pain was crawling up his spine like a living thing, feeding off the muscle and tissue of his body until it reached his neck and split in two. One branch of the pain slithered toward his left ear, the other toward his right, and when they met in the center of his brain the pain changed into a sound he had not heard in almost forty years.

High and shrill, the sound of the earth screaming.

"HELP!"

Joseph blinked and saw his son, cowering and still under attack.

"Uncle, dammit, uncle!"

"Daniel, mind your language!"

"Then stop hitting me," his son said. "Don't you know that Native American women are supposed to be subservient to their husbands?"

That got him a cuff to the back of the head. "In what century?"

"Dad! Help me, will you? Call off this wildcat!"

Joseph managed to smile as he retrieved his spoon from the plate and filled it with beans. He could continue the pretense only as long as he didn't actually eat anything. The thought of food right now made him sick.

"You only have yourself to blame, Daniel. A man should know better than to poke a stick into a beehive."

Estralita's glittering dark eyes shifted toward him.

"A beehive?"

"Full of honey, but protected by sharp stingers," Joseph said, trying to motion his giggling grandsons into silence.

"Boy, that's the truth," Daniel muttered, and the boys began giggling again.

They had no school that day and were determined to get as much enjoyment from every precious moment that they could. They hadn't even bothered to get out of their pajamas and slippers, and Joseph envied them more than just a bit. He had gotten up and dressed at the usual time, forgetting he wouldn't have to walk them to school . . . but now he had the feeling he might be walking somewhere else before the morning was gone.

Without thinking, he set the spoon down and kneaded his hands together.

The sudden silence that followed alerted him that they were all watching.

"I'll get you that sweater now, Father," Estralita said, and hurried away as quickly as her condition allowed, opening the oven door to give its trapped heat a better escape into the small kitchen.

"You kids eat up before everything gets cold," Daniel said, a familiar code to let the boys know the grown-ups were going to talk and they weren't. "So, Dad, what's up? 'Lita says you haven't been acting like yourself in the last couple of days."

Joseph waited until his daughter-in-law had come back into the room with the greased wool cardigan she'd knitted for him before answering.

"I see our little beehive has been busy." He smiled up at her as she helped him on with the sweater, a blush working into the premature lines beneath her eyes. "But it's nothing more than a foolish old man who doesn't think of the cold when he's out in it, telling stories. She has told me a hundred times a day, it seems, not to sit out in the cold, but I am an old man, and old men never think of the cold until the aches and pains begin, and then it's too late to do anything but suffer. There's nothing wrong, Little Star, except that I don't have your wisdom."

His daughter-in-law beamed at hearing his pet name for her and settled slowly back into her chair. The baby inside her belly turned, and she giggled.

"Your new little one is always hungry," Estralita said, taking a bite of a rolled tortilla. "You boys had better be careful—the way she's eating, she'll probably be able to beat both of you up before you know it."

The boys smiled, knowing that could never happen, but Daniel only shook his head in what looked to be amazement.

"Is there something wrong, Daniel?" Joseph asked.

"Only this," his son said, motioning to his wife. "Is that how you handle women? By telling them they're right?"

Estralita and his grandsons looked at Joseph.

"Of course," he said. "That's the *only* way, my son, and your sons should memorize that one rule right now. It might save them from having as many aches and pains when they're as old as I am."

His son nodded and tapped Joey, who was sitting closest to him, on the side of the head. Joey, in turn, elbowed his younger brother slightly harder than was necessary and was immediately scolded by their mother. The world, at least the part that was protected by the thick kitchen walls, was once again filled with the natural clatter of everyday life.

Joseph smiled, but listened to the sound that rode the wind beyond the adobe walls.

The spirit whistle sang its hollow song above the silence, and he trembled as it passed, covering the spot just above his belly with both hands. It was foolish, he knew, but he'd already confessed to being a foolish old man, so he closed his eyes and allowed his invisible self to reach for the sound.

Dizzy . . . lost . . . he rode the back of the wind and felt the world spin in on itself beneath him. But he didn't ride alone—another spirit rode next to him.

Gideon.

"Been a while since yah been here, ain't it?"

Joseph looked down from the wind's back and saw himself as he once was—years younger and on his knees, weeping in a secluded grove of aspens next to the mutilated body of his firstborn son, Daniel's older brother. It was spring, but the quaking leaves were bright red, blood red.

Gideon had torn his son apart.

"Ah had a right t'kill him. He stole mah Glory from me."

"He stole nothing from you."

"Dad?"

Joseph blinked and watched Daniel's face swim into focus. The kitchen looked smaller somehow.

"Grandfather, are you okay?"

His namesake was standing next to the sink, a load of dishes in his hands, his younger brother dawdling over the last inch of milk in his glass. *Is breakfast over?* Joseph looked down at the congealed beans and eggs on his plate and felt his stomach turn over.

"I'm . . . fine," he said, and didn't even convince himself.

"You sure, Dad?" Daniel asked. "You sort of spaced out, and then you mumbled something."

"It was just a story I hadn't thought of in a long while . . . about an old man who lost a son." Joseph shook his head when he noticed the gleam in his grandsons' eyes. "No, that is not a story for children. But perhaps I'll tell your father one day."

"Well, it'll have to be later, Dad," Daniel said, draining the last of his coffee as he stood. "You and the kids might have the day off, but I still have to get to work."

Joseph picked up his cup and held it close to his lips. His stomach was still too queasy to even think about taking a sip, but he found it calming somehow to savor only the deep brown scent and feel the warmth of the steam against his face. It felt so natural.

"Where do they have you today?" he asked, watching his son slip into his orange safety vest. Daniel was a crew chief for the Department of Highways, a job that made Joseph very proud of his son.

"Up near Third Mesa. Board finally got approval to pave the access roads out there. Should be worth a couple of weeks of work at least . . . and thank God it's still cool. I hate pouring blacktop in summer."

Third Mesa was north of them. The bile in Joseph's stomach churned.

"Be careful, Daniel," he said, "there's a storm coming."

"Yeah? Weather station said it was supposed to be cool and clear." Walking over to the window over the sink, Daniel leaned down and scanned the sky from horizon to horizon. "Looks okay to me. Just a few clouds over the ridge, but it doesn't look like they'll be moving this way anytime soon."

"Just be careful."

His son was smiling when he turned around. "Hey, I always am, you know that."

"I know." His brother had said the same thing about being careful, right before he went up to the ridge that last time. "But take a raincoat, just in case."

Daniel's smile swept into his round cheeks. "Okay, I'll take a raincoat. Just in case. Now, good-bye, see you tonight. And you two"—he pointed to Andrew and Joey—"behave and mind your mother . . . and don't wear out your grandfather."

A wave and hurried rush of good-byes and he was gone.

"All right, you heard your father," Estralita said, reclaiming control. "Joey, when you're finished with the dishes, I want you to get dressed. You're coming to the laundromat with me."

"Aw, Mom."

"And Andrew, I need you to get dressed and clean your room."

"It's *his* room, too."

"And this is *our* house, but I clean it. So you can do this one thing, can't you?"

"Yeah."

"Good. Now hurry up."

Joseph listened a while longer to the grumbling and mutters coming from his grandchildren before he was able to force down the now cold coffee and stand up. Andrew, despite being the more vocal of the two, immediately took the cup from his hand and carried it to the sink, where Joey washed it, wiped it, and put it away.

They were good boys, both of them.

The pain Joseph felt earlier returned, but this time it had encircled his heart.

He found Estralita in the adobe's main room, sorting laundry, by color, into three Army-surplus duffle bags. Her face was glistening with sweat, but offering to help would only fall on deaf ears.

"Can I speak to you for a moment, Little Star?"

Her smile eased the pain around Joseph's heart. "Of course, Father. Can I get you anything?"

"You can sit," he said, motioning her to the one spot on the couch not covered with laundry. "And put your feet up. You're keeping my granddaughter-to-be awake—let her rest a minute."

Estralita rolled her eyes as she maneuvered herself onto the couch, but sighed when she sat back. Besides the few random moments at the kitchen table, Joseph knew his daughter-in-law had been on her poor swollen feet most of the morning.

"It feels good to sit, doesn't it?" he asked.

"It feels lazy," she argued, but didn't move. "You are feeling all right, aren't you?"

"Fine. I am fine, Little Star. I just wanted to talk a moment."

Nodding, his daughter-in-law leaned back against the cushions and waited. And now that he had her full attention, Joseph didn't know where to begin.

So he told her a story.

"When I was a child, there was an old man—much older than I am now, I think—named Raymond Tewawina who spoke to animals and understood their words. It was accepted by all on the reservation that he could do this, and no one ever questioned his ability. Except one scrawny little boy who would one day grow up to be a foolish old man who doesn't know when to come in out of the cold."

Estralita giggled behind a cupped hand, understanding who he was referring to but not wanting to embarrass him with the knowledge.

"I didn't believe the old ways then, so one day I followed Raymond Tewawina into the hills just to see what would happen. And do you know what I saw, Little Star?"

She shook her head slowly from side to side, already caught up in the story—like the child she once was.

"I saw him sitting on a rock, in a canyon, talking to a coyote. I thought I'd lost him in the rocks and was about to turn around when I heard him singing. I'd never heard the song at any of the dances, but I followed it until I found him. He was singing to the coyote, and the coyote sang back to him. I hid among the rocks and listened. When they were finished singing, he spoke to the coyote, asking him about the rains to come and if the summer would be long or short—and the coyote answered him with yips and barks each time he stopped. That evening, Tewawina told the council that the summer would be short but the rains would come late. And they did.

"Do you believe that, Little Star? That a man may understand the language of an animal?"

"Yes."

"And do you believe that the Kachinas come down from the sky to dance with us?"

Estralita's eyes widened at the question. "Of course I do, Father."

"Why?"

"Because . . ." She shrugged. "I just know."

"Good," Joseph said, and felt the pain diminish, "I'm glad. This means there will be someone to tell the stories when I'm gone, and that makes me glad. As long as there is one person to keep the legends alive, our people will endure. Little Star, I think it's time that you and my son and my grandchildren leave the reservation."

"What? Why?"

"For a better life. Daniel can get a good job anywhere, and my grandsons . . . my grand*children* will be able to see places they've only read about."

"And so they can learn firsthand what the white world thinks of Native Americans?" There was a bitterness in her voice that Joseph had never heard before. "No. They can learn about that later, when they're adults—if they choose to leave the reservation."

Her voice softened again when she cradled her belly in her hands. "If they choose to leave. It's not easy here, Father, both Daniel and I know that . . . but this is our home, and this is where my children will hear the stories of our ancestors and be able to look out at the mountains and canyons and desert and see where those stories took place. This is our home, Father, our land."

This is mah land, Joseph. All of it.

The sentiment didn't sound any better coming from his daughter-in-law's lips.

"Of course," he said, "you're right."

"You know," Estralita said as she struggled back to her feet, "if you keep saying that, Daniel may just have to accept it."

"Then I'll make sure I keep saying it."

He left her laughing while she sorted laundry, and it was a good sound, one that Joseph struggled to keep with him while he put on his coat and hat and left the house. The wind was from the north—again from the mountains—and on its back rode the piercing cry of the spirit whistle. A dozen dogs howled at its passing and the dusty brown sparrows suddenly took to the air, flying south as fast as their wings could beat. Perhaps a few others on the reservation would sense something in the air, or tremble for a moment and nick their face as they shaved, or drop a plate or yell at a child for a minor thing . . . The sound made a man's soul itch, but the prickling went too deep to scratch.

Joseph had learned to live with the itch a long time ago.

He pulled the fleece collar up over his neck and nodded. "I hear you, little brother. I hear you."

Gideon slipped the whistle into his pocket, then wiped the bitter taste off his lips. Used to be a time when he liked the flavor of willow . . . 'course, that was around the same time when he could climb the switchbacks and forty-degree slopes without breaking a sweat. Or only just a small one.

Back when lowlanders knew their place and, more important, knew his.

Twenty, hell, ten years ago no man would have had the balls to talk to him like that company man. Sky's lover . . . shit, who would have thought she'd take up with something like that? Just goes to show she hadn't any more sense than her mama did.

Poor little Glory, she never even got a chance to learn from her mistake.

Her face suddenly came back to him, swirling into his mind all pale and still, her golden hair matted down with sweat.

Gideon ran his thumb down the pocket's stitching.

"It shoulda been slower," he whispered. "She died so fast, Ah shoulda killed him slower'n Ah did. Made him pay in hours for what he took from me . . . mah land, this is mah land, company man, and if Ah catch yah up on it again yer gonna pay for what yah did to mah Glory. Ah mean, Sky . . . no, Ah mean . . . Aw hell, Ah don't know what Ah mean."

The wind rustled the grass at his feet as he eased the rifle down off his shoulder and massage the depression it had left in his skin. Damn, it was depressing to get old. Back when he liked the taste of willow, he could have carried a wooden cross-beam across that same shoulder from sunup to sunset and still be able to dig a couple postholes before supper.

At least that was how he liked to remember it.

The truth might be a bit different, but he didn't think by much. He'd been a hell of a scrapper in his day; he had to be to turn his back on the society of his kind and take up a life on the ridge. It'd been a hard choice to make—the ground had been too steep and rocky to do more than plant out a couple of plots of vegetables and berries, couldn't keep a cow or chickens alive for more than a season most years— but he'd had no choice. If he'd done like his wife had wanted and stayed around people, he would have gone crazy.

Or killed more than just that one damned Indian rapist.

Damn, his shoulder hurt.

Leaning the rifle up against a tree, Gideon rotated his arm until pain and the grinding of joints told him he was doing more harm than good. If he was lucky, he'd still be able to use his arm the rest of the way to the spring. And he *had* to get to the spring. When he'd seen the company land man drive away, he'd acted like a peach-faced kid, blind drunk for the first time on his daddy's best sipping liquor—he'd taken off across the ridge, tootin' on that damned whistle like there was no tomorrow, neglecting to put the heavy rifle back over the mantelpiece where it belonged and to fetch a canteen.

The hike up to the sacred pool once had been nothing more than an hour's stroll up and back, with either a bandanna full of prickly roses or currants as a little peace offering for having been gone so long.

Gideon left the rifle against the tree and walked past a budding wild rose without stopping. There was no one he wanted to bring flowers to anymore, not now . . . not when he saw the way she looked at the man . . . Sky—acting like she didn't know him when all the time she'd been . . . she was . . .

"Goddamned half-breed . . . yer mama died givin' yah birth, and this is how yah treat the man who raised yah up and tried t'teach yah . . . tried t'show yah the . . . the . . ."

Wherever the thought was going got bumped from his brain when thunder rumbled overhead.

"Don't yah even think about it," he shouted.

The clouds answered, low and deep, not willing to let the threat go unanswered. Gideon could smell the rain on the wind's breath as a dusty brown quail burst from the brush directly in front of him, squawking and playing broken-wing to the front of his boots. The bird's sudden appearance had startled him, and that alone would have been enough reason to add her to the evening's stewing pot. One command— that's all it would take.

Gideon's hand was inching toward the whistle in his pocket when his lungs suddenly forgot how to breathe and required more than just a little effort to remind them what it felt like.

The little quail didn't notice; she kept right on playacting.

Although he didn't hear the following rolls of thunder or smell the sharp scent of burning insulation, Gideon watched the series of bright flashes drain the world of color. Had to be lightning ... couldn't be anything else.

The wind lapped at the sweat pouring down his face.

"What?"

It tugged at his coattails.

"What is it, dammit? Leave me 'lone."

The wind held him up while he made sure his lungs were back in working order. They were, and so was his belly. It emptied itself nice and easy all over the little bird. Gideon wiped his mouth as he straightened back up and nudged the bile-sodden pile of feathers with the tip of one boot.

"Damn."

He really hadn't meant to kill it.

And he sure as hell wasn't going to take it back with him now. Just the thought of it threatened to make him sick again. Although, if she'd been acting that hard to keep him away, that meant a clutch of eggs had to be close by.

Gideon found the nest just off the path, tucked into a small, leaf-lined, water-filled depression between two rocks. Four chicks, white-eyed and bloated, bobbed against one another.

His belly didn't much like the idea of scrambled chicks either.

"Sorry," he told the dead brood, and then told the hen the same thing, "Sorry," as he nudged her back into the brush. "Sometimes yer better off bein' dead."

The wind picked up a pinecone and dropped it in front of him, wanting to play. Gideon picked it up and threw it as hard as he could. It fell short of the granite outcrop he was aiming at and rolled harmlessly down into a small water canyon.

He didn't even hear an echo.

The wind dropped a second cone, and this time Gideon walked right by.

"Get on back t'the cabin. Ah need t'be alone right now."

The wind gusted, closing around him in a tight swirl of dead leaves. There were other things tucked into the whirlpool of leaves, harder things that left thin scratches on the sleeves of his coat.

"I SAID GET!"

He was reaching for the whistle when the dust devil slipped over the edge of the trail and spun itself out in a shower of debris.

Gideon didn't look back when he heard the unmistakable sound of a tree being uprooted, but he did quicken his pace as much as he was able.

He had to get to the spring before the wind decided to come back on its own. If he didn't, it wouldn't be long before the Old One figured out just how little control he still had over it.

CHAPTER 7

If the spring had ever had a name, it was forgotten long before the first storyteller sang its song, and there was still evidence that the Ancient Ones, the Anasazi, had known about the deep artesian pool and worshiped there.

When he was little, Gideon's hand had been a perfect match to the pale, ancient handprints outlined in red ocher. By the age of fifteen, his hand was twice the size of the ghost prints. The Ancient Ones had been such a small people to have been so feared.

And Gideon had feared. Once.

The first time he'd seen the spring after being told the story of the Ancient Ones, and the one who had first ridden the wind, Gideon had shivered with fear. Now he shivered from exhaustion.

It had taken him three more hours—walking, resting, resting, walking—to reach the lip of the natural basin and another twenty minutes to slip and slide down the narrow footpath to the water, and by then his strength was gone.

Crawling on hands and knees, Gideon panted out the song of blessing and plunged his face into the icy pool. The water had a slightly oily feel against his tongue and tasted a bit like a rusty nail wrapped in dead leaves. It was the best water he'd ever had in his life.

Always had been.

Always would be.

Gideon drank until his belly cramped and curled him into a tight ball on the ledge of stones that Joseph told him had been laid by Yaponcha himself. Of course, he hadn't believed Joseph then and he certainly didn't now, but whoever the mason had been—Kachina or man—he had Gideon's undying gratitude.

He was going to close his eyes only for a moment. Only a moment.

And when he opened them, the light was different, softer, the shadows were deeper, and the wind was searching for him. He could hear it, moaning above him.

Gideon ignored it.

"Hear me, Old One," he whispered, and saw the ghosts of his breath dance across the dark water. "Ah'm in need of yer help. They're tryin' t'take mah land . . . our land. Yaponcha . . . help me."

The sun continued to cross the sky, lengthening the shadows as Gideon waited for an answer. And waited. And waited.

* * *

Sam Reynolds popped three aspirins into his mouth and dry-swallowed them as he openly checked his wristwatch. 11:40—he'd been waiting two hours and thirty minutes, the last fifteen of which had been spent sitting in an uncomfortable chair and watching his employer, Jennet Mackay, verbally glad-hand a prospective investor over the phone.

"Hey, what can I tell you, Phil? This is an opportunity waiting to happen. Both the Grand Canyon and Flagstaff are within driving distance, and I just picked up some prime ridge land just north of town. . . . What? Oh yeah . . . hadn't thought of it, but we might just be able to put a couple of ski runs in. Once we clear the slopes, of course."

Jennet Mackay winked at Sam and lifted a finger in a *be right with you* motion. Sam downed another aspirin before closing the tin. His head ached like a son-of-a-bitch and the skin beneath the large adhesive-pad bandage itched, but neither compared to the pain in his ego.

Sam looked at his watch again. Two hours and thirty-*four* minutes.

Mackay ignored him, swiveling his leather executive chair toward the wall of smoked glass and the view of downtown Richland six stories below.

Sam had been impressed when he'd first walked into Mackay's office—with its museum-quality Native American art decor, inch-thick mahogany paneling, Navajo throw rugs over slabbed pink-marble flooring, recessed track lights, and that goddamned wall-to-wall, floor-to-ceiling window.

Of course, now that he knew the man he was working for, Sam was even more impressed.

And envious.

One day, Sam promised himself.

And then Jennet Mackay turned around and winked at him.

But not today.

"Okay, then, Phil," Mackay said into the hands-free headset, "see you soon. Right. And don't forget, you still owe me a dinner for setting you up on the Internet deal. What? Yeah, definitely. All right—talk to you later."

Mackay tapped a button on the headset and nodded to Sam to indicate that, for the next few moments until a more important call came in, he had the Great Man's full attention.

"So how much were we bilked out of?"

To prolong the inevitable, if only for another moment, Sam lifted his briefcase to his lap and snapped it open. Inside were four, and only four, bright blue Sun Country Homes file folders containing the signed and sealed transactions that would add another couple million smiles to the company stockholders. But only to the stockholders. Sam watched Mackay's eyes as the folders landed on the glass insert that covered the middle section of the rosewood desk. Beneath the glass was a grid map of Richland, Arizona, done in multiple colors—monkey-vomit green for current Sun Country Homes sites, bright yellow for future Sun Country Homes sites, pink for prospective Sun Country Homes sites, and gray for everything else. There was very little gray left on the map.

The side of Mackay's thumb began stroking the glass above a narrow sliver of pink near the directional north edge of the map as he leaned forward to study the names and property numbers on the cover of each folder. A casual observer might think the action nothing more than a random movement, but Sam knew better. Jennet Mackay hadn't become a thirty-eight-year-old real-estate wunderkind by doing anything at random.

"You seem to be missing one," Mackay said, looking up. His eyes matched the gray on the map and were just as inaccessible.

"Really?" Sam straightened in the chair and patted his coat. "Hmm, don't seem to have it."

Mackay's hand stretched out over the glass, and his fingers covered Richland's gray heart.

"I really don't think this is the time for levity, Reynolds, do you?"

Sam dropped his hands to the briefcase and snapped the lid shut.

"Forgive me for saying this, Mr. Mackay, but you're acting as if I came back empty-handed. SC Industries has just acquired another hundred thousand acres. I think that would be worth at least a grin."

"And instead, that isn't worth shit." Mackay's hand closed into a fist. "If I send a man out to close on five properties, I expect him to do it and not wander into my office with his tail planted firmly between his legs."

The throbbing pain in his head wasn't going away, despite the aspirin. If anything, it was getting worse the longer he sat there and stared at the self-made-millionaire land-baron prick.

"I hired you because you were supposed to be the best acquisition agent in four states. Generally, I don't make mistakes about people or land, but I guess there always has to be a first time . . . and you're it."

Mackay raised his hand when Sam started to stand up, then hit another button on his wireless headset.

"Sit down, Reynolds, and save the dramatics. Addie, hold my calls until further notice. I have a schedule to keep, and this negligence on your part is endangering that timetable. I believe you were simply to make an offer on this property as a gesture."

Mackay's cold gray eyes grew colder.

"*Only* as a gesture. I thought I made myself clear on that point."

"You did," Sam said, feeling the same tight-gut tremble he used to feel when he got called down to the vice principal's office in high school "for a little talk." "And I will close the deal the next time, but I still don't understand your attitude. The tract has a nice view and all, but it will take a hell of a lot of excavating before you can even think about planning out foundations . . . and you know that."

The left corner of Mackay's mouth twitched, but Sam couldn't tell if the direction was up or down. And he didn't really care, one way or the other. The man was only his employer, not God.

"So why is this particular piece of land so important to you?"

Mackay smiled.

"It's not any more important than any of these," he said, motioning to the four folders on the desk in front of him. "But I want it, as do at least five very wealthy and influential techno-wizards, and *that's* what makes it important. Does that answer your question, Mr. Reynolds?"

Sam thought it best only to nod, and this time it was the right answer.

"Very good. I'm glad I was able to enlighten you . . . so perhaps you can return the favor. I offered you a position in my company, Mr. Reynolds, after speaking with a number of your past employers. I must say you have a very impressive record, both professionally and on file with a number of police departments across the country."

The knot in Sam's gut twisted just a little tighter.

"Very impressive, indeed, Mr. Renyolds . . . up until today. You're a human bulldozer, so tell me, did you forget how to use force?"

Sam returned the briefcase to the carpet next to his chair, then folded his left leg over the right. Calm, cool, and collected—at least on the outside.

"No, but there were complications."

"Ah, so that explains the bandage. I guess the old man must be a lot stronger than he looks."

Sam smiled and felt the ragged edges of the wound scrape against the gauze pad. He could and had taken a lot over the years from many men—employers, police, and clients—but the mocking tone in Mackay's voice was almost enough to make him forget his professionalism.

And the lifestyle to which he'd become familiar.

"That old man couldn't go a round with his own shadow and come out the winner." It was a struggle, but Sam managed to keep the smile as natural as possible. "No, a freak windstorm kicked up some gravel and I got tapped."

"That was the complication?"

One punch, Sam thought. *No, not even . . . just a tap, that's all it would take to push Mackay's rhinoplasty-perfect nose right through the back of his less-than-perfect head.*

111

"No," he answered, still nice and natural, "his granddaughter showed up, and I know how you feel about witnesses."

"His granddaughter." Mackay's gray eyes lightened up. "I thought you'd already taken care of that problem."

"Almost," Sam said.

When Gideon opened his eyes again, the shadows were halfway across the water, creeping toward him like a thick mist. And Yaponcha still hadn't answered.

"What's the matter?" he asked as his eyes drifted shut. "Yah gettin' old, too?"

Sky had listened to three presentations on how to increase a child's self-esteem in the classroom, watched two videos dealing with aggressive behavior in children ages seven to twelve, taste-tested samples of six new cafeteria items, and voted on seven separate issues pertaining to the continued quality of education in her school.

And couldn't actually remember one detail of anything that happened after she left the ridgeline and pulled into the school's parking lot. She remembered shaking, and someone—it could have even been Dave Kershner, her beloved principal—asking if she was all right, that she looked worried.

Sick was more like it. She remembered that much, that she'd felt sick enough to have to excuse herself halfway through a panel discussion on "The Early Discussion of Head Lice," and run for the nearest bathroom, where she vomited for almost fifteen minutes straight into a tiny, child-size toilet.

It hadn't helped much, not one tiny bit.

The churning, sick feeling continued throughout the day, but had finally begun to ease somewhat by the time the 3:30 dismissal bell rang and she'd gathered up the stack of handouts and piecharts and folders that were supposed to make her a better teacher. She even felt almost good enough to joke about it to some of the other teachers as they walked to the parking lot . . . until she saw him standing next to the Tracker.

Then all she wanted to do was run back inside and get sick all over again.

Maybe even die, curled up in a ball on the floor next to the miniature toilet, if she was lucky.

But she couldn't do that to poor Mr. Willis. He already had more than enough around the school to clean up.

Sky said good-bye to her friends and tightened her grip on the papers as she walked toward him.

He was still wearing the dress slacks and shiny business loafers he had worn earlier that day, but he'd replaced the bright blue blazer and button-down shirt for a pale yellow turtleneck and brown leather bomber jacket. A large bandage covered most of the left side of his forehead. He smiled and winked at her when she reached the Tracker, then flinched and gently touched the bandage.

"It's okay," he said as if she'd asked, "nothing serious. Sky, we have to talk."

"I don't think so, Sam." She waited for him to move, and when he didn't she went ahead and opened the door into him. He still didn't move.

"Sky, please." His voice was deeper than she remembered it. *Funny how things can change in such a short time.* "I don't want it to end like this. Hell, I don't want it to end at all. Please, just let me try to explain."

She tossed the papers onto the passenger's seat and looked back toward the school. There were still too many of her coworkers milling around—and most of them seemed more interested in watching her and the big Anglo than getting home. If she made any sort of a scene, it would become schoolwide gossip by morning.

"Okay," she said, and watched him smile, "but I need to know which one of you is going to do the explaining—advertising executive Sam, or Sun Country Homes Sam. That was so I can gauge my answers accordingly."

"Sky."

"Darn, I can't tell the difference—you *both* sound so much alike.'"

"I deserve that," he said.

Sky made a sound in her throat to let him know she agreed with him wholeheartedly.

"Okay, here's the truth . . . and the reason why I didn't tell you about working for SC Industries. God . . ."

He puffed out his cheeks and looked down, scuffing the heel of one of his fancy shoes against a crack in the blacktop. Sky folded her arms over her chest to stop herself from reaching out to touch and comfort him.

Idiot, she told herself. *Stop acting like an idiot. He's just trying to get sympathy.*

And he was succeeding.

Sky saw three of her coworkers, women she'd grown up with, watching.

"Ah hell, hon, I lost the advertising job."

"What?"

"Yeah, a couple of weeks ago." He glanced up at her from beneath his lashes. "I made the biggest mistake an advertising executive could make—I told the client exactly what I thought about his product. Truth really will set you free if you're not careful. Sun Country was the only place hiring . . . for close to the same amount I was making, so . . ."

Sam shrugged and let the rest of the statement die in silence.

Sky took him into her arms before she'd even realized she'd moved. He hugged her back, warming those areas of her body that had felt frozen since that morning.

"Oh God, Sam, I'm so sorry. But why didn't you tell me?"

He laughed, and his breath tickled the side of her face.

"Pride," he said. "Which is another thing a *real* advertising executive can't afford to have—at least not self-pride. We really haven't been dating all that long, and I couldn't bring myself to tell you." He squeezed her like a favorite toy and let go, held her out at arm's length. "I'm sorry. I underestimated you without ever giving you a chance, but I was worried how you'd react when you found out your boyfriend had lost his job. I've known a few women in life who would have dumped me for losing a single account . . . and I didn't want to take the chance of that happening."

Sky pushed past his hands and reclaimed her spot next to his chest. "It wouldn't have. You should know by now that it wouldn't have mattered."

"I know now," he said, "and that's all that matters. God bless you, Sky Berliner."

"Berlander," Sky said automatically, and then looked up. "You thought my last name was Berliner?"

A look of horror crept across his face. "Um—yeah. So when you showed up today and called him grandfather, I . . . Oh, boy."

"You didn't know my last name."

"I . . . ah."

Sky reached up and tugged the right side of his mustache. Hard.

"Ow!"

"That really *will* cost you, Reynolds."

"Yes, ma'am."

"Dinner, *dessert*, and a movie. My choice."

"Yes, ma'am."

"Good." Sky pushed him away and got into the Tracker, leaving the door open between them. "I think Sandra Bullock's newest chick flick is playing over at the Rialto."

Sam nodded, resigned to his fate. "Shall I come with you or follow?"

"You follow . . . that way you can use that wonderful cell phone of yours to make dinner reservations. Not too fancy, but nice."

"Anyplace you had in mind?" he asked, his hand already reaching toward the jacket's inside breast pocket.

The answer came easier to her lips than she expected.

"Surprise me," she said. "This has been a day of surprises, hasn't it?"

Sky pulled the door closed before he could say anything. It *was* a day of surprises, and she'd suddenly had a bad feeling that the day was far from over.

Joseph sprinkled the last of the blue corn kernels onto the ground, finishing the small circle, as wide as his hand could stretch, already outlined in white, blue, and red kernels. It was a small calling circle, but he had no intention of staying out in the cold any longer than he had to. The temperature had fallen twenty degrees when the sun set, and the smell of the lamb stew Estralita had been simmering all day kept calling to him to hurry up and come inside.

His breath warmed his hands as he recited the Night Blessing over them, hurrying to thank Skyrawaka, the Celestial Kachina, for one more day because it was cold and his joints hurt and his belly ached and . . .

Joseph stopped and sat back, acknowledging the grinding pain in his knees with a sigh. He was acting like a white man in church, repeating a litany of words without hearing them.

"Forgive me," he whispered, and watched his breath envelop the apology and carry it to the sky. "I have grown thoughtless with age, and frightened. My brother is right about that."

The wind brushed a strand of hair across his face. Joseph lifted his hand and felt the air rush past his fingers.

"Thank you, but he's right . . . I am afraid, Old One. You knew that when You brought us together. I could never have been the Chosen One alone . . . I am too frightened of the power."

An owl hooted in the distance as the wind dropped to the ground, swirling into a tiny dust devil that stumbled across the winter-hard ground like a newborn foal.

It was the most pathetic thing Joseph had ever seen.

The perfect thing for a man terrified of the power he had been given.

Joseph nodded, accepting the sign

"Thank you. Sleep now, little sister."

He waved a hand at the miniature whirlwind and watched it collapse in on itself, sprinkling the dried twigs and dead leaves it had gathered on top of the corn. The night was silent again, and Joseph listened to it, shivering in the cold until his son came looking for him.

"Dad?"

Joseph bit the inside of his cheek to keep from groaning as he pushed himself to his feet.

"What were you doing on the ground, Dad? Did you fall down?"

Brushing off the knees of his jeans, Joseph walked over to his son and patted him lightly on the arm. He could feel the tight muscles under the younger man's flannel shirt and allowed himself a moment of fatherly pride. If he could just talk Daniel into leaving the reservation, there was no telling what great things his son could accomplish.

"Dad?"

"I'm fine," Joseph said. "I was just . . . being old."

His son looked confused but nodded. "Okay, I guess. Come on—'Lita said if we're not washed and at the table in two minutes, she's going to feed our portions to the chickens."

Joseph didn't have to feign terror at the thought— he just let the real fear he had lived with for most of his life show on his face.

Gideon was right.

Gideon was always right.

Gideon.

Someone called his name.

Gideon's eyes jerked open into darkness. Where was he? What the hell was going on?

Gideon.

"What?" His voice echoed back at him from the dark; nothing and no one else answered him. "Where are yah?"

Nausea doubled him over as he got to his feet.

GIDEON.

The voice came out of the darkness, everywhere and nowhere. Gideon turned and stumbled and fell backward into the pool. The last thing he heard before the icy water closed over his head was the echo of his own stupidity splashing against the granite walls.

He broke the surface less than a moment later, sputtering and squalling like a half-drowned possum as he hauled himself back onto the rocks as the world returned to him in shades of gray.

The voice had been part of a dream, just remembered as he shivered—he'd been running from something high in the air, something he couldn't see but that called his name over and over, louder each time because it was getting closer. He'd still been asleep when he *dreamed* he was awake.

"D-d-damn ol' f-fool." Gideon couldn't feel his lips move as he spoke. "G-g-goddamned ol' fool . . . yer gonna kill yerself 'fore anyone else gets a chance, yah keep doin' things like this."

He chuckled, thinking about that, until the laughter turned rancid and bubbly in his throat and something—something much larger and more important feeling—broke loose in his chest. Whatever it was, it had left a taste of copper on his tongue.

"Called me a goddamned squatter," Gideon muttered, and felt his knees inch up toward the scalding pain in his chest. "Damn."

He hurt, god-*damn* he hurt. He hurt like a son of a bitch.

Gideon moaned before he could stop himself, and the wind answered—a little too quickly and a whole lot too loud. The sound of it echoed down the steep rock walls and landed on top of him with an almost physical force.

That was all it took.

Gideon opened his mouth to curse, but instead spewed bile and the remains of the boiled fawn and mashed carrots he had had for breakfast out into the pool.

Blasphemy.

Ribbons of steam rose from the vomit as it floated on the surface of the sacred water. Christ, he'd done it now. Overhead, the wind howled like a wolf.

"Forgive me, Yaponcha." His tongue trembled around the ancient language he'd learned as a child. "I meant no disrespect, Old One, but I have become weak within this skin."

The wind raced above him. Whistling. Impatient.

120

Gideon could feel the Kachinas moving in the air around him.

"Yaponcha, grant me the final right of the Wind Caller . . . allow me to pass from this body to become the true spirit of the Chosen One. Grant me this so that I may defend Your land from those who would take it. Yaponcha, hear me."

Gideon lifted his face toward the stars just as the wind swept down over him like a flood . . . suffocating . . . drowning him in a sea of air . . . thick . . . burning . . . acrid . . . the taste of smoke to replace the copper on his tongue.

The taste of smoke.

Gideon let the wind haul him to his feet. "Oh God."

Smoke.

This ridge was on fire.

Sky watched Sam's face harden as he snapped the cell phone shut. They were standing in line at the box office, surrounded by trolls and elves and wizards of various sizes who'd come, by broom or some other magical transport, to see Hollywood's latest "classic fantasy epic"—which was playing on six of the theater's ten screens.

"Problem?" she asked, and hoped to God it wasn't. They'd had a wonderful evening so far, and she wanted it to continue.

Sam had not only gotten reservations at a semi-fancy restaurant, but had taken a detour on the way to her apartment and shown up with two dozen roses and a pound of chocolate-covered cherries.

Sky was a sucker for chocolate-covered cherries,

and somehow, although the morning had shown how little she knew about him, Sam had known that much about her.

"Nope," he said, and smiled. "So are you really going to make me watch a chick flick?"

Sky laced her arm through his and smiled—and hoped it looked like the real thing.

"You owe me, remember?"

CHAPTER 8

The kerosene-basted fire lapped at the cabin's seasoned wood like a starving kitten going after a dish of milk. The end product, which would be a smoldering pile of ash and rubble, was coming quick . . . but still not quick enough for the two arsonists.

They had things to do and people to see, and waiting for the owner of the property to show up was not high on their list of the evening's priorities.

The fire itself, however, was pretty damned cool, and they did try to spend their downtime constructively, marking the passage of time by tossing pinecones into the inferno and applauding the sudden whoosh and pop when they ignited.

It had been seventy-three cones in just under an hour, which was, they decided, a personal best for both of them.

Josh and Will. Quiet men who preferred dark beer

over light, enjoyed country music, and were, in their humble opinions, the best head-breakers, rib-crackers, and groin-stompers SC Industries had.

Or ever would have, modesty notwithstanding.

Pinecone number seventy-four sailed through the night in a perfectly descending arch, igniting like a meteor a full yard before it reached the flames.

Will and Josh cheered like kids at a circus. Even though they hated waiting, they really did love their work.

The next pinecone, heavy with sap, exploded in a shower of sparks.

"Yeah!"

"Beautiful."

Will threw number seventy-six into the flames with an over-the-shoulder, backhanded lob. It was impressive, but not as impressive as when they had started. The fire had reached its pinnacle and was winding down, and no amount of pine sap was going to induce it to stay.

High-grade gasoline, enclosed in a bottle that had held one of the finest Merlots Will had ever tasted, and corked with a dollop of plastique and green cherry-stem fuse, was another matter entirely.

The fuse hissed at the touch of the Bic lighter—the starving kitten full and feisty and raring to go.

"One Mississippi," Will said as he reared back John Elway–style.

"Two Mississippi." The bottle flew in a nice tight, overhand bomb.

BANG. WHOOSH.

"Three Mississippi."

Fighting the fire with fire, it was a standard technique. The already charred wood crumbled under the new assault, smothering the newer flames. It was a beautiful thing to watch.

"'The moving finger writes,'" Josh said as he lifted the shovels out of the back of the pickup and handed one to his partner, "'and having writ, moves on.'"

Will's smile was golden in the firelight. "Was that your subtle way of telling me you're getting tired of waiting, Omar?"

"Well, just a bit. Besides, I think we should tidy up a bit before the old man gets here."

A twig snapped where it shouldn't have and the fire-warmed grins widened.

"Sounds like our guest has finally arrived."

Josh leaned his shovel against the truck's "SAVE THE BABY SEALS" bumper sticker and turned to face the ragged collection of skin, bones, and clothing that not even the Salvation Army would have accepted for donation. The old man wearing them looked to be in his late seventies, which matched the age on the files both he and Will had been given, and looked about as sturdy as a marshmallow that had been left out in the rain. And as wet. The old man was soaking wet and shivering.

There was only one thing interesting about him, and that was the shotgun he was leaning on like a walking stick. It was the most beautiful thing Josh had ever seen outside of a museum.

Or the Las Vegas Gun Show.

Josh looked at Will, and Will nodded, silently relinquishing the honor of spokesman. The nod also accepted the role of "bad cop," should it be required.

Which, considering how they operated, it probably would be.

"Mr. Berlander," he said, not bothering to extend his hand, "that's a beautiful gun you have there."

The old man stared back at him, then looked at Will, then looked at the fire. When his gaze returned, Josh nodded.

"Mr. Mackay couldn't stand the thought of a man your age going through the emotional trauma of moving . . . you know, trying to decide after a lifetime what to take and what to toss." Josh sighed. "This way you won't have to decide—just think of this as a gift."

The old man's jaw tightened beneath the sagging jowls as he snapped the shotgun into firing position.

Josh felt himself grow hard just looking at it.

"Look at that, Will. It's an early-thirties Parker, number-two model, is it, Mr. Berlander?"

The old man tightened his shoulder in against the butt plate as an answer.

"It's just beautiful," Josh continued, "and obviously well taken care of. I'll give you twelve thousand for it."

The muzzle twitched and realigned on his face.

"Okay, fifteen-five, but that's as far as I can spend."

Both hammers clicked back. Josh put his hands up in front of him.

"Hey, no need to get mad. . . . Okay, so maybe I can go up to twenty, but for that I'm going to have to have proof of authenticity."

The old man tried to steady his aim, but he was shivering so much, the muzzle kept bouncing from Josh to Will—which really wasn't making Will very happy. Josh could tell his partner was just about ready to call it an evening.

"G-g-get off mah l-land."

"We're not on your land, Mr. Berlander," Bad Cop Will said, and instantly became the shotgun's primary target. Playing Bad Cop always had its disadvantages, not that Will seemed to notice. He circled around to the right of the cabin and didn't even seem to care that the old man was leading him like a dove about to take wing.

"*That* was your land, Mr. Berlander," Will said, jerking a thumb toward the smoking ruins. "This isn't. In fact, you're trespassing, sir. *This* land belongs to SC Industries for . . ." He pressed the light function on his Timex Indiglo watch. ". . . almost six hours now. Back taxes can really be a bitch, can't they, sir?"

"Y-y-y-y-y-yah g-g-g-goddamn-n-n-n."

Will turned around and smiled, his Lands' End thermal parka open just enough for the old man to see the .38 in the holster on his belt.

"But don't you worry, Mr. B, with the money my friend will give you for that old gun . . . on top of what Mr. Mackay is still willing to give you for your plot, you're going to come out smelling like roses. Instead of just smelling."

That was it, the final straw. Josh knew it the second after the words left Will's lips and acted accordingly.

He jumped the old man from behind, making sure the shotgun was safely in his hands before its previous owner hit the ground.

The only thing Josh miscalculated was the brittleness of old bones.

"Aw, fuck."

* * *

The wind sounded funny—like it was inside his head instead of outside where it belonged. Gideon could hear it, moaning inside his head while the fire that destroyed his cabin began doing the same thing to his shoulder. For the life of him, he couldn't figure out how the fire had jumped that far, or how it could take, considering how wet his shirt was.

He also wished the wind inside him would quiet down a bit. He was having the devil's own time trying to hear what the intruders were saying to each other . . . something about . . .

The second man, the man Gideon had been planning to serve a double load of rock salt, knelt down and grabbed his right shoulder, wiggling it back and forth.

Gideon's scream—long and loud—released the wind that had become trapped inside him.

"Holy shit, Josh," the man said, lifting his hand for his partner to see. Gideon saw too, even though the fire in his shoulder had spread all the way down his arm and into his neck. The tips of the man's fingers were covered in something dark and drippy. "His shoulder is all torn up, and at least one bone went through the skin."

"It was an accident. Honest to Christ, I just went after the gun—it was his fault he didn't let go. The report never said his bones were like matchsticks. Fuck."

"I know," the other man said. "It's okay, it wasn't your fault. I'll testify that you had to grab him to pull him out of the fire. You'll be a hero."

"Thanks, I appreciate that. Now, fess up . . . isn't

this the most beautiful shotgun you've ever seen?"

"It is pretty sweet, I'll grant you that."

Gideon closed his eyes as a shooting star bolted across the night sky directly above him, going north to south. It was a bad sign, but at least the fire in his shoulder had done some good. He was warmer now . . . and sleepy . . . maybe if he could just sleep a bit he'd feel better, stronger, and he'd . . . he'd be able to . . .

Pain woke him up. The fire wasn't out yet.

"Don't go to sleep, Mr. Berlander." The man who'd stolen his gun was squatting down next to him. "We still have a little business to take care of. Okay?"

Gideon discovered he couldn't move when the man reached out and patted his cheek. His arms and legs were all atingle, and it felt like someone had dropped a boulder on his chest and left it there.

"Good." Smiling, the man held two slips of paper up for Gideon to see. "This first check is for the land, which my compatriot and I feel is a very generous offer for a smoldering pile of ash. The second is my personal check for the shotgun. Eighteen-seven—which, again, is very generous given the condition of the weapon. It's a sin the way you kept this gun, Mr. Berlander, but rest assured, I'll restore it to its original glory."

Glory . . . mah daughter. She's buried here, next to her maw.

"The hell yah will."

Gideon struggled against the invisible boulder and managed to lift his head just enough to project the wad of spit where he wanted. Bull's-eye. The man looked at the glob for a moment, glistening in the light of the dying fire, then flicked it off the second, personal check.

And this time, when the man grabbed Gideon's broken shoulder and twisted, both of them knew it wasn't an accident.

"We'll talk later, and don't worry about signing—we have samples of your handwriting on file and, given the nature of your injury, no one will question the sloppiness." The man sat back and sighed, and Gideon watched the wind snatch the tiny breath-cloud away. Good. "Hey, Will? Come on, let's get him in the truck—he's not supposed to die up here, and I'm not too sure how much longer he has."

Gideon couldn't keep the scream inside when they lifted him off the ground and tossed him, more or less carefully, into the truck bed. It was a good thing, maybe the first good thing to happen since he fell into the pool . . . the wind escaped when he screamed, and he could hear it, rustling through the burned bones of the cabin . . . building up anger . . . building up speed.

"What about the shovels?" the other man shouted above the rising windstorm. "We can't leave them. I'm the one who signed them out."

"Okay, get them, but hurry. I don't like the way the old goat is mumbling. I think he's getting delirious. Hurry it up. I'll call Mackay and let him know what happened . . . and don't worry, I'll ask him to tell the papers *you* spotted the fire first and gave up a night's worth of fishing to play Smokey the Bear."

Gideon didn't catch the man's answer, but it must have been funny, because his partner chuckled and shook his head as he flipped open a gleaming little phone, no bigger than a transistor radio.

"Clown," the man said, but Gideon had a hard time hearing that, too. The wind was howling now, circling in from the trees along the northern ridge and coming fast, like a shark scenting blood in the water. It was the only thing Gideon could hear, but that was enough.

When the first blast rocked the truck on its tires, the man had to grab on to the side panel to steady himself. The phone wasn't as lucky. The wind snatched it from his hands and carried it off.

"Shit!"

"What?" The wind carried the sound of the other man's voice in its teeth.

"Lost the phone . . . you call Mackay."

"Okay! Wow, this is some wind, huh? Tell that old man he should be thanking us. Man, if I had to live up here, I'd die."

"All right," Gideon said.

The man, Will, never saw what killed him. But his partner did, and it was the look on the man's face that made Gideon fight to stay conscious despite the pain in his arm and chest.

"What the—"

The wind screamed like a woman being raped, a sound Josh was well familiar with on a professional level, but it sent shivers racing down through the marrow of his bones. There was something in the sound that triggered an immediate response in his primitive back brain: *Run.*

And he was all for taking that advice.

"Will! Come on, man! Leave the damned shovels . . . we can get them later! Shit!"

The wind was coming the wrong way, blowing his words and the rushing, screaming sounds back at him. A tree splintered somewhere out in the shrieking darkness. It was like being in the eye of a tornado.

"No," he said just to hear himself, "more like the stomach."

A cold hand suddenly latched itself to his wrist. The old man was barely conscious; Josh could tell that just by looking at the rolling eyes below the half-closed lids . . . but he still had enough wherewithal to try and sit up. If that little voice in the back of his head hadn't still been yelling at him to *Go, run, get away*, Josh might have even been impressed.

Or something.

As it was, he was pretty sure he broke at least one gnarled finger, maybe two, when he pulled away. He couldn't be sure, though; it might have just been the sound of limbs snapping in the wind.

"Let go of me," he shouted. He had to shout to hear himself now.

The old man's lips moved, but nothing came out.

"What?"

The lips moved again.

"SHIT!"

Standing on tiptoe, Josh leveled himself up over the side of the truck until his face was inches from the old man's. Sheltered from the wind, it was quieter in the flatbed, although, without the wind, the smell coming off the old man was enough to make Josh's eyes water.

"What?"

"Ah said, yah best say g'bye to yer friend."

Josh could feel his lips trying to form a smile as he strong-armed himself back to the ground. The old man was delirious, just like he thought. . . . Will wasn't going anywhere. But there'd been something in the old man's voice that made Josh turn and cup his hands around his mouth to make sure he was heard.

"WILL! GET YOUR ASS OVER HERE. WE'RE LEAVING RIGHT— NO!"

Will had turned around when he heard Josh, raising the shovels over his head like a victory banner . . . and then the wind hit him, sucking air and blood out through his mouth and nose, sucking the face right along with it.

Josh felt his own guts threaten mutiny when a debris-filled whirlwind settled down over the closest thing he had to a friend and began to rip him apart . . . piece by piece by piece.

By piece.

One minute, Will had been a man; the next he was a rag doll with the stuffing pulled out of it. The only trouble was that Will didn't know he'd been reduced to a toy; he kept screaming as if he were still alive.

"Noisy bastard, ain't he?"

Josh stumbled as he turned. The old man had pulled himself up just enough to see over the side of the truck. His face was so pale it seemed to glow in the darkness.

"But don't worry, Ah'm sure he'll quiet down . . . right 'bout . . . now."

The old man tipped his head, and Josh whirled

133

around to see an uprooted aspen, as thick as a man's arm, tear through Will's spine and exit through his belly, pinning him like a bug to the earth.

The wind died right after Will did, and the night got quiet. Except for a soft whistle.

When Josh could move again, he followed the sound back to the truck where the old man was playing a little tune. *Not much in the way of a song*, Josh thought as the wind began to blow again, *just one note played low and soft.*

The old man stopped playing when their eyes met.

"Ever hear the ol' sayin' 'Ya gotta pay the piper'?" Josh nodded.

"Well, just think o' me as the piper. Mah little sweetheart took yore friend on 'er own, but yer mine, boy."

The old man put the whistle to his lips again and blew a sound that almost split Josh's head in two—and probably would have if the wind hadn't suddenly hit him from behind and slammed him into the side of the truck. Opening his mouth in pain was a mistake: The minute he did, the wind began to pour down his throat. Josh could feel his lungs swelling against his ribs.

It took every ounce of strength he had to cover his face with his arms, but the wind wasn't giving up. It tugged at his sleeves and pulled his head, trying to get at his face.

"God!"

The whistle stopped and the wind faltered.

"That's right, boy," the old man said, "but not yours . . . mine."

Josh peeked out from under his arms and saw the

old man wink. That was when the primal brain took over and struck out, as hard as it could.

He didn't even remember pulling the little snub-nose that Will had always made fun of. A late-nineteenth-century derringer just wasn't a "man's gun," Will had been overly fond of saying, not like his own sweet "Dirty Harry Special." Maybe not, but Will was dead, and having a big old gun of his hadn't done him any good.

The smoke from the hand-loaded black-powder round hung in the air above the truck—that was how Josh knew the wind had died again. The old man could have been dead, too, for all he knew or cared, and he wasn't about to check until he was off the damned mountain and standing in the bright sodium glare of the nearest hospital's emergency-room entrance.

Maybe not even then.

Josh's primal back brain just didn't give a damn, one way or the other.

CHAPTER 9

Joseph woke to a searing pain in his right shoulder and knew he was dying.

Eyes opened to the soft darkness of his room, he grabbed at the core of the pain and felt his fingers slip into an oozing hole of torn flesh and shattered bone. The scream lifted him from the warmth of his bed and hurled him across the room. Images without form swirled around him as he fell to his knees while two voice sang a death song.

His voice and another's becoming one as life oozed from him.

Covered with gray ash, his long white hair dancing in the streams of air that rose from the whirlwind that girdled his lower half, Yaponcha glided toward him from the darkness.

"Forgive me, Old One," Joseph whimpered, cowering as he always had, "I have failed you. I'm dying and—"

"Jesus Christ, Dad, what's the matter?"

Joseph blinked and saw his son standing in the doorway, illuminated by the coyote-shaped nightlight in the hall. He was wearing pajama bottoms and a thermal top, and carrying Joey's Little League baseball bat.

"I thought," Daniel said, and then looked sleepily at the bat in his hands. "I don't know what I thought. Are you okay? What were you shouting about?"

Joseph rubbed his right shoulder through the nightshirt's heavy flannel and exhaled slowly when his fingers felt only solid flesh. *It was only a dream.* A dream that held power.

He could feel himself shivering as he got to his feet, and it had very little to do with the temperature of the room. Even so, Joseph pulled the heavy winter quilt over his shoulders as he sat down on the edge of the bed. The thought of crawling back under the covers and falling asleep almost made him physically ill.

"It was a leg cramp . . . you know, the kind Little Star gets. I think I did too much walking today."

Daniel yawned loudly and scratched his head, almost giving himself a concussion with the bat. Joseph felt the tension ease from him as he smiled. *Maybe it was only a dream, after all. Old men dream of nothing sometimes.*

"'Lita only gets those in the last month of pregnancy," his son said as he laid the bat over one shoulder. "Is there anything you want to tell me?"

"No," Joseph said, "I'm not pregnant."

"Good. I'm too old to have a baby brother. You want something?"

Joseph shook his head. "I'm fine. Go back to bed."

Daniel nodded and turned away, his eyes already half closed. Estralita wouldn't have been that easily satisfied; she would have made him promise to see Dr. Hernandez the next morning for a checkup. Joseph quietly whispered a prayer of thanks to the Kachinas for having sent his son instead of his daughter-in-law.

Joseph waited until he heard the door of the master bedroom thump shut before wrapping a blanket around his shoulders. It was only a dream—a bad one, yes, but no worse than the ones he had as a child after eating too many pieces of his mother's sweet potato candy.

"Only a dream," he mumbled softly, only loud enough to convince himself as he stood and walked out of the sleeping porch.

Still shivering beneath the heavy wool, Joseph moved as quietly as he could down the hall to his grandsons' room. When he reached the door, he paused and listened. Other than Daniel's muffled and rhythmic snores, the house was silent—which made the click of the doorknob when he turned it seem all the louder. Estralita might still be awake, but she was used to him checking on the boys and, although she wouldn't go back to sleep until he was in bed, she wouldn't get up.

The painted doorknob grew hot in his hand as Joseph stood in the doorway and looked at his grandsons. Joey was bunched into his customary lump near the foot of the bed while his younger brother slept flat on his back, head nestled against that of his favorite stuffed toy, a threadbare blue-and-white panda his father had won for him at a ringtoss game.

Warm again, Joseph let the blanket slip from his shoulders as he walked to the narrow space between the beds. The boys were fine, sleeping soundly, but that still didn't stop him from reaching beneath the covers and pulling his oldest grandson into a more appropriate—head on pillow, body straight, covers tucked in—sleeping position.

That would last an hour, maybe less. Joseph never knew how long, but in the morning, or—like tonight, if he came in to check again—Joey would be curled up and under the covers at the foot of his bed, as if hiding from something in the night.

The thought sent another shiver down Joseph's spine as he turned to study his youngest grandson's face. He looked so much like his uncle, Daniel's lost brother, that it always made Joseph's heart tremble.

But only for a moment, and only a little.

Joseph took a deep breath to calm the tremble as he touched the boy's cheek. Grunting in his sleep, Andrew pulled the stuffed bear to him and whispered something under his breath.

A name.

"Yaponcha . . ."

Joseph grasped the headboard to steady himself when Joey, his voice muffled by blankets, answered.

"Yaponcha . . ."

". . . hear me, Old One . . ."

". . . the time is almost come . . . and I beg You . . ."

". . . grant Your servant the power to protect the land . . ."

". . . as You have always protected it. Help me, Old . . ."

"One. Yaponcha, hear me . . . make me as You . . ."

". . . are. Release me . . . set me . . ."

"Free!"

Pain erupted in Joseph's shoulder and across his chest, driving him to his knees in the center of the pale blue rug Estralita had woven when Joey was still an infant. The words his grandsons spoke were ancient, and the single voice that spoke them belonged to another.

Gideon.

Joseph hunched forward and sang another type of prayer while the wind rattled the windows and sought a way in.

A child was crying in one of the first-floor apartments.

Sky stopped at the top of the stairs and leaned over the railing, trying to decide where the sound was coming from. Most of her downstairs neighbors had children, so there always seemed to be at least one child crying about something. Hunger, sadness, pain, loneliness—there was always a reason behind a child's tears. Not so easy when you grew up, though. A child could cry and know an adult would come to find out what was wrong, to soothe the boo-boo and make everything all right with a kiss.

Sky felt her own eyes begin to fill and blinked them dry. She had nothing to cry about; the evening had been perfect and Sam had dutifully explained everything—even how he was going to have a flower lei made to keep alive the fantasy about him being a highly paid advertising executive. For a while longer, he said. And winked. The same old Sam, her lover . . . the man she really didn't know anything about. Good old Sam Reynolds, late of the advertising game, currently employed as a blue-coated real-estate agent.

Not that it mattered what he did, and she told him that, slipping it in every chance she got while he'd been attentive, witty, generous, and understanding when she claimed a sudden headache on the way back to the apartment.

Of course, she'd had a hard day, he understood. Long day for him, too. Take a rain check. No problem. Maybe check another movie on the weekend. Action flick this time. Hah, hah. Love you. Get some sleep. Call you after work. 'Night.

Understanding to a fault.

Even though Sky had gotten the impression he'd been looking for an excuse to leave since getting the phone call . . . *from the telemarketer*.

Right.

The sound of weeping echoed up from the empty courtyard.

Damn, it was so easy for a child to cry . . .

. . . but Grandfather didn't like it when she cried, so Sky scrubbed the tears off her cheek with the sleeve of her red calico work shirt/dress and watched the wind pluck a flower from the bunch she'd just put on her mama's grave. The wind always seemed to like the yellow ones best, stealing at least one buttercup or dandelion regardless of how big a rock she used to hold down the flowers as her grandfather had taught her.

It was always windy by the graves, she knew that,

but she just couldn't figure out why the wind stole only the yellow flowers.

"Ah won't bring any next time," Sky shouted after the flower as it tumbled and danced along the ground. "Yah just see if Ah don't."

The wind circled back at her in a tiny dust devil, pelting her with gravel and weeds.

"Ain't funny!" she yelled back at it, and heard a crested jay squawk at her from the branch of a nearby aspen. Sky stuck her tongue out at the noisy bird and tasted dirt on her lips.

Ain't funny a'tall.

"Little gal, yah ain't gettin' dirty now, are yah? Ah got someone here wantin' t'meet'cha."

Sky immediately stood up and dusted the red dirt off her knees and the back of her dress. Her grandfather never liked it when she got dirty, and especially didn't like it when there were other people around—said it made her look too much like the red-dirt man, who killed her mama. Sky hated the red-dirt man even though she wasn't real sure what a red-dirt man was or what he looked like. Red, a'course, and dirty . . . and probably nothing like the tall man who was walking up the hill next to her grandfather. This was a city man, his face and hands almost as blinding white as the shirt he wore.

He had on a bright yellow tie, and the wind kept tugging at it. That made Sky laugh.

"That's my little gal," her grandfather said, nodding to her.

The city man looked surprised for a moment, then smiled. His teeth *were* the same color as his shirt, and his eyes were green. As green as new spring grass. Sky fell in love.

"I didn't know she was part Native American."

She didn't know what that meant, but she knew it couldn't be anything bad, even though she heard her grandfather grunt low in his throat. The city man wouldn't have said anything bad about her; a man with eyes that pretty wouldn't say bad things about nobody.

"Ain't her fault."

"Oh no, Mr. Berlander, I didn't mean that. It's just that . . . Well, we can discuss that at a later time." And then the man looked down at her and smiled. "Hello there, young lady. You must be Sky."

Sky nodded and squeezed her toes into the dirt at the edge of her mama's grave. It was too hot for shoes, too hot for the long-sleeved dress her grandfather had told her to wear, too, but he'd wanted her to look nice and not look like some wild Injun.

"Little gal, where's yer manners?"

"Ah'm Sky," she said. "Pleased t'meet'cha."

The city man's laugh was as soft as cat-tail down; it didn't sound anything like her grandfather's gut-busting cackle. She could have stood there and listened to it all day.

"The pleasure is all mine, Sky," the man said, and she felt a funny little burning feeling that started at the bottom of her neck and quickly spread into her cheeks. "Let's see . . . you're what? About eight years old?"

"Yes, sir. In four days." And Sky held up four fingers to make sure he knew.

The man seemed impressed; his eyes were all sparkly. "Did your grandfather teach you to count and read?"

"Yes, sir.

"But you've never been to school, have you, Sky?"

"No!"

Sky backed up so quickly she almost took a tumble. Schooling was good, fun sometimes when her grandfather didn't get mad at her for not knowing things as fast as he wanted her to, but *school* . . . *school* was the bad place where the red-dirt man had caught her mama and tore her open and stuffed something inside her and then killed her. Sky wasn't exactly sure how it all happened or what the exact sequence of events was, but she was sure of one thing: *School* was where it all started. If she went to *school*, a red-dirt man would kill her, too.

Her grandfather said so.

The city man's green eyes narrowed as he took a step toward her. "What's wrong, Sky? Mr. Berlander, what's the matter with her? Sky, it's okay. Don't you want to go to school and be with other children?"

Other children? Did they know about the red-dirt man? She bet they didn't . . . she bet the red-dirt man was killing them right now.

"NO!"

The city man looked at her grandfather and then back at her, and Sky decided his eyes weren't that pretty after all.

"Sky, honey, it's okay. School's a wonderful place where you'll make lots of friends and—"

The only one who didn't seem surprised when she

threw the marble-sized clod of dirt was her grandfather. In fact, he was smiling, as happy as you please.

"NO! GO 'WAY!"

The city man finally backed up, brushing off the dark brown spot on his bright white shirt.

"I can't understand your granddaughter's reaction, Mr. Berlander, unless you've been giving her the wrong impression about school."

"Just told her the truth, s'all. Ah hauled her mama down t'school 'cause Ah promised her mama 'fore she died that's what Ah'd do. If Ah hadn't taken her down there, she'd be alive right now . . . tellin' yah the same thing her daughter's tellin' yah. Go 'way."

The man shook his head and took a deep breath. "We know what happened to your daughter, Mr. Berlander, but you can't blame the educational system for that. I'm afraid girls get pregnant and die in childbirth with or without education . . . as you may find out in a few years."

"You threatenin' us? You plannin' on sneakin' up here and doin' her yerself?"

"Good God, man, how could you say something like that?"

Sky watched her grandfather shrug, but she could tell by the way the muscles stood out on his neck that he was angry, angrier than she'd ever remembered seeing him. And that scared her almost as much as the *school* talk.

"I was talking about your granddaughter's right to a decent education, Mr. Berlander. You've kept her in virtual isolation. She obviously has no social skills to speak of, and that, as studies have shown, is due to her lack of peer-group interaction. There are laws, Mr. Berlander, and what you've done—are still doing—to this poor child, is . . ."

The man stopped talking and looked at her grandfather the same way her grandfather looked when he was telling her stories about the red-dirt man. Like he had just stepped in something long dead.

"I'm through talking, Mr. Berlander, but unless you enroll Sky in school by the end of the week, I'll see to it that you will be facing charges of child neglect and endangerment and have Sky placed into the protective custody of Social Services."

The wind had gotten cold while the city man talked. Sky hugged herself, shivering when the man turned and winked at her.

"Don't you worry, Sky, everything's going to be fine. You may not think so right now, but just wait until you get to school and see how much fun it is. Really, you're going to love it there.

"As for you, Mr. Berlander . . . I hope we understand each other. Good day. Sky, I'll be sure to stop by school and say hi."

And then Sky knew: The city man with green-grass eyes and the bright yellow tie was really the red-dirt man. She should have known the minute he smiled at her. When he reached out toward her, Sky vaulted over her mama's grave and ran to her grandfather, pressing her face against his rock-hard side.

"Don't let 'em take me," she howled. "Don't let 'em."

"God, you poor little thing—what's he done to you?" Sky could hear the red-dirt man's shoes scuff against the ground as he walked away. "School or not, Mr. Berlander, expect a call from Social Services. You're not fit to be her guardian."

Her grandfather didn't move until the wind had carried the sound of the man's shoes down-canyon, and then he held her out at arm's length as he kneeled down in front of her.

"Did yah hear that, little gal, that man's gonna steal yah and drag yah off t'school."

"NO! Grandfather, don't let 'em . . . no! Please don't. NO! NO!"

"Hush now, child, hush and listen." His fingers tightened a little on her arms—not much, but the warmth of his hands took away the cold and made her feel safe again. "Ah ain't gonna let him take yah. Ah can protect yah and keep yah here, but yah gotta help me. Yah willin' t'do that?"

Sky nodded so hard she heard her back teeth clink together.

"Good. C'mon, then, we gotta get down-canyon a ways."

Taking his hand, Sky followed her grandfather through the trees beyond her mama's grave to a high ridge overlooking the snaking dirt road that led down from their mountain. The red-dirt man's car was just coming to the edge of the longest curve, creeping along the ruts and washouts more slowly than Sky could skip; its long black hood was already covered in a thin layer of dust.

Standing that far above the road, Sky could see only the tops of the man's hands as they gripped the steering wheel. The knuckles were almost as white as his shirt had been.

"Bold as brass and twice as shiny, ain't he?" Sky

giggled and felt a soft thump against the back of her head. "Hush now, little gal, this ain't no laughin' matter. Now, pay attention . . . one day yah might have t'do something like this yerself."

When her grandfather motioned her closer to the edge, Sky nudged a rock over the side with her big toe and felt her belly hitch up a little when it hit the road below. The red-dirt man in the car didn't seem to notice.

"Think o'this just like if yah was out huntin'," her grandfather said. "First yah gotta trap the prey."

Sky was about to ask how a person went about trapping a car when her grandfather started humming. It wasn't like any song Sky had ever heard before, and it made the skin on her back and arms pucker up under the heavy cotton dress. If it hadn't been for the wind picking up, she would have been real uncomfortable.

On the road below, the red-dirt man misjudged a shadow and buried the right front wheel of his car into a long, narrow rut. Her grandfather's humming changed into a chuckle.

"Easy as shootin' fish in a barrel," he said, and handed her a small willow whistle. It was the prettiest thing Sky had ever seen, not anything like the plain old white whistles her grandfather whittled for her. It was painted bright red, like an autumn apple, with circles of yellow and blue at both ends.

"Can Ah have it?" Sky asked.

"Nope, it's just a loaner, but Ah'll make yah one when yer ready. Think a'this as a test. Now, look down there. That man's gonna try t'take yah away from everything yah know and love and drag yah on down to *school*, where the men'll come at yah like wolves after a spring lamb. That man's gonna make sure they do t'yah like they did t'yer mama. Yah want that t'happen, baby?"

"N-NO!"

"Well, yer gonna have t'do something 'bout it, then, ain't'cha?"

Sky clutched the whistle against her chest and nodded, even though she had no idea what she could do about it. Until her grandfather knelt down behind her and helped her carry the pretty little whistle to her lips.

"Yah got the power t'stop 'em, child. . . . Go on, give it a good hard puff and see what happens. Ain't no one gonna take yah away from me like they did yer mama. No one."

The whistle tasted bitter against her lips, but Sky barely noticed it as she took a deep breath and blew as hard as she could.

The sound tore at her ears the same way the sudden gust of a wind tore at the hem of her dress as it raced past. If her grandfather hadn't been holding on to her, Sky knew, the wind would have swept her down into the giant dust devil that had suddenly covered the red-dirt man's car. She couldn't see much through the swirling dirt and leaves, but she saw the inside of the windshield go red, as if someone had thrown a bucket of paint on it, right before the roof caved in and the glass shattered.

"That's it, little gal . . ." The wind was so loud her grandfather had to yell into her ear, but it still sounded like he was a million miles away. "Keep goin' . . . that's right, clear that mess off our land."

Sky blew the whistle again, even though the insides of her lungs were burning, and watched the dust devil engulf the car. The windows were either blown out or scratched so badly by flying debris they were white, like the eyes of a fish left out in the sun too long, and there didn't seem any place on the once-shiny black surface that wasn't dented. It was a mess, a real mess, and it didn't belong there.

Sky knew that—her grandfather had just said it, hadn't he?—but it still made her feel funny inside when the wind started pushing the twisted lump of black and red metal and man off the edge of the road. She knew it was a mess, and that the man was . . . *had been* a red-dirt man who would have come back and taken her, like another red-dirt—dirt-red—dirty red man had come and taken her mama.

The wind died when the whistle slipped out of her mouth. Sky thought her grandfather would be angry about it, but he didn't say a thing, just picked it up off the ground and put it back into his pocket without even dusting it off. In fact, he seemed as happy as if the chicken had started pooping gold nuggets.

"Ah knew it," he said as he stood up. "Ah knew it was in yah from the moment yer mama squirted yah out. Didn't want t'see it, 'specially when she died, but Ah couldn't help it. Ah knew right then it was born in yah, that's why Ah run him off when he came t'see yah that first time. He would'a stole yah and yer power an' used 'em both against me . . . but Ah saw yah first."

The sound of metal hitting wood came from somewhere down among the trees. It would take a long time for someone to find the red-dirt man and his car. A long, long time, if ever.

And it was all her fault somehow.

When her grandfather reached out to hug her, Sky shied away as if he'd been holding a switch.

"Nothin' t'be scared of now, little gal," he said, talking soft. "Yah done real good . . . ain't nobody come lookin' for him gonna think it weren't nothin' but an accident."

He was smiling. Sky had never seen him smile so much before.

"Ah'm real proud of you, Sky, yah proved yerself. Now Ah can teach yah things no school'd ever think of. Ain't no one gonna take yah from me. No one."

But her grandfather had been wrong.

Another red-dirt man showed up one morning when her grandfather was off hunting, and Sky got into his long black car without a word, sitting still and quiet in the backseat, waiting for him to kill her like he had her mama. But it never happened, not then and not later when her grandfather had come blasting into the school like a storm, shouting and demanding and waving the piece of paper the red-dirt man had left stuck in the front door.

Her grandfather wanted her back, demanded her back, but then one of the other red-dirt men asked her what *she* wanted and Sky told them: She wanted to stay. They never asked her why, just got all puffed up like a banty rooster and told her, 'Yes, of course you can stay, no one's going to take her away,' so she never had to tell them why she wanted to stay.

He knew, though, her grandfather—she could see

it in his eyes when they got hard and cold, but he never said a word about it.

Not then, not even after she returned from the outside world to teach at the reservation school. It had taken years and a number of psychology classes, but Sky had finally managed to convince herself that the man had been killed by accident, by a freak wind. That part was easy; the harder part was accepting the fact that her grandfather had tried to put the blame on her. He was the worst kind of child abuser—but he was her only living relative, and for some reason even she couldn't understand, she just couldn't abandon him.

As much as she wanted to.

The sound of crying grew louder, and Sky realized it was only the wind. Only the wind.

Pushing away from the railing, Sky felt a sharp pain in her right shoulder and gasped. She couldn't remember doing it, but she must have pulled a muscle. Her whole shoulder felt like it was on fire.

Sam Reynolds watched the suds dribble down the neck of his fourth beer in little under thirty minutes and signaled for a fifth. The Hispanic bartender nodded and cracked open the Bud where Sam could see it. He knew it wasn't impossible to water down beer, even when it came in bottles, so he kept as clear an eye as he still had on it until the bartender set it down in front of him.

Half a bottle later, he wondered just how good an eye he still had left: Four and a half beers—that on top of most of the split of wine they'd had with dinner—and he still didn't feel the tiniest bit buzzed.

Hell, he didn't even feel bizzed. And he really needed to feel something.

Sam finished off the rest of the bottle and took a moment to look around before ordering number six; he didn't want the bartender to think he was just another Anglo lush who'd wandered into the place because he was too drunk to notice where he was. Sam knew where he was, all right: He was in a neighborhood dive a block away from Sky's HUD-subsidized apartment complex. He could even draw a map back to her place if he wanted to. Which he didn't. What he wanted to do was get drunk, as quickly and effortlessly as possible, which had been the *only* reason he'd stopped in the first place.

Unfortunately, the beer just wasn't doing it.

"Gimme a double of Jose," Sam said, pointing to a row of bottles behind the bartender, "gold."

One of the man's bushy eyebrows lifted just a bit, as if to question the judgment of mixing cactus with barley and hops, but it didn't stop him from pouring out the order. That was the one thing he liked about the bar; the second was that the tequila had done the trick—it finally started up the old buzz machine.

It also washed away the bitter taste that had been clinging to the back of his tongue since Mackay's call.

"Just thought you'd like to know that I transferred the Berlander account to two of your associates this afternoon, and I'm happy to say the problem has been solved. William and Joshua are excellent workers, don't you agree? As for you, Mr. Reynolds, I have a rather large investment in you, so why don't we just put all this behind us? There's some property I've had my eye on for some time now for a private airfield; the current owner has a

verbal agreement with the native sheepherders to let them use it as grazing land. You have one chance, Mr. Reynolds, and one chance only, to show the owner that private jets make more sense than sheep. I'll expect the signed contract on my desk by close of business tomorrow."

"Bastard," Sam said into the hollow of his empty glass. The tequila fumes washed back at him and made his eyes water. "One day . . . bastard gives me one day. Shit."

He set the glass down and wiggled his fingers. When the bartender was less than quick with the re-fill, Sam dug into his pocket and peeled off two tens and a five—more than enough to keep the buzz machine fed for a while longer. The glass filled as if by magic.

And just as magically disappeared.

"Gives *me* one day—hell, that's not the way I work. I'm not like those two knuckle-draggers. Willy and Josh, big men on campus. Yeah, I'll just *bet* they closed the account. Goddamn liars . . . they're nothing but goddamned liars."

The bartender nodded and moved quickly to the other end of the bar. The wound on Sam's forehead was itching like crazy, and that didn't help improve his mood. The growing buzz was okay, but what he really needed was to find Willy and Josh and bash their heads down into their big bull necks.

Pulling off the bandage, he looked at the seeping yellow and red stain.

"See this?" he yelled at the drunk sitting next to him. The man was a 'breed, like Sky, with long gray-ing black hair that hung past the shoulders of his K-Mart flannel shirt. "You see this, Chief? I gave my skin for that account, and that goddamned bastard takes it away from me and hands it to two monkeys. You think that's fair, Chief?"

The bartender dropped out of sight when the drunk turned toward Sam.

"Why don't you get back uptown, white boy, before you get hurt?"

Sam flipped the bandage off the 'breed's nose.

He'd found his fight.

Outside the wind wept like a lost child, frightened and alone. Day and night, for a week.

CHAPTER 10

The land was being torn apart, piece by bloody piece, and there was nothing Gideon could do but stand there and yell and threaten and be ignored by the pack of ravening earthmovers that surrounded him.

"This is mah land! Yah got no right t'do this!"

The ground shook under his feet when a bulldozer fed the charred remains of his cabin into a dump truck's groaning belly. They couldn't hear him.

"AH SAID STOP IT!"

They didn't.

They wouldn't.

But they would. By God he'd make them stop.

A backhoe dug into his daughter's grave—"NO! GLORY!"—then lumbered away with its prize: bones and a scrap of dirt-red calico. A grader followed the backhoe like a puppy, sweeping away all evidence of the sacrilege.

"Goddamn yah!"

Gideon could feel his heart seize up as he grabbed a lantern from the mound of smoldering wood and stones at his feet. The lantern didn't have a scratch on it and it was still lit. The rich smell of kerosene helped clear Gideon's head and he raised the wick. The flame hissed like a snake as the light flared, blinding him for a moment. The light was so bright, he thought he could hear the angels talking to him from the other side: *Can you hear me, Mr. Berlander? What are his blood gases? No other choice, I'm afraid. Keep reading out his numbers. Have to take it if we don't want to lose him. Too much blood loss, start an—*

Gideon shook the voices out of his head—didn't make any sense anyway—and flung the sizzling lantern at the nearest 'dozer. The lantern exploded against the edge of the windshield, bathing everything from the hood down in flames.

"Told'cha! Get off my land!"

His words echoed in the sudden silence. The drivers had turned off the engines and were crawling down the sides of their machines like bright blue ants. Each one of them identical to the other— bright blue faces etched with wide, toothy grins, bright blue uniforms with the words SUN COUNTRY HOMES embroidered across the back and front in gold.

Bright blue men with bright blue smiles.

Company machines dressed like men, coming straight for him. . . .

Can you hear me, Mr. Berlander? one of the man-machines asked. Gideon threw a roundhouse punch and shattered the smiling face. Beneath the bloody plastic hide was a gleaming silver skull. The man-

157

machine didn't seem to notice, and held up a blue-gloved hand, extending two fingers.

How many fingers am I holding up, Mr. Berlander? it asked.

Gideon swung at it again. Another of the man-machines grabbed him from behind, pinning his arms to his side.

He's delusional. Prepare a sedative. Please try to control yourself, Mr. Berlander.

"Goddamn yer silver hides . . . let GO of me!"

Blood pressure's rising. Please, Mr. Berlander, try to relax.

Gideon kicked out and connected with something soft. It grunted, so Gideon kicked it again.

"Ah said LET GO!"

Blood pressure 196 over 130. Get that into him, NOW!

Gideon saw the knife coming at him and tried to dodge to one side. Other hands, cold and hard, held him steady as the knife was plunged into his shoulder up to the hilt. One of the man-machines caught his arm as it fell and carried it away. Gideon stared at the seeping wound in his shoulder. There was so little pain it almost felt as if he were dreaming.

He wished to God he was as he blinked his eyes and saw two pale fingers floating in front of his eyes. Gideon tried to swat them away and gasped in pain as fire tore through his right shoulder.

"Mr. Berlander, are you in pain?" The voice belonged to the ugliest woman Gideon had ever seen. Her face hovered just beyond the raised fingers.

"Two."

The face got closer, and Gideon squeezed his eyes shut. "What?"

"Fingers," he said. His throat felt as raw as a gutted fish. "Two fingers."

A peppermint-scented sigh hit him in the face.

"Oh. Good, that's very good, Mr. Berlander. You got it right. Two fingers."

Gideon heard a soft scratching sound and pried his left eyelid open just enough to see that the ugly woman was writing something down on a big metal chart. The metal was silver, the pencil she was using bright blue. Gideon closed his eyes, and would have kept them that way if the ugly woman hadn't nudged him none too gently.

"Can you open your eyes for me, Mr. Berlander? Good. Do you know where you are, Mr. Berlander?" She didn't even give him a chance to guess, even though he would have been wrong. "You're at Memorial Hospital, Mr. Berlander, in the ICU. Do you understand?"

Gideon started to answer and felt the raw edges of his throat rub together. He nodded as carefully as he could without waking the fire demon in his shoulder. There'd been a fire at his cabin, and the blue man-machines came and . . . He nodded again and started to close his eyes.

"Oh, please stay awake if you can, okay? There's someone who's been waiting a long time to see you."

The ugly woman backed away and another woman, one Gideon recognized immediately, took her place. Sky couldn't meet his eyes, so he closed his to save her the trouble.

"How long?" Gideon asked.

"Um." There was a flurry of hushed words beyond the barrier of his eyelids, and then: "A week. You've been here a week, Grandfather."

Gideon's eyes flew open as he tried to jerk himself upright—and screamed at the pain that ricocheted off every bone and muscle in his body.

More voices joined in as someone strong, with cold hands, pushed him back down, but Gideon could still hear her, Sky, pleading and begging for them—whoever *they* were—to save him, help him, to do something for him.

If he'd had the strength to do anything but writhe in pain, Gideon would have told her to save her breath. But since he couldn't, he added his own agonizing howl to the commotion.

"Mr. Berlander, listen to me."

This was a new voice, male, the same one he recognized from this dream. It was one of the man-machines. Gideon tried to throw a punch the way he had before. In the dream, reality came in waves and with much the same outcome: He lost.

"Everything's going to be okay now, Mr. Berlander—just try to stay still. I'm going to give you a shot for the pain and then put you on a morphine drip. Can you hear me, Mr. Berlander? Just try to relax and let the . . . drug . . . take . . . effect."

Gideon took a deep breath and felt the pain sink beneath a tingling gush that started at his toes and legs and swept up into his belly-chest-neck before he could wheeze it back out again. There was a slight ringing in his ears, but it wasn't much and wouldn't keep him awake. Hell, he'd slept through windstorms and blizzards and fire . . . he'd slept through fire and man-machines and bulldozers eating his poor dead daughter . . . he'd slept through worse things than a little ringing in his ears.

He just needed a little rest, and when he woke up he'd show 'em . . . he'd show 'em all . . . every last . . . one of . . . 'em.

Sky folded her arms across her chest and leaned back against the curtain-draped glass wall that separated the small room from the ICU's main corridor. It wasn't anything like the intensive-care rooms she'd seen on TV or in the movies. It was quieter, for one thing. There was only one monitor directly above the bed, and if it was beeping at all, Sky couldn't hear it above the soft *plop plop plop* of the IV drip and the old man's rasping breath . . .

. . . and the phantom sound of his screams that still echoed inside her head.

She'd never heard him in pain before, and it made her feel small and frightened—and guilty, as if it were her fault. Again.

"Ms. Berlander?"

Sky blinked the doctor's face into focus. He was young and handsome and blond—a golden boy, the kind of doctor who would have fit in perfectly on a sound stage, with a lot of noisy, beeping machines and a director yelling, "Action." He was new to the area; she would have remembered seeing him before.

"I'm Dr. MacMillan." His hand was warm and soft as it closed around hers in a gesture that already conveyed sympathy at her loss. "I'll be handling Dr. Forsythe's cases while he's on vacation."

Sky smiled at the explanation and tucked her hand under her arm when he released it. It suddenly felt colder in the room.

"The nurses tell me you've been here every day since they brought your grandfather in. How are you holding up?"

A shrug was enough. "He's dying, isn't he."

It wasn't really a question, and it would have been so much easier for both of them, she thought, if he had just nodded and said, "Yes, he's dying. I'm so sorry." But, like his theatrical counterparts, he had to play doctor.

"It's still a little too early to speculate about that, Ms. Berlander," he lied, then quickly covered all the potential malpractice bases. "Your grandfather is surprisingly sturdy for a man of his age, although . . . we are concerned. Aside from the obvious physical trauma he suffered, your grandfather's preexisting condition has severely weakened his system."

Sky shook her head. "What condition?"

The golden doctor's face took on an ashen hue. "D-Dr. Forsythe didn't mention the cancer?"

The room's temperature dropped to absolute freezing. "No, he didn't mention the cancer. Where?"

"Both lungs, and the CAT scan showed malignant masses in both the liver and spine. I'm . . . sorry to have to be the one . . . you know."

Sky knew. "So he is dying."

"I really don't feel too optimistic about your grandfather's prognosis, no. But—"

She hoped her sign hadn't been *too* loud.

"—he's in no pain at the moment and should be out of it for a while. You can wait, of course, but I don't expect him to wake up until this evening. We'll call you the moment he does if you'd rather leave."

Sky looked past the doctor to the unconscious old man tethered to the bed by IVs and monitor leads. Beneath the wrinkles and weather-hardened skin, the old man's slack face was almost as pale as the thick bandage that encompassed his right side from shoulder to belly. Drugged up and peaceful, he didn't look anything like the Gideon Berlander who was her only living relative, and that made his . . . the prognosis easier to accept.

Somewhat.

"I do have some things I should take care of," she said, and let the doctor escort her from the room. A small gust of air from the room's ventilation system rushed past her ears as she stepped into the hall and sent a shiver down her spine.

No one could ever tell her why they kept hospital rooms so chilly.

The golden doctor walked with her as far as the circular reception desk and stopped.

"Here," he said, handing her a cream-colored pamphlet. "This will explain about our hospice program in greater detail, but basically it's about providing whatever care the long-term patient desires so their final days can be spent at home with as much dignity and ease as possible."

The cover showed a sepia-colored sun setting behind sepia-colored hills. There wasn't one sepia-colored cloud in the cream-colored sky. It was all very peaceful, if the "long-term patient" was into sepia and cream—if not, there was a line from a James Whitcomb Riley poem that undoubtedly would put all reservations about dying, death, and dignity to rest: "The sun that cheers our pathway here / Shall beam upon us—*there*."

Unless the patient, like the old man her grandfather had become, didn't believe in *there* and no longer had a *here* in which to live out those last days. Except with her, naturally. She'd have to move out of the bedroom and sleep on the couch until he . . .

"Thank you," Sky said, and folded the pamphlet into the front flap of her purse. "I'll come back later, then."

The doctor smiled and hugged the file to his chest. "You may want to call first . . . just in case he's still asleep."

Or dead, she thought. *That could happen. He's old, sick, maimed . . . people die in hospitals all the time, and he was dying.*

He was dying. Gideon was dying.

It didn't seem real, but it was. Gideon Berlander was dying.

Finally.

Sky nodded and felt a burden lift off her shoulders. "Thank you, Doctor."

Joseph leaned back against the hard plastic chair and tried to concentrate on the *Reader's Digest* story he'd been staring at without reading for the past hour. Just like all the other stories in the various other magazines he'd stared at and not read over the past week. He'd gotten a lot of nonreading done since Sky called to tell him about Gideon.

The story he was currently not reading was about a

man who found God while lost in the Adirondacks. Or at least that's what Joseph gathered from the illustration above the byline.

He was getting so used to pretending to read, he didn't even look up until something in his mind realized that the footsteps echoing in the corridor outside the waiting room were made by boots and not rubber soles.

Joseph felt the tension across his shoulders ease when he looked up and saw the small smile on her lips. It was the first time in a week that Sky didn't look frightened.

"It's good news, Cielo?"

"Good news?"

Joseph's muscles began to tighten again.

"Cielo, how is he?"

"Oh," she said, and nodded as if she finally understood his question. "Dying. He's dying."

The word came so easily to her.

"No," Joseph said. "The injury was bad, yes, but he's strong."

"He's got cancer. There's nothing they can do for him but make him comfortable. See, they gave me a pamphlet about the hospital's hospice program." Sky's gaze never seemed to fully reach his eyes as she held out the brochure. "I have to go now, Joseph. My class is . . . we're going on a field trip after lunch, and I have to . . ."

Sky's odd smile faded when Joseph grabbed her arms. The hospital's brochure fell from her hand, but only he seemed to notice.

"Sky, listen to me—this is very important. Are you sure he's dying?"

A frown appeared between her eyes. "Yes, that's what the doctor told me."

"Then there are things I must tell you before he dies . . . and things you must do. Cielo, I know this will be hard for you to understand, but you must believe me: You were born to reunite what was divided by accident."

Joseph stopped and took a deep breath, feeling his stomach turn from the stench of disinfectant and floral offerings. This was not the way he'd planned to tell her, having to explain things in haste that should have taken years of careful, gentle training, but he had no choice. If Gideon *was* dying—and the very thought made him tremble—then she had to know how to defend herself.

"Cielo, listen to me. When Gideon was only a boy, he wandered into a ceremony that wasn't meant for him and—"

But Sky was already pulling away, silencing the rest of his words with a shake of her head.

"I have to go now, Joseph. We'll talk about this later, I promise."

"Cielo, it's important."

She backed up another step. "Later, please. Okay?"

There was a look in her eyes like that of a foal caught in its first downpour. If he didn't give her the answer she wanted to hear, she'd run blind and he'd lose her to the approaching storm. Joseph nodded and watched the frown between her eyes vanish.

"All right, Cielo. We'll talk later."

Sky gave him one last, quick smile before turning and almost running down the corridor and past the elevator bay to the stairs. Joseph understood completely. Waiting, even for those few moments for the elevator doors to open, would have been just long enough for her to think about everything that had happened and was going to happen.

She had to run from that now, just as he had run miles into the desert the day he found what was left of his son. He'd run blind, just as she was, but it hadn't helped.

The next day had come, as it would for her, and he'd had to think about it.

He had no choice, then or now, and neither did she.

Joseph tried not to breathe the hospital scent any deeper into his lungs than he had to, as he walked into the pool of bright light that surrounded the ICU's nurses' station. Surrounding it, and him, in a semicircle were the patient's cubicles. Only three of the glass-fronted rooms were vacant, their sheer privacy drapes pushed open to reveal narrow beds and silent life-support machines; the other rooms were hidden, their occupants and machines only shadows behind the curtains.

Gideon was a shadow in one of those rooms, a dying shadow.

Joseph waited until the nurse, young and blond— although he didn't think naturally—was finished writing something down on a chart before he cleared his throat. Her eyes were shining and her smile genuine when she looked up.

"May I help you?"

"Yes," he said, wishing now that he'd dressed better than in an ancient wool shirt. The flannel-lined denim coat was newer, so he pulled it closed across his chest. "Gideon Berlander, please."

The bright young nurse looked down at another chart and frowned. When she looked up again, her eyes were no longer shining.

"Are you a relative?"

"A friend." Joseph lied, because he knew what her eyes would say if he told her the truth, that the dying old white man and he were brothers in every way but blood.

"I'm sorry, Mr.—?"

"Longwalker. My name is Joseph Longwalker."

Her smile became a little less genuine and much more sad.

"I'm sorry, Mr. Longwalker, but it's against hospital policy for anyone but the relatives to visit critical-care patients in the ICU. I hope you understand."

"I do, but can you tell me his condition?"

A curtain parted and another nurse, not quite so bright and lovely, stepped out of the room carrying a depleted IV bag. The bright nurse at the desk didn't answer until her colleague pulled the curtain back into place and hurried away. Joseph wasn't sure, but guessed his question was also against hospital policy.

"Mr. Berlander is under sedation right now," she said, "and I really don't think he'll be allowed visitors for a while."

"He's dying?"

She didn't nod so much as drop her chin, but it was more than enough of an answer for Joseph.

"Thank you," he said. "May I come back?"

"It's like I said, Mr. Longwalker—he's not allowed visitors."

"I know, but if I brought something, would you see that he gets it?"

The bright smile was back, as if at last he'd asked something that didn't go against hospital policy.

"Certainly, sir. Of course, the patients aren't allowed flowers in the units, but if you leave them with whoever is on duty at the desk, we'll make sure he knows they're for him."

Her eyes moved to the second curtained room on the right. Gideon's room, Joseph was certain of it, but he felt nothing when he looked at it. It was almost as if Gideon's spirit had already left his body.

The thought made Joseph shiver.

"I know," the nurse said, "it's a little cold in here."

"Yes," Joseph said as he stepped back from the desk, "it is. Thank you for your help. Could I ask just one more thing?"

Professional and bright, she smiled at him. "Of course."

"Keep him alive."

He was dying. Her grandfather was dying.

Gideon was dying.

"He's dying."

Sky steadied herself against the side of the Tracker and let the wind blow the hair out of her face. Even saying the words out loud didn't help.

"He really is dying."

No, it still didn't sound right.

The wind turned as Sky got into the car, carrying the sound of a train's whistle in its teeth. It was the morning freight heading south to Holbrook. She'd heard that whistle every day, but this was the first time she stopped to listen to it. At school, the whistle meant there were only ten minutes left in the first recess period. On Saturdays it meant she had only two hours before the banks and post office closed. On Sundays it meant missing ten-o'clock mass to stay in bed with Sam and cuddle.

At least that's what it used to mean. Last Sunday, Sam was away on business and she slept alone. Last Sunday was only two days after her grandfather's "accident."

"Ms. Berlander? Yes, this is Memorial Hospital. I'm afraid your grandfather's been in a serious accident."

"No, I'm sorry, I don't know the details, but there are strong indications that he may have attempted suicide."

"Do you know if he was depressed?"

It was impossible, she told them. Gideon Berlander was not the sort of man who'd try to kill himself.

And then they told her a few things about his injuries and how two fishermen had found him, raving and bloody from an apparent self-inflicted wound. A psychologist suggested she consider having her grandfather committed for observation once he recovered.

Of course, now she didn't have to worry about that. *He's dying.*

Sky closed the door before the sound of the whistle faded. Nothing would change after he died: The train would still sound its whistle as it passed through town, and the kids at school would hear it and scurry to get in one more game of hopscotch or tetherball before the end of recess. The wind would continue to blow and night would follow day.

Babies are born and old men die.

Sky turned the keys in the ignition and gasped as frigid air blasted her from the vents. The Tracker's heater had gone cold. God, she didn't think she'd been in the hospital that long . . . *time flies when you're having fun, doesn't it?*

Sliding the heater vent closed, Sky leaned her head against the window and listened to the wind sniff along the top of the doors like a dog on a scent. It was a soft, furtive sound, not meant to disturb but only to let her know it was there. If she needed it.

"He's dying," she whispered, and the wind moaned.

CHAPTER 11

The wind plucked a discarded white plastic shopping bag up off the side of the road and wrapped it around the car's radio antenna. Sam watched it flap and flutter for a few seconds before another gust of wind pulled it free and sent it careening into oncoming traffic. He caught sight of it again in his rearview mirror just as a minivan ran over it.

"Ashes to ashes, trash to trash," he said, and turned up the radio to the familiar sounds of pounding hooves and steel guitars playing an old western melody about a young cowboy who knows he's done wrong. Sam remembered the tune from school, singing it with the gusto only a kid who'd never seen a real cowboy in his life could.

He preferred the new lyrics, especially the last line of the chorus: "Oh, I'm a lone cowboy in search of a home."

"Well, cowboy, if you're looking for a home, you don't have to look any farther than a bright orange and yellow Sun Country Homes sign." The announcer was an oldtime B-Western star whose voice had lost none of its legendary drawl. "That's right, pardner. Look for the Sun Country Homes sign and you'll find the home you've always wanted. Starting in the low two hundred thousands, Sun Country Homes has the home for you. See our ads in the New Homes section of the Sunday paper, or check out our website at triple double-U dot Sun Country Homes dot.com. We'll be watchin' for you, cowboy. Yee-HAW."

Sam turned the radio off when another voice, younger and without a hint of drawl, began to fast-forward through the disclaimer. He knew the spiel by heart, just like every other one of Mackay's employees.

It was part of the job, and there were pop quizzes to ensure quality control. Although Sam had never heard of any employee using that knowledge to keep them from getting fired.

Jennet Mackay required only one thing from his employees, besides coming in with a minimum of three new property leads per month, and that was blind loyalty to the company. If an employee was given an assignment, it, or the employee, would be finished by a certain time.

No one in the eighteen-year history of SC Industries ever got a second chance.

With the exception of Mr. and Mrs. Reynolds's little boy, Sammy.

And then only because he'd had more than an ace up his sleeve. He'd been holding the queen of hearts.

"Which reminds me."

Sam pulled out his cell phone and flipped it open, punching the preset memory button six times. The first preset was Mackay's office, the second his "open" home line. The third and fourth were private, not-to-be-given-out numbers; the fifth, his favorite Chinese takeout place. He'd added the sixth number out as insurance.

And bumped Sky down to seventh.

The electronic warbling filled his ear as he pulled to a stop beneath a gaudy red-orange-and-yellow billboard:

LIVE THE WESTERN DREAM!
SUN COUNTRY HOMES IS PROUD
TO ANNOUNCE

PIONEER RIDGE
Executive Homes
Breathtaking views, endless vistas
Another SUN COUNTRY HOMES
Planned Development
Starting in the Low 700's
Home sites still available

Pioneer Ridge, aka the old Berlander property. Sam ran his little finger over the thin scar on his forehead as a voice came onto the line.

"Memorial Hospital, how may I direct your call?"

"ICU, please."

Soft music whispered in his ear as the transfer was made.

"ICU."

"Ah, yeah—hi. This is Sam Reynolds and I just wanted to check on Mr. Berlander's condition."

A city bus displaying a Sun Country Homes poster rolled through the intersection as the nurse's voice became less professionally distant. He'd made it a point to call the hospital at least once a day to ask about the old man's condition. He didn't mention it to Sky, but knew the hospital staff would.

"Oh, hi. Let's see . . ." Sam heard the rustle of paper. "Mr. Berlander is resting comfortably right now. He was in a little bit of pain this morning, but that's only to be expected given his condition."

Sam exhaled against the phone, knowing it would sound like a sigh. "Is he . . . Mr. Berlander getting any better?"

The nurse's long pause said that Mr. Berlander was not.

"I really can't say. You should talk to his granddaughter."

The light changed and Sam nodded as he eased the car forward. Lunchtime traffic was heavier than usual.

"Oh. I see. Poor Sky."

"Yeah, it really is a shame."

That sounded like the old man was dying, but he had to be sure.

Sam hung a right into an access alley, then made an almost immediate left into the tollgated underground parking structure. He nodded to the attendant on duty as he passed.

"Can anything be done?"

"I don't think so," the nurse said. "His condition is too advanced, I'm afraid, but—"

Sam did a quick mental rundown of all the likely "conditions" that might be too advanced for recovery: heart disease, cirrhosis of the liver, cancer, arteriosclerosis, tuberculosis, AIDS, if the old man had ever gotten lucky.

"—you really should talk to his granddaughter."

"I will, tonight." *Have to make sure the nurse doesn't forget my relationship to Sky, no matter how strained that might be at the moment.* "I was just hoping it was better news."

"I know, and I'm sorry."

Yup, he was dying.

Sam pulled the car back into its parking slot and turned off the engine. Without the tiny engine and heater sounds to complement it, his voice sounded hollow and flat.

"Well, Sky and I both know you and the doctors are doing your best for him by keeping him comfortable. And I'm sure some part of him understands exactly what's going on."

She took it as a compliment. "Thank you. I'll let him know you called again when he wakes up."

"You do that," Sam said, and flipped the phone closed. "And I would love to see his face when you do."

Joseph tightened his grip on the metal pole as the bus pulled back into traffic. The bus was crowded, the streets were crowded, but everywhere he looked through the tinted window glass he saw people he didn't recognize, and it made him feel lonely.

And hungry.

Usually, he'd be home by now, sitting in front of

one of Estralita's wonderful midday meals and talking about small, unimportant things. Never mentioning Gideon except in small, unimportant ways: "The nurses say he's resting comfortably." "The doctors are hopeful." "He's off the respirator." "His heart is strong."

The truth was always harder to face.

"He's dying," Joseph whispered out loud, and immediately regretted it when he felt the person who'd been standing next to him back away. He was on a crowded downtown bus, talking to himself like he was one of those poor souls who wandered the streets of the city, happily carrying on two-way conversations with the air.

Foolish old man, he thought, *where do you think you are? Home?*

Joseph cleared his throat and pretended to find things of interest out the window. Home was exactly the place he should be—preparing for what was to come.

Estralita was probably already worried about him, wondering what had happened to him and where he was. Even with the temporary addition of the hour-and-forty-minute-long bus trip to "visit a sick friend," his routine had not significantly changed from year to year or season to season. Joseph was usually as constant as the northern star.

Usually, but not today.

He probably should have called to tell her he'd accidentally missed the bus, but that, even as small as it was, would have been more lie than he was willing to tell. Poor Estralita—she didn't deserve to be treated like that.

He should be home.

To get ready.

And pray that Gideon didn't die until he could speak to him.

Go home, old man.

Joseph moved to let a woman pass. He couldn't go home, not yet. From the moment that morning when Sky had told him about Gideon, Joseph's skin had suddenly felt a size too small for his body. It was all right as long as he kept moving, but every time he stopped he could feel his skin tighten like wet leather. If he went home now his skin would strangle him, and he didn't want Estralita to see that.

Just a few more hours, he promised himself, *and then I'll go back and begin. Maybe stop by the trading post for a bag of hard candy to show how sorry I am. Maybe—*

The bus veered to the right, and Joseph was snapped out of his thoughts of penance as an eddy of men and women in business clothes surged toward the front and back doors. When the bus finally stopped and the doors opened, an equal number of people similarly attired got on.

Joseph was the only one who wasn't wearing the camouflage costume of Richland's financial district. He watched them through the window and smiled. It was like a scene from one of those television shows his son watched, where well-dressed policemen and -women managed to solve unthinkable crimes in just an hour. With commercial breaks.

The bus lurched back into traffic as Joseph continued to watch. None of it was real—not the people, or the cars, or the skyscrapers of glass and steel. Reality was hidden behind a curtain in a hospital room across town, trapped inside a dying old man.

"Enough," he said out loud, not caring who heard him this time, and pulled the bell cord.

Joseph was one of many who got off at the stop— but the only one who stepped aside and let the flow of office workers and corporative executives pass by. He had one stop to make before catching the right bus back to the reservation.

Moving through the crowd at an angle, Joseph walked over to a canvas-sided newspaper kiosk in front of a bank and bought two chocolate bars. It was a very poor peace offering for the worry he'd undoubtedly caused her, but he knew Estralita would forgive him that, too. He would have liked to find a candy store or even make do with a box of overpriced chocolates from some hotel's gift shop, but he didn't have the time.

He had to get home and prepare the way for the next Chosen One.

If he still had enough time.

Sam watched his employer wrap a smile around the butt of a $75 see-gar as he leaned back into the crushed velvet of his executive throne. The smile, like everything else in the man's office, was overdone and only 10 percent genuine, but it was a hell of a lot better than the look Mackay usually reserved for the hired help.

"Well, things like this happen, don't they?" Mackay puffed a perfect smoke ring toward the recessed ceiling lights. "Don't suppose he'll get better, do you?"

The question was in reference to the update Sam had given him on Gideon Berlander's condition.

"I wouldn't think so."

"Um. Did they say how long he had?"

"No, but I'll ask Sky at dinner tonight.

"Must be hard on her, since he's her only living relative and all."

"For a while."

Mackay stopped smiling. "Oh. Does this mean we'll be hearing the toll of wedding bells soon?"

Sam retrieved his employer's smile and added a couple more volts of energy to it without actually opening his mouth. It was a salesman's smile, full of promises and false advertising, but Mackay apparently didn't realize that and Sam wanted to keep it that way. As long as the great and powerful Jennet Mackay thought there might be a chance of a wife not being able to testify against her husband—if the truth about blunt-force trauma as a negotiating tool ever reared its ugly little head—Sam knew he wouldn't have to live off his unemployment insurance.

Besides, he wanted his promised "starting in the low 700's" executive mansion up on the ridge, and he wasn't going to do anything—short of marrying the half-breed—to jeopardize that.

Hell, he'd earned it. Even if he hadn't been the one who supplied the final muscle in the transaction, his name appeared on the closing papers, and that's all a court of law would need.

Should that need arise.

When the corners of Sam's mouth began to ache from the pressure of holding the smile, he dropped one side and shrugged.

"You never can tell," he said. "Sky's a wonderful woman, and you can tell she'd make a great mother just by watching her with those kids out on the reservation. I think we'd be very happy together."

Mackay set his cigar off into a cut-crystal ashtray, then picked up a bright blue paper SC Industries pocket folder. "Don't try to bullshit a bullshitter, Reynolds, especially not someone who's made it his life's work. But if you are going to see her tonight, I guess you might as well handle the last bits of paperwork."

Sam let the other side of his smile drop as he took the folder and flipped it open. The left pocket, above the empty business-card slot, held the standard copy-in-triplicate closing contract. The right pocket held the very lucrative check, minus his commission, made out to Sky Berlander, acting as Gideon Berlander's authorized power of attorney.

Sam checked the amount and caught himself before he whistled. It was much more than the offer he'd been authorized to give and would more than cover the medical bills and funeral expenses, with maybe enough left over for a comfortable little nest egg—if the stubborn old man didn't hang on longer than another week.

"Very generous," he said, closing the envelope. "Sky will appreciate it."

"I'm sure she will. In fact, why don't we plan to meet up on the ridge to celebrate."

Sam had already decided that it might be nice to have a little housewarming once he had a house to warm, but he hadn't considered inviting either Sky or Mackay. Once her grandfather was dead and buried, he'd let their relationship follow suit . . . and Jennet Mackay just didn't look like the type of man who'd enjoy chowing down on barbecued ribs and coleslaw, no matter how imported the beer was.

"Problem?"

Sam felt a twinge along the length of the scar on his forehead when he blinked. "Pardon? No, no problem . . . I was just planning the menu."

"For what?"

"The . . . celebration?"

Mackay retrieved his cigar from the ashtray and puffed life back into it as he settled back into his chair.

"You won't need to. After looking at the property myself, I decided it was high time I did something I've been thinking about for years."

The twinge in his forehead became a slow throb. "You're going to live up there."

"Oh, hell no." The words were clouded in rich smoke. "I love my condo—houses are too much trouble. No—I'm going into the restaurant game. Can't you just picture it, Reynolds? A five-star gourmet restaurant on the top of that ridge, looking down on the lights of the city and surrounded by millionaires?"

"Where on the top of the ridge, exactly?" Sam asked, although he had a twisted-gut feeling he already knew where. Exactly.

Mackay smiled. *Shit*, Sam thought. "From the site of the cabin back to the drop. Of course, I'll have to put up a retaining wall and fencing along the walkways—can't have customers sliding down the mountain, can we? And get this: I'm thinking of making the wall overlooking the city out of glass. Won't that be something?"

Sam rubbed his forehead.

"Yeah," he said. "It's abso-fucking-lutely something."

CHAPTER 12

Joseph pretended not to notice his daughter-in-law watching him from behind the kitchen curtain as she nibbled the second of the two chocolate peace offerings he'd brought her from the city. She'd blushed when he put the candy bars into her hands and denied that she'd been worried, but she hadn't taken her eyes off him for more than a moment or two since he'd come home.

As if she expected him to disappear.

Soon perhaps, he thought, *but not yet.*

"I have too much to do," he told his hands as they stripped the bark from a green willow branch, "and all of it should have been done years ago."

The wind rearranged the strips of bark at his feet, restless, like a child that had been ignored too long. Joseph peeled off another curl with the bone-handled knife and held it out to the gusting air. The bark twisted and turned against his fingers.

"Men lie to themselves," he said when the wind snatched the bark out of his hand and flew it into the sky. "We always think we have just a little more time than we do. I should have demanded we perform the ceremony when she came of age . . . but I always thought there'd be more time."

The wind caressed his cheek and brought him the sound of footsteps crunching on hard-packed dirt. A moment later, he heard his grandson's voices.

How late *was* it?

Joseph closed the pocketknife carefully against his knee and looked toward the house. Estralita met his eyes and smiled, a little sheepishly, before waving at the group of children walking up the road. Two broke away from the group as it passed; but one lingered, talking to a sweet-faced girl with long, shimmering hair, while the other dashed up the gravel sidewalk.

Andy's cheeks were red from the cold. Seeing him reminded Joseph of how cold it was . . . and how late.

"Where were you, Grandfather?"

Joseph slipped the knife into the pocket of his jacket before accepting the eight-year-old's bear hug.

"I lost track of time," he said honestly.

The little boy nodded as he let go, then sat down in the pile of shavings and played with the curls of willow the same way the wind had. His dark eyes never left the willow branch in Joseph's hand.

"What'cha making, Grandfather?"

Joseph ran his thumb along the strip of bark still on the branch. "A whistle."

"For me?"

"No."

"Oh." The disappointment in the child's voice was almost physical. "For Joey."

Joseph pulled the knife out of his pocket and flicked it open. "No, it's not for Joey. It's for a friend of mine."

"Oh. Your friend in the hospital?"

Gideon Berlander, a friend? "No, I'm making it for another friend, who needs it more."

To avoid any more questions along those lines, he nodded toward the road as he stripped off another curl of bark. "Who is Joey talking to?"

And the distraction worked, at least for the moment. Andy went back to playing with the shavings and shrugged.

"Oh, that's only Cindy Nampeyo. She's in Joey's class, and he likes her. He's in love with her."

"He is?"

"Yeah," Andy said, raising his voice to match his older brother's approach, "everybody in school knows that. They kiss all the time. 'Joey 'n' Cindy sittin' in a tree, k-i-s-s-i-n-g!' It's gross."

Shoulders hunched, head down, Joey glared at his brother. His cheeks were a brighter red than Andy's had been, though Joseph suspected it was from more than just the cold.

"Don't listen to him, Grandfather," the older boy said, "that brat doesn't know what he's talking about."

"I'm not a brat," Andy countered, "and I do, too. Everybody in school knows you two *love* each other."

Joseph stripped off another long curl. "That's good."

"Huh?"

"That your brother is in love. I met your grandmother when we were both younger than you are now and knew even then that we would get married one day."

Joey's blush deepened. "I don't know about getting married. . . ."

"And you shouldn't," Joseph said, letting him off the hook. "It's a different time and different world. Your grandmother and I knew, but our time is over."

"You still miss her, don't you, Grandfather?" The question was from Joey, who had been just old enough when she died to remember her.

Joseph stripped the last of the bark away and used the bare willow to tap the center of his chest.

"I miss her here, but that's all right, for that's how it should be. Now . . ." Rolling the stiffness out of his shoulders, Joseph measured out one hand's length on the willow and began to whittle the shape of a mouthpiece. He could feel his grandson's eyes on him. "Who has homework?"

"I only have to read a chapter in geography."

"And I only got spelling words to study, but I know them real good."

"I'm glad to hear it," Joseph said.

"What are you making, Grandfather?" Joey asked as he and his school books joined his younger brother at Joseph's feet.

"It's a whistle," Andy said, quick to let his brother know he already had that information. "Right, Grandfather."

"Yes," Joseph said, "but it's not an ordinary whistle. This will be a spirit whistle."

187

From the direction of the house came the rattle of pipes as Estralita began another load of laundry, but outside was only the sound of the wind.

"Like in the stories, Grandfather?" Joey asked.

"Yes, and I want both of you to pay attention, because one day you may both have to do this. Now hush, both of you, and watch."

But he might as well have told the wind to stop blowing. The possibility that they might get to make a spirit whistle seemed to remove every last shred of self-control his grandsons had. Joseph ignored the gibbering and jostling as he freed the shape of the mouthpiece from the wood. The boys only grew quiet again when he produced a small box of wooden matches and tossed it to Joey.

"Ooo, he's not supposed to play with matches, Grandfather."

"He won't be," Joseph assured the younger boy. "Joey, gather up the willow bark and burn it. Then keep the fire going until I tell you to let it die."

While the balance of sibling power shifted back to the older boy, Joseph began scraping the pulp from the whistle with a pick made from the right wing bone of an owl. When the fire was burning steadily, he held the hollow whistle above the flames until the greasy smoke covered it.

"Hear me, Old One . . . I send the spirit of this wood to you on the smoke, grant it a new spirit and voice."

The wind swirled the smoke into a tight column. Andy's eyes widened as he watched it spiraling upward.

"Wow."

"Hush," Joseph scolded, then winked. "Thank you, Old One."

The smoke had turned the wood to the color of old bone. It had been so long since he'd made a spirit whistle, Joseph couldn't remember if the bone color was a good sign or bad, so he didn't think—tried hard not to think as he drilled out the sound hole with the knife tip. *It has been too long.*

The fire had finished with the willow and began nibbling the dry grasses and twigs Joey had added to it.

"Nice whistle, Grandfather," his grandson said as he fed a small pinecone to the flames, but it was clear, by the sound of his voice, that he wasn't impressed. Joseph had been making both boys willow whistles since they first learned the difference between breathing in and breathing out. "Is it finished?"

"No, this is still just a whistle. Now we need the magic. Andy, take this empty soda can and fill it half full of water from the garden hose. Go on. Joey, keep the fire going."

While the brothers concentrated on their tasks, Joseph cut a thin plug from the remaining willow and pressed it into the mouthpiece to act as a reed. The "magic" had already been done—the Old One had given the whistle a new soul—but that didn't matter. Children needed ceremony as well as stories in their lives, especially those children who may be chosen to carry on the traditions.

He'd already let one of those children slip through his fingers; he couldn't let it happen again.

Andy reappeared—arm outstretched, staring at the aluminum can in his hand, water droplets burbling over the rim with each stiff-legged step—as

Joseph pulled the medicine pouch out from beneath his shirt. He had worn the pouch for sixty-three years, taking comfort and strength from the feel of it against his skin. His own grandfather had given it to him the day he was sent to the Old One.

The pouch, and the powered medicine plants it contained, had been his bridge from the world of earth to the world of the Kachina, but his grandsons, and son, saw it only for what it appeared to be: a relic wrapped in faded blue calico.

"Put the can here," Joseph told the boy, pointing to a spot far enough back from the crackling fire so there could be no mishaps. "When the ceremony is finished, it will be your job to put out the fire, all right?"

Andy nodded and sat back on his legs, his chest already puffing with pride.

"Joey, you keep the fire going."

The older boy tore a sheet of paper out of his notebook and fed it to the flames a piece at a time.

"Good, now how many birds shall we call down?"

Both boys smiled. It was the first story he had ever told them.

"Four!" Andy blurted out even before his brother could open his mouth. "Four birds—

"And the medicine man said,
'Send me one bird, one . . .
One bird to send to the Sun.'"

Joey grunted, and his brother fell silent.

"Then," he continued, "then the medicine man said,

190

'Send me two birds, two . . .
Two birds to the River that runs.' "

Both of the boys looked at Joseph.

"And then the medicine man said,
'Send me three birds, three . . .
Three birds to send to the sky.
And finally the medicine man said,
'Send me four birds, four . . .
Four birds to say who will die.' "

But hear me, Old One: Don't let me be one of those four.

"Old One," Joseph said, holding the medicine pouch tight in his fist as he watched the smoke from the fire rise, "we seek your guidance in this as we do in all things. Make the voice you have given this whistle speak only of good and peace. Make its voice a lullaby to those seeking rest and a song of memory to those who are lost."

And give its voice strength to protect, should it be needed.

The material made dry creaking sounds while Joseph worked the drawstring top open. The sound reminded him just how long it had been since he'd made a spirit whistle; if the pouch itself had suffered from the passage of time, would the medicine inside still have any power?

He didn't know, but he prayed silently as he gathered a pinch of the fragrant herbs and rubbed them into the body of the whistle.

The change was instantaneous.

"Wow, cool! It's like those color-changer toys."

Joseph smiled at the eight-year-old's comment but secretly exhaled in relief. The whistle in his hand was now the color of the morning sun—bright yellow, the color of the Northwest. It was the strongest sign he could have gotten, but even now he wasn't sure if the sign was good or bad. Northwest meant the mountain and the cave.

Northwest meant Yaponcha.

But the direction also meant Gideon.

"Yeah, that really was cool, Grandfather. Can you make us ones like that?"

Joseph closed the medicine pouch and slipped it back beneath his shirt. "Maybe, but not right now. Now Andy must put the fire out—and make sure it's out—then we must find two feathers, one from a hawk and the other from an owl, so that the whistle may have power both during the day and night. After that—"

"Joey, Andrew." Estralita's voice, though gentle, was unexpected and made Joseph and the boys jump. "Stop bothering your grandfather and get inside and do your homework. You have homework, right?"

"But ma'am," Andy whined, "we have to help Grandfather find feathers for the—"

"Don't argue with your mother," Joseph interrupted before the boy could tell his mother what they needed to find feathers for. He didn't need to give his daughter-in-law anything else to worry about. "Doing your homework is more important."

"But Grandfa-ather."

"Hush now. Go do as your mother says, both of you."

The boys grumbled but gathered up their dusty schoolbooks and stood up. Joseph stayed seated, holding the whistle tight in his hand and watching the soggy ashes seep into the ground. Come morning there'd be nothing left but a dark spot in the dirt.

"Father?"

Joseph looked up to see Estralita standing at the back door, huddled in an oversized work shirt that barely stretched over her swollen belly. His new grandchild was going to be big.

"I just made a fresh pot of coffee, Father, and some oatmeal cookies." She smiled and the wind caught her hair, fanning it around her face like a blue-black halo. "I'll bring you some, if you like, before the boys eat them all."

"No, I'll come get some. Oatmeal cookies sound good."

Slipping the whistle into the pocket of his coat, Joseph stood up and walked to the house. Halfway there, the wind gusted from the northeast and deposited two feathers, one from a hawk, the other from an owl, at his feet.

It was a good sign.

When Sky heard Sam's recorded message on her answering machine, apologizing that he'd be a couple hours late for their planned six-o'clock dinner date, but with the promise of a *big* surprise, her reaction was not that of a woman in love.

"God, why couldn't he have just canceled?"

And to make matters worse, she had no idea why she felt that way.

Their relationship was seemingly back on course;

he told her he was looking for another job—in advertising—and the ICU nurses gave her glowing accounts of his daily phone calls inquiring about her grandfather.

Sam was a charmer, all right, but ICU nurses are generally easily impressed.

Sky pressed the message erase button and sighed.

Her head had begun pounding an hour into the field trip and only gotten worse as the day dragged on. The three extra-strength Tylenols she'd begged from the school nurse had managed to reduce the pain to a dull, constant throb behind her right eye, but now the headache was back and all she wanted to do was crawl into bed—*alone*.

Sleep. All she wanted to do was go to sleep and forget the fact that Gideon was dying and her head was splitting and her lover would be late for dinner but still show up, flowers and candy as the surprise . . . and all she wanted was fourteen straight hours of oblivion.

Or, at the very least, a good four-hour catnap on the couch that, with any luck, would leave her looking so puffy and haggard that Sam would take one look and leave her in peace.

Sky was heading for the couch when the doorbell rang.

He had lied on the phone. He was right on time.

"Oh . . . shit."

Sky managed to narrow the list of possible reasons for canceling their date to one credible excuse by the time she crossed the room and opened the front door.

"Hi. Hey look, can we just—Grandfather Joseph?"

194

The wrinkles in the old man's face deepened when he reached out and touched her cheek. His fingertips felt like sandpaper.

"Cielo, are you all right?"

"It's been a long day," she said, and stepped back, holding on to the door for balance. "Please, won't you come in? I was . . . just going to make coffee."

He gave her a look that told her he knew she was lying, but thanked her and made himself comfortable on the couch while the headache accompanied her into the kitchen. While Mr. Coffee gurgled and belched, Sky got down the bottle of generic aspirin-like pain relievers and poured three of the white pills into her hand.

"I apologize for dropping in on you like this without calling first," Joseph said from the other room, "especially since you aren't feeling well."

Sky looked at the pills in her hand and quickly dry-swallowed them. He must have heard her shake the pills out of the bottle.

"No, I'm really all right, Grandfather," she said, grimacing at the bitter taste on the back of her tongue. "It's just a little headache."

To prove it was nothing more, Sky walked to the doorway and leaned against the jamb. Joseph was sitting on the couch as if he were in church—back straight, hands folded in his lap, feet together. He looked out of place, and it took Sky a moment to realize why that was. He'd never been to her apartment before, and the place was a mess. There was a week's worth of newspapers, still bundled, beneath the coffee table, unfolded laundry still in its basket on the chair. Uncorrected tests on the desk. Unopened mail on the end tables. Takeout food bags, empty soft-drink cans, lions and tigers and bears. Oh my.

Since Gideon's "accident" she'd let the place, and herself, go to hell.

The ache in her head was nothing compared to the sudden self-loathing she felt.

"I really am glad you're here, Grandfather," she said, bending down carefully to remove an empty pizza carton from where it sat on the pile of newspapers. The carton wasn't empty. Sky caught a whiff of rancid cheese when she lifted the carton. *God.* "But I wish you would have let me know you were coming. It would have given me a chance to clean up."

Joseph looked around as if he hadn't noticed the mess. Or the smell.

"I came to see you, Cielo. Sit down, I need to tell you something."

"Sure, but let me get you some coffee first."

The old man patted the cushion next to him—at least the couch was relatively neat—and shook his head.

"Later. Come."

Sky dropped the carton back onto the papers and picked her way to the couch. "I'm usually much neater than this."

"I know," he said when she sat down, "it's been a hard week for all of us, and it will be harder still when he dies."

Sky didn't expect the sudden tightness in her chest and belly and gasped in surprise . . . only in surprise. She knew it couldn't have been anything else, but Joseph took her hands in his and squeezed them gently.

"I know. You have heard me tell the stories of our people to the children, but do you remember a story about the Old One, Yaponcha?"

Sky took a deep breath and frowned. She'd heard so many of Joseph's stories over the years, she couldn't be sure. But it *sounded* so familiar.

"He's a Kachina, isn't he?" Since most of the stories the old man told were about Kachinas, Sky knew she had at least a fifty-fifty chance of having guessed right.

And Joseph's smile proved it. "Yes, he is the Kachina of the Wind and Dust Devils, but he is never seen at any of the dances and he has no mask. He is a deity beyond all the others. Do you remember the stories?"

Sky shook her head. "Not really."

"It's all right, I'll tell you one now."

"Now?"

Sky glanced at the clock on the VCR. Sam would be showing up later, if not sooner, Gideon was dying, the place really did look like it had been hit by a small but violent tornado, Gideon was dying, her head was still pounding, and—

Gideon was dying.

And all she wanted to do was hear a story.

Sky curled her legs under her and settled back into the cushions.

"Many years ago," he began, "the Old One, Yaponcha, called out to the world because the time had come to pick a new Wind Caller. It was a hard thing for the medicine men and chiefs to decide, but finally the Chosen One was found and brought to the sacred cave high in the mountains. But the Chosen One was weak and afraid, and he failed many of the tests the Old One put before him. He would have been rejected had there not been someone else in the cave—an outsider, not of the people, who had wandered in by accident.

"But the Old One didn't know this. To him, the souls of both looked as one—so he joined them. They became the Two-Together, and together the Old One taught them the secret ways and the words of the wind.

"But the other, the outsider, didn't understand the meanings of the words he learned. He knew only the power he controlled, and it twisted him inside. Soon it became clear to all that Yaponcha had made a mistake in accepting the outsider."

"I didn't think gods could make mistakes," Sky said.

"Why not? The gods are much like men."

"That's depressing. But if Yaponcha saw he'd made a mistake, why didn't he just correct it?"

"How?" Joseph asked. "By killing an innocent child? He was in the cave by accident—it wasn't his fault that he'd been given a power he never knew existed. He was simply in the wrong place at the right time."

"Then why didn't Yaponcha make the real Chosen One stronger?"

Joseph smiled and patted Sky's hands. "He did, by creating a third from the blood of both."

Either the aspirinlike pain relievers were stronger

than the real thing, or Sky was more tired than she thought.

"You lost me."

His answer didn't help.

"Do you know why your name is Sky?"

Sky leaned her head against the back of the couch. She still had no idea why the old man had decided to pick today for a visit, and whatever the reason, he was going to take his time before he told her. It was like the "Guess Who I Am" game she played with the children at school—you could guess, but unless you guessed correctly the game would go on and on.

"No, but I always thought it was short for Skyler or something."

"No, it's not." Joseph let go of her hands and took a deep breath. "I named you Sky because that's where I found you—under the evening sky, alone and trembling in the cold."

"Joseph, what are you talking about?"

"When your mother died giving birth to you, your grandfather Gideon saw in your face the reason why his daughter died. He saw only your father, so he took you outside and left you under the sky.

"You were so cold when I found you, you didn't even cry, but you grabbed my finger, this one . . ." Joseph held up the little finger on his right hand and shook it at her. "And you wouldn't let go. I named you Sky, Cielo, and would have taken you back to the reservation with me if he hadn't come back to his senses and taken you from me."

"What?" Sky scooted as far away as she could

from the man she'd always thought of as gentle and kind, everyone's grandfather. He'd witnessed a child being abused—her—and hadn't done anything. "He tried to kill me, and you didn't even try to take me away? Why?"

"I was weak."

"Weak? Joseph, I was helpless and you left me with him."

"But it was all right, Cielo, I knew he wouldn't harm you after that. Once his mind was clear of the grief, he saw you for what you are."

The memory of wind and a red-dirt man tried to form itself around the pain in Sky's head, but she shook it away.

"What am I, Joseph?"

Only the old man's eyes followed her as she paced back and forth like a caged animal; the rest of him was still as if carved from stone.

"My granddaughter as much as you are his. My son, Thomas, was your father."

Sky heard the heater kick on as the room got cold. Not red-dirt man, dirty Redman. She'd misunderstood as a child. She'd been waiting for a red-dirt man all these years; no wonder he never showed up.

"Your son raped my mother."

"No, your mother and father were in love. I remember the first time Thomas told me about her. . . . He'd come home from school at the beginning of his freshman year and told me about a girl in his chemistry class, a girl with golden hair and eyes like the morning sky. They were only fifteen—too young to think of circumstances or to be careful, but Thomas never raped your mother. Gideon said it was rape to justify murdering my son."

"You're lying. He couldn't have murdered my father and gotten away with it. There are laws in this country, Joseph. No court would let a murderer raise a child."

Sky felt bile rise in the back of her throat. "Not even a child he tried to kill."

"No court knew about it, Cielo."

Joseph stood up and began to walked around the coffee table, but she matched his advancing steps with steps of her own. She'd backed all the way to the bedroom hallway when he finally stopped.

"When they realized she was pregnant, Thomas told me he wanted to marry her but that Glory, your mother, was too frightened to tell Gideon. . . . I told Thomas I would speak to Gideon myself, make him understand, but that he was not to go see Glory again until I had. He said he wouldn't . . . but he was young and in love.

"Gideon must have followed your mother when she left the house that afternoon. He found them together, I suppose, and called the wind. While your mother watched, the wind tore my son to pieces. I'd heard the wind and knew what had happened, but by the time I got to the ridge, there wasn't even enough left of your father for me to bury."

Sky leaned her forehead against the hallway's cool plaster and closed her eyes. A new image merged with her memory about the wind and the red-dirt man—an image of blood dripping from green aspen leaves while a girl with blond hair and eyes the color of the morning sky rocked back and forth and screamed.

"I told the reservation police Thomas had run away. I might have saved him, Cielo, if I had been willing to call the wind—but even then I was afraid. That is my weakness, and that's why the Old One had no choice but to link my spirit to Gideon's. He was never afraid of the power given to him. Come, sit down. There's more."

Sky shook her head but let him lead her back to the couch. *More? How could there be more? It is already a nightmare.*

"But I don't understand, Joseph . . . *Grand-father.* . . . Why are you telling me this now?"

"Because Gideon is dying, Cielo, and before that happens he must release his power over the wind. If he doesn't, if he dies as the Wind Caller, the new Chosen One will have to take the power from him by force."

The three aspirins she'd taken had no chance against this kind of nonsense. Sky leaned back and stared at the ceiling. *What the hell is going on? Okay, I can believe the part about Joseph being my grandfather and his son dying by Gideon's hand, but not the way he was supposed to have killed my father. . . . No, that couldn't have happened, it just isn't possible for someone to*—blow into a whistle and watch the wind destroy a long black car—*control the wind. Jesus . . . it's a story—just another story like the ones he told the kids at school.*

"Cielo? Sky here. . . . I have something for you."

When Sky looked down at what Joseph was holding in his hand, a small jolt, like a static discharge, lifted the hairs on her arms and at the back of her neck.

The whistle lay diagonally across his palm. It was beautiful—bright yellow with four consecutive bands painted dark blue just below the mouthpiece. Two feathers, one pale gray, the other banded tan, tied together by a thick braid of white thread, spun lazily in the heater's warm breeze.

"Cielo, take it."

Sky crossed her arms over her chest, tucking her hands in tight against her ribs.

"Joseph, I lied to you, I really am tired, and I think . . . You should go now, Joseph. I mean, Grandfather."

He didn't move except to lay the whistle on her knees. The whistle wasn't heavy, but Sky could feel its weight through the heavy corduroy weave of her pants.

"It's yours, Cielo. I made it for you when I got back from the hospital."

"It's . . . very pretty, Joseph, but—"

"I know, it's all coming too quickly and I'm sorry for this . . . and for everything that I should have done and didn't. I should have taken you from him that day; the Old One sent the wind to tell me of your birth, so I should have known from that moment that he'd had a hand in giving you life. He brought my son and Gideon's daughter together to make what had been divided whole again. In you."

Sky tried to pull away when he grabbed her hands, but the old man wouldn't let go. She stopped struggling when the whistle rolled down her legs to nestle against her belly.

"You were born the Chosen One, and both Gideon and I saw it. I should have taken you—I

203

think now that Yaponcha had sent the wind because
that is what he wanted. I failed him as I failed you
and let Gideon keep you. I thought he would have
trained you to call the wind, but now I know he
didn't."

But he did, Joseph, she wanted to tell him. *He
showed me how to call the wind once when a red-dirt man
came in a long black car.*

Both of them jumped when the front door rattled—but it was only the wind.

"I don't have much time, Cielo," Joseph said,
tightening his grip on her hands. "If I can't convince
Gideon to give you his half of the power before he
dies, you will have to fight him. I have already given
you mine. You are already braver than I ever was."

Sky shook her head. "This is crazy, Joseph—really,
I can't listen anymore. I don't believe in any of this.
It's just . . . these are just stories. Please, Joseph, take
the whistle and go home. I'll talk to you Monday after school—I promise, okay?"

Her hands tingled when he finally let go. "We'll
talk, Cielo, but the whistle is yours."

"No! Listen Joseph, I—"

The knocking woke her up. Someone was knocking on a door somewhere in the complex.

Sky could feel her heart trying to pulverize itself
against the inside of her ribs as she sat up—on the
couch, covered by the ratty pink-and-black afghan
she knitted as a home ec project her senior year in
college and still used to hide behind when she
watched horror movies at night.

She didn't remember falling asleep, and if the time
on the VCR clock was right, she had been asleep for

only twenty minutes. But, of course, that wasn't possible. Joseph had to have been talking to her for longer than that.

Pushing the afghan aside, Sky stood up just a little too quickly and woke up the remnants of the headache she'd had all afternoon. God, she needed some aspirin.

But I took some . . . three of them when I went into the kitchen to make Joseph coffee.

Another green-tinted minute on the VCR elapsed by the time she reached the kitchen and stared at the empty coffeepot. She must have dreamed making coffee the same way she dreamed she'd taken aspirin.

It was only a dream.

Sky was reaching for the aspirin bottle when two more knocks echoed through the darkened living room. That wasn't a dream.

She opened the door very slowly.

"Hey, how's my best girl? Did I wake you? I must have—you still look half asleep."

Sam's grin was subdued as he handed her flowers—peppermint-striped carnations—and a tin of hand-dipped chocolate-covered cherries. The aspirinlike pain relievers rattled when she accepted the offerings, but he didn't seem to notice the sound or the bottle she was holding.

In fact, he barely looked even at her as he walked to the couch and sat down in exactly the same spot where Joseph had been sitting. In the dream.

"I'm sorry, I know I should have called first, but when the meeting broke up early I took it as a sign to get my tail over here, a-sap. I called the hospital this morning, and they told me about your grandfather."

Sam leaned forward over his knees, hands clasped. "God, I'm so sorry, I can't begin to imagine what you must be going through . . . but if it's any consolation at all, I had the check that was supposed to go to your grandfather from Sun Country Homes made out to you. If nothing else this will give you some peace of mind concerning hospital bills. And whatever other expenses should arise."

Like my grandfather's funeral, she wanted to add, then silently corrected herself *My grandfather Gideon's funeral . . . Have to keep the grandfathers straight now that I have two of them.*

"But that was a dream," she said, and realized she'd spoken out loud only when Sam answered. And misunderstood.

"It's not a dream, honey—you'll have enough to take care of your grandfather for as long as he needs it. Really, you don't have to worry."

Sam reached into the breast pocket of his coat—charcoal gray instead of bright blue—and pulled out an oversized check. *It* was bright blue and carried the familiar SC Industries trademark setting/rising sun logo in the upper left corner.

It took her a moment to realize he was holding it out to her—and him a moment longer to realize her hands will full.

"I'll just leave it here on the table and you can forget about it until the banks open up in the morning, how's that? So, what do you feel up for tonight?"

Tonight? Oh, right—their date.

"Let me just put these in water, first," Sky said, nodding to the flowers as she backed into the kitchen, "and then do you know what I'd really like to do?"

Sam's smile widened. "No, what?"

"I'd like to get blind, stinking drunk."

"That can be arranged, m'lady."

Sky set the candy down next to the sink as she filled a plastic mini-mart tumbler with water. The carnations waited until she used some of the water to wash down three of the bitter white pills.

"Hey," he called, "what's this?"

Sky stuck the carnations into the tumbler without taking them out of their green paper wrapping and took them with her as she walked back into the living room to see what he was talking about.

"What's what?" she asked, and heard the plastic squeak under her fingers as she pressed it against her belly to keep it from falling.

"Pretty little thing, isn't it?" Sam asked, holding the bright yellow whistle up for her to see. The two feathers, tied together on their white cord, spun lazily in a gust of warm air as the heater came on. "You get this out at the trading post?

"Sky?

"Honey?"

"No," she finally said, "someone gave it to me."

Joseph folded the newspaper and set it aside when his son came into the sleeping porch.

"Heard you had yourself a little adventure today," Daniel said. He was wiping his hands on one of Estralita's dish towels. "And I'm sorry to hear about your friend."

"Thank you. It was wrong of me to worry Little Star in her condition, but I just needed to be alone for a while."

"In the middle of the city?"

Joseph smiled as he stood up to take the towel from his son's hands. "Haven't you ever been alone standing in the middle of a crowd?"

"Yeah, well, I guess. Is there anything I can do?"

"No, but thank you for asking. Old men die . . . it's just hard for other old men to accept this sometimes. So, is dinner ready?"

Joseph asked the question as if he hadn't been sitting quietly on his bed all afternoon, reading the paper. He asked the question because a part of him had been away for hours.

" 'Lita's serving it up, but I think you still have a couple of minutes if you want to wash up first."

Joseph looked down at the yellow dye on his fingers and nodded. "I'd better, Little Star might send me to bed without any supper if I don't."

"And I would, too."

Estralita's voice, followed by the sound of his grandson's laughter, echoed softly from the kitchen.

"You'd better hurry," Joseph said as he tossed the dish towel over his son's broad shoulder. "I'll be right there. And tell those greedy magpies of yours to save me at least one slice of fry bread."

Daniel winked. "I'll try. Oh, that reminds me: Andy wanted me to ask you if a jay's feather would be okay. You two making something?"

"A willow whistle. But we'll have to start a new one after dinner—I broke the one I made this after-

noon. Old hands aren't as steady as they used to be."
Joseph walked into the bathroom. "Tell him for this
whistle a jay's feather is fine.

"And remind him about the fry bread."

CHAPTER 13

Gideon woke to find a vulture sitting in the middle of his chest, lapping the raw stump of his shoulder with a long pink tongue. He'd never seen a bird with a tongue like that—especially not a scavenger—and he had to admit it was mighty interesting just to watch it dip its bald, wrinkly head down to slurp the pus and blood that had seeped through the thick wad of bandages.

It reminded Gideon of the times when his mama would hand him the bowl she'd just made cornbread in so he could lick up the leftover.

"Mighty sweet," he muttered as the vulture turned to look at him. "She put a little sorghum in with the meal—makes it real sweet."

The vulture pondered this and nodded. "Ah could do with a drop o'sorghum mahself—yah ain't the sweetest man Ah ever gnawed on."

Gideon snorted at the bird. "Well, so sorry Ah'm dyin'."

"We try our best, Mr. Berlander," another voice on the foot of his bed crooned, "but you are a stubborn old goat."

There was a strange, prickling feeling along the back of his neck when Gideon tried to lift his head up so he could see who his newest enemy was. The vulture on his chest winked at him when a hand covered with dusty black feathers pushed his head back down. A raven wearing a pink nurse's coat cocked its head to one side and stared at him.

"Try not to move, Mr. Berlander," it cawed, "you'll tear your stitches open again."

"Mmm-mmm." The vulture on Gideon's chest smacked its beak. "G'on, Giddy, move about—yah ain't got much meat on yah, and Ah would surely love t'suck on them stitches."

Gideon jerked away from the raven and startled the smirking vulture into flight.

"Get off me!"

The raven was a lot stronger than it looked and had help. The room was full of carrion birds—vultures and ravens mostly, but with a few magpies and turkey buzzards hovering in the shadows around the bed. Gideon squirmed a foot out from under the tight sheets and kicked one of the smaller magpies in the belly. It screeched and took off in a cloud of white and black feathers.

"Mr. Berlander, please, lie still!"

"Go t'hell!"

One of the larger vultures swept down and clamped a callused talon over his remaining arm.

"Increase the morphine drip," it snapped at the raven. "Mr. Berlander, you have to stay st—"

"LET GO!"

The scavenger's dead eyes widened in surprise when Gideon pulled his arm free and backhanded it across the beak. A deep crack appeared in the loose skin at the top of its head.

"Yah shouldn'ta done that," the first vulture said as it clucked its long pink tongue. "Now yah went and made it mad."

As Gideon watched, the crack in the vultures skin continued to grow until the pink flesh fell away from the gleaming silver skull beneath. The metal eyelids clinked together as it blinked at him. A bright blue "Come Home to a SUN COUNTRY HOME" bumper sticker covered one side of its razor-sharp beak.

They were machines.

"Well, what did you expect, Mr. Berlander?" the vulture asked him. "Okay, everyone . . . dinnertime."

Gideon tried to beat them off him, but the first vulture just laughed and helped tie his arm down while the raven nurse ripped off her feathers and shoved a thick tube down his throat.

Another machine . . .

. . . just like the ones pumping air into his lungs . . .

. . . just like the ones sucking puss and piss out of him . . .

. . . just like the ones that tore open his land . . . and now tore him apart.

Machines.

Gideon screamed long and hard, but the machines didn't hear him.

"That was close."

"I don't know what happened—one minute he was breathing and then he just coded."

"Well, we got him back and he's on the respirator, so I think we're okay, but you'd better keep a sharp eye on this one."

"After this little scare, you'd better believe we will."

"Great. Page me if anything changes, okay?"

"Of course, Doctor."

Sam nursed a sip from his second beer and winked across the table to where Sky sat, licking salt off her lips from her third double margarita. He'd seen a lot of people set out to get drunk, himself included, and might have applauded her effort if he thought the other diners would understand.

If they had gone to the Tex-Mex dive near the highway that Sky suggested, a little whooping and hollering and losing brain cells wouldn't be a problem, but Sam had wanted to show off and obtained an instant "$100 Greased Palm" reservation at the fanciest restaurant in town.

At least until Mackay built his five-star place on what should have been Casa de Reynolds.

It also hadn't hurt that the overly posh eatery was known around the office as Mackay's favorite Friday-night dining spot. Sam had wanted to add another layer of credence to his claim of close personal involvement with Gideon Berlander's only remaining relative.

Of course, now, as she finished off the dregs of the third margarita and signaled for a fourth, he was beginning to regret that decision.

Mackay hadn't shown up yet, and if he was lucky, he could get Sky out of the public eye—and ear—before that happened.

She hadn't stopped jabbering nonsense since halfway through her second drink, and there were no signs of her stopping anytime soon.

"—which I thought was pretty peculiar until I heard you knocking and—"

Sam caught the advancing waiter's eyes and nodded him away.

"Not that I'm not impressed," he said as he reached over and manually lowered Sky's hand. Most of her lobster dinner was still in its shell and was beginning to crust over. "And I'm sure the *Guinness Book of World Records* people would be equally fascinated by you trying to consume your body weight in tequila, but don't you think you should slow down just long enough to catch your breath?"

"I can breathe, see?" Sky opened her mouth and panted like a dog. Her breast jiggled beneath the stupid paper lobster bib the waiter had tied around her neck.

"I see you're going to pass out if you keep that up."

She stopped panting and giggled. "I'm fine. Besides, I'm celebrating, so stop being such a tight-ass, okay?"

The fox-faced matron at the next table shot them a dirty look. Sam reached for his beer and took a much larger sip while Sky just kept on rambling.

"I'm rich, I just found out I have a new grandfather to replace the old one, and best of all," she toasted herself with the empty glass, "I've been chosen."

"For great things, no doubt."

"For better than great things . . . I can break wind— Oh God, I mean . . ."

Sky covered her mouth and started to laugh until tears began rolling down her cheeks. It took Sam almost a full minute before he realized she wasn't laughing and the tears were coming faster.

The table was just a little too wide, so he had to stand up and move the chair around to her side while people and the waitstaff stared.

"Here." He untied the lobster bib and pressed it into her hand. "Shh, come on now—wipe your eyes and tell me what's wrong."

Sky took the bib and kept her head down while she mopped up the tears. Fortunately, unlike a lot of women he'd dated and dumped over the years, she didn't wear a lot of water-soluble makeup, so there was very little smudging around her eyes when she looked up.

"I—I'm sorry." The tears had stopped, but her voice sounded so scratchy it made Sam's throat ache. "I guess I'm more upset than I thought."

"Jesus, honey, you have a right to be, with everything you've been through." He gave her a quick hug, almost brotherly, and began to slide his chair back to its original position. "Having a loved one in the hospital is bad enough, but finding out that your grandfather's . . . condition is terminal can—"

"Only the white one," she said.

"Only the white one what?"

215

The corners of Sky's mouth tightened, then relaxed into a parody of a smile. Sam had seen his employer do the same too many times to be fooled, but in this case his career wasn't involved, so there was no need to pretend he cared. The deal was closed and she had her check, and except for the possibility of some drunken pussy, his job was over.

He sat back and signaled the waiter before she had a chance to say anything else. The twenty-something-year-old cast only one fleeting, though disparaging, look in Sky's direction as he hurried to the table.

"Yes, sir?"

"The lady and I are finished. Would you please bring the bill."

Sam had to admit the kid was good and probably deserving of the 20 percent tip he would get. He didn't ask if Sky would like the leftovers wrapped or if they'd be wanting coffee, dessert, or an after-dinner aperitif. He just took the plates and Sam's platinum-plus credit card and ran.

Sam suspected the entire restaurant—staff and customers alike—would be much more comfortable when he and his drunken half-breed companion left. He hoisted the beer and downed it. She might have wasted her dinner, but he'd be damned if he was going to squander a $7 Belgian dark.

"Sam?"

Uh-oh. Better head 'er off at the pass. "Oh, I'm sorry. Did you want to finish that?"

"What? No, I just—"

"God, I didn't even ask. . . . Do you want coffee? How about dessert?"

Her big brown eyes got a little bigger, but they weren't focusing any better than they had a moment earlier. She looked so confused, Sam had to bite the inside of his cheek to keep from smiling.

"Did you want something else, honey?"

"No." Her hair shimmered like oil under the lights. "It's okay. You wouldn't believe me if I told you."

"Well, maybe it's best that you don't tell me," he said. "Besides, things may look better in the morning. Right?"

Any answer she might have had was derailed by the waiter's return. Sam added the 20 percent tip to the bill and signed his name without bothering to do the math. He'd seen Mackay do that and immediately adopted the practice—it just screamed class.

Sam smiled the waiter away as he stood up and walked to her chair.

"Ready?" he asked.

For as much alcohol as Sky had consumed, Sam was impressed by how well she moved through the warren of tables with only the occasional wobble. It really was too bad they had no future, but unless he planned to hawk real estate all his life, he needed a wife who was more of a genetic match.

Gotta think of the future generation and all that shit, he thought, and watched her almost miss the step down to the waiting area. A group of the well-dressed white-eyes glared at both of them. Sam gave them the tiniest *What're you going to do?* shrug as he grabbed Sky's arm and led her to the door.

"Are you going to be all right?" he asked. "Do you want to go to the ladies' and splash cold water on your face or something?"

217

Sky shook her head and smiled. "No, I'll be okay. But would you mind taking me home? I think . . . I'm sorry, I didn't mean to ruin dinner."

He gave her a quick hug to conceal her from another group of Richland's richest and walked her to one of the plush velvet chairs in front of the telephone alcove.

"You didn't ruin anything," he said. "I should have known you probably wouldn't feel like doing much, but . . . it's this damned male ego I got stuck with. I thought my smiling countenance and sparkling personality would do the trick. I'm sorry, Sky, I blew it. Sit tight and I'll go get the coats, okay?"

He gave her knees a little squeeze, just because he liked the feel of her skin encased in nylon, and winked.

"Be right back."

It took him only ten steps and another $20 tip to get their coats—his cream cashmere, hers synthetic gray—but she was gone when he turned around. The scar on his forehead began to itch.

"Dammit."

"I, um." The hat-check girl was young and cute, good breeding stock. "I think, um . . . the lady went outside."

Sam heard the wood-and-glass door click and nodded his thanks.

The wind bitch-slapped him across the face before his mind registered what the hell Sky was doing.

"Ah now."

She was bent almost in half over the entrance railing, vomiting up what little she had to eat and most of the tequila into the restaurant's illuminated reflecting pond while two valets and half a dozen customers pointedly ignored the show.

Sam put his coat on as he walked down the stairs to hand one of the valets his parking stub.

"Take your time," he said.

His forehead itched like a son of a bitch.

It was only a few minutes past eleven, but as was usual on Friday nights, the boys had managed to stay up longer than their parents, although Joseph didn't think their victory would last much longer.

Joey was draped lengthwise over the recliner, his head propped against one palm, his eyelids at half-mast. Andrew wasn't even pretending that hard to stay awake. Curled up next to Joseph on the couch, he stared unblinkingly at the television until the commercials, when he'd give a little jump and mutter "I'm awake."

Joseph laid his hand gently on the younger boy's shoulder and turned his head toward the darkness beyond the television's flickering blue-white light. Inside, the house was warm and quiet, peaceful despite the sounds of Daniel's snores and the refrigerator motor's labored churning. Outside, the wind howled and moaned, rattling windows and doors and kicking up the dust like an angry child.

No, Joseph corrected himself, like a frightened child who knows something is going to happen but doesn't know what.

The windstorm had begun just after sunset, sweeping down from the northwest with the taste of winter on its breath. Joseph had stood at the front window and watched it sweep across the land. Angry, *fright-*

ened, it hurled tumbleweeds down the road and beat the dry ground with small cottonwood branches—and there was nothing he could do about it.

It was part of the cycle of life and death and rebirth, but he hated hearing her cry in the night.

"Hush," he whispered as the wind wept along the roof.

"I'm awake," Andrew muttered.

Joseph looked down at the sleepy boy, then over to his brother, and shook his head. "No, I don't think either of you are. Come on, now . . . off to bed."

There was some grumbling from the recliner as Joseph outdrew the desperado on the screen with the remote control. Without the soundtrack to compete with, the wind sounded even more lost and alone.

"Hey, we were watching that."

"It's an old movie," Joseph said as he hauled Andrew to his feet and nodded for Joey to do the same, "the bad men lose and the hero rides off into the sunset. No real Indians or horses were injured in the making of the movie. Come on, all of us need our rest—we have a big day tomorrow."

Andrew wrapped his arms around Joseph's rib cage and looked up. "We're going to make whistles, right?"

"No, something better than whistles."

"But you promised," the little boy whined at the same time his older brother, still in the recliner but hunched forward with his stocking feet on the floor, asked, "What could be better than whistles?"

Joseph lifted one finger to his lips when he reached the hallway that led to the bedrooms.

"Shh. Come on, I'll tell you in your room."

Andrew made a detour to the bathroom while Joseph and his older brother tiptoed past.

"Do you have to go?" he asked Joey as the boy clambered beneath the covers.

"I'm okay. So what's better than making whistles?"

"Don't tell! Don't tell! Don't tell until I get there." Andrew was still hoisting his pajama bottoms up when he ran into the room. His bed protested loudly when he jumped on it. "Okay, tell."

Joseph sat down on the foot of Joey's bed and reached into the breast pocket of his shirt. The two cylindrical shapes overlapped each other, the larger of the two on top. Until that night when he'd taken them from the back of his sock drawer and removed the yellowed tissue paper he'd wrapped them in, Joseph hadn't seen the pocketknives or even thought about them in almost forty years.

He kept his fingers closed around the knives as he lowered his hand. Both boys leaned forward, eyes shining in the glow of the small table lamp between the beds.

"What's that, Grandfather?"

Joseph looked from one boy to the other and opened his hand. The larger knife had a white bone handle, the smaller a handle of red stone. He'd traded three baskets of pine nuts for them the Christmas Thomas was twelve and Daniel eight.

"This one," he said, handing the smaller knife to Andrew, "belonged to your father. And this—"

Joseph took the older boy's hand and laid the knife across it. "This was your uncle's. You remember me speaking of him?"

Joey nodded, but his eyes never left the knife.

"Yeah, Uncle Thomas was dad's older brother. He left the reservation and died." He stopped and looked up. "Sorry, Grandfather."

Joseph ruffled the boy's hair. "It's all right, that was a long time ago. Yes, he left the reservation and died. Now, I'm giving you these knives because I think it's time you boys learned how to carve."

Whispered shouts of joy—"Oh wow!" "Oh, cool!" "Yeah!" "All right!"—ricocheted off the walls despite Joseph's best efforts to control them.

"Hush! If you wake your father, he might not let us borrow the truck in the morning."

"Where're we going to go, Grandfather?"

The wind rattled the window as Joseph stood up, but it wasn't enough to drown out the sound of his knees crackling.

"Out to the tules to find a good piece of dead cottonwood. This is the first lesson: Always use cottonwood when you carve Kachinas."

"Kachinas?"

"You're gonna teach us to carve Kachinas? Wow!"

"But only if you get quiet and go to sleep right now. And put those knives on the table and promise me you won't play with them or even open them until I show you how to do it. All right?"

Joseph stood there until both knives were on the table before bending down and turning out the lamp. The room instantly filled with a soft, pale light filled with dancing shadows.

"Remember," Joseph said, hugging first one and then the other—although the *other* had complained he was getting too old for good-night hugs. "Don't touch the knives and get right to sleep. We'll leave right after breakfast."

"Promise."

"Promise. G'night, Grandfather."

He remembered the same sort of promises from Thomas and Daniel when he'd given them the knives—and it hadn't done any more good than his telling the wind to quiet.

"Good night."

The wind met him as he entered the sleeping porch.

It had crept in through the cracks in the plaster walls and around the weather stripping, waiting like a puma in the shadows until his back was turned. But he couldn't let it attack, for both their sakes.

"Sleep, little one," he told it, holding his hand out to her cold breath, "it will be all right. I have talked with the Chosen One . . . you won't be alone."

The wind withdrew and fled back into the troubled night as Joseph got into bed and pulled the covers up over his ears. But the heavy wool didn't help very much—he could still hear the wind and the sound of stockinged feet running for the bathroom.

"Joey," he whispered, and smiled and fell asleep.

Someone was pulling her leg.

Literally.

Sky pried both sets of eyelids open and watched the blurry shape of a man strip off her panty hose, one leg at a time.

"Halt," she said, then waited for the three extra inches of tongue to make itself comfortable in her mouth. "Who goes there?"

"Where?" the shape asked, one dark eye winking above a Cheshire-cat grin that seemed much too large and brilliant to be real. "Do I get my choice?"

Sky lifted her head to discover two things: one, that she was lying in the center of her own bed in her own bedroom, and, two, the blurry man was actually blurry Sam.

"Excuse me, but what do you think you're doing?"

Sam's face came into a little better focus when he pulled her into a sitting position so he could pull her dress off over her head. When her hair fell over her eyes, Sky flipped it back away with a head toss . . . and felt the entire room begin to spin. Clockwise.

"Uh-oh. Room's spinning."

Sam pushed her back onto the mattress and stood up.

"Don't close your eyes, you'll only feel worse. Well, I was hoping to get you undressed and into bed before you got sick again, but that may be a long shot."

Sky dug her fingers into the bedspread and hung on for dear life as the room continued its waltz.

"I . . . was sick?"

He touched her head with something cold and damp—*a washcloth?*

"Yeah, you gave yourself a bad case of the tequila-urps. You don't remember?"

"Oh, God, I threw . . . I got sick in your truck, didn't I?" Sky closed her eyes, then flung them open an instant later when the slow waltz became a mambo. "I was hoping most of that was a really bad dream."

"Nope, but don't worry. I know a great car wash that does upholstery."

"Shit."

"It's okay, really . . . with everything you've been through . . . don't worry . . . about it . . . these things . . . all the time."

His voice was doing funny things, going up and down like the room . . . up and down.

"Bathroom."

And she might have made it, too.

If the floor hadn't suddenly come up and popped her one right on the nose.

Gideon opened his mouth to scream and gagged around the pipe or hose that had been jammed down his throat. He hadn't seen them do it, but he knew the carrion birds were responsible—they were trying to kill him, to turn him into carrion so they could feed on him.

He could feel their dead doll eyes staring at him . . . waiting . . . licking their shiny metal beaks with those long pink tongues.

No! Ah ain't dead yet. Not yet!

A little black-and-white magpie swooped down and pecked at his right eyelid.

"Arugh!"

Gideon's left hand had never been as strong as his right, but he snatched the bird off and crushed it in a shower of sparks and broken gears. That was one Sun Country machine that wouldn't be bothering him again.

He wished he didn't have the damn tube down his throat.

"Aruggggh!"

The vulture on his chest looked down at him and shook its gleaming metal head.

"Think yer hot shit, don't'cha? Well, yah ain't nothin' but ripenin' meat, and yah know what Ah'm sayin' is true. What's the matter? Cat gotcher tongue?"

Gideon threw the dead magpie at the vulture's head. The bird ducked and clamped a taloned foot down on the center of his chest. "Yah didn't answer me . . . Berlander . . ."

Mr. Berlander?

Can you hear me, Mr. Berlander? Open your eyes, Mr. Berlander.

Gideon wondered why the damned vulture was suddenly so polite and what the hell it was talking about. His eyes already were open . . . weren't they?

Come on, Mr. Berlander . . . open your eyes.

Gideon did, and the white ruff of feathers around the vulture's bare neck lengthened into the shoulders of a sparkling white doctor's coat. The gleaming metal head cocked to one side and blinked. The silver eyelids made a soft grinding sound.

"Hey, you're awake," the vulture said.

CHAPTER 14

Gideon blinked and the metal bird turned into flesh and bone. Maybe.

The man in the white doctor's coat had steel-gray eyes that sparkled just enough to make Gideon flinch at his touch.

"Are you in pain, Mr. Berlander?" the maybe man asked, then nodded as if he already knew the answer. "Nurse, increase the drip by another milligram. There you go, Mr. Berlander, that should help. Just try to relax and let the morphine do its job.

"No, don't try to bend your arm. We have you on an arm board, Mr. Berlander, do you understand? Just keep it straight—that's right. Good."

Gideon looked down at the molded plastic board strapped to his arms and frowned. *How'd I catch and kill that damned mechanical magpie with this thing on my arm?* It was a puzzlement . . . but then he felt a warm trickle move up his arm to the center of his chest, and then up into his neck and shoulders. The world got soft around the edges as the warmth oozed on down into his legs. It wasn't a bad feeling, as feelings go, but he wished to God the maybe man would just go away and let him die in peace.

He could handle it from here on out, as long as the vultures didn't come back.

"I'm Dr. Winegardt," he said, moving closer. Gideon tried to move away, but the warm feeling had done something to his muscles and he didn't have any more strength than a newly hatched chick. "You suffered a little respiratory distress last night, so we had to put in a breathing tube. You're still on it, but I'd like to see if you can breathe on your own. Are you willing to try?"

Gideon nodded his head and felt the tube rub against the inside of his throat. If he could have, he would have gagged.

"Okay, I'm going to turn off the machine now."

The doctor nodded to the nurse standing on the opposite side of the bed. The woman nodded back and flicked a switch on a pumping machine. The machine stopped pumping, and Gideon felt his lungs collapse in on themselves.

"And now I'm unhooking you. Okay, Mr. Berlander, try to take a breath."

Gideon forgot he was dying and sucked in air as fast as his lungs could pull.

"Great. Okay, now comes the fun part. Mr. Berlander, I want you to take a deep breath, hold it, and then cough as hard as you can when I pull this out. You understand?"

Gideon nodded and took a breath. Coughing wasn't hard to remember to do when the doctor pulled out the clear plastic tube. He vomited air in the doctor's face, but the maybe man didn't seem to hold that against him.

In fact, he seemed downright pleased.

"That's great, Mr. Berlander, you're doing fine. Just take nice slow breaths . . . that's right. Would you like some ice chips?"

He would have rather had a cold beer or even a cup of 'shine, but Gideon ran a tongue that felt like raw liver over lips that felt like sandpaper, and nodded. It still felt like the tube was in him.

The nurse who turned off the machine leaned over the bed and spooned a tiny sliver of ice out of a paper cup. Gideon opened his mouth like a baby bird.

A baby vulture?

He pushed the images of birds from his mind as the cold, artificial spit dribbled down his throat.

"So," the doctor said, waving the nurse and the cup of ice away, "how do you feel, Mr. Berlander?"

Gideon kept his eyes glued to the paper cup. It was easier than looking into the steel-gray eyes.

"Like shit," he said, and heard a low, grumbling chuckle as the nurse fed him another ice chip.

"Well, that's to be expected, Mr. Berlander," the doctor said. "You gave us a little bit of a scare last night. We think you suffered a reaction to the sedative that was administered to you yesterday when you became agitated. Do you remember the incident? Your granddaughter was here and—"

"Ah remember," Gideon said, and got another chip of ice. He felt a little like a dog being rewarded for doing tricks, but as long as his throat was sore and they had the ice, he was more than willing to perform. "Yah took mah arm."

The doctor took the cup of ice from the nurse and fed Gideon the next couple of chips himself—one right after the other, to keep him from talking.

"We explained that to you in the ER when you first came in, Mr. Berlander. You'd lost a lot of blood and you were very disoriented, so I'm not surprised you're having trouble remembering the conversation, but when you came in your right deltoid and trapezius looked like hamburger." The doctor smiled, just a little, and fed Gideon another ice chip. "In layman's terms, Mr. Berlander, the shoulder was gone and you were in danger of bleeding out your subclavian artery, and to be honest, I'm surprised you didn't. But, like I said, we told you this."

Gideon swallowed the ice chip whole. "When? When did yah tell me?"

The doctor's steel eyes locked onto his. "Every time you woke up for the last eight days."

"Eight days?"

The next ice chip froze itself to Gideon's tongue.

"You've been drifting in and out of consciousness, Mr. Berlander—seemingly lucid one moment, then either raving in a paranoid delirium or slipping into unconsciousness. Last night, though, that was the first time you ever . . . the first time we ever had to put you on the respirator. But don't you worry, Mr. Berlander, I think that was the turning point. You should be just fine now."

Gideon opened his mouth for another ice chip and immediately spit it back in the doctor's face. It hit just a little low, glancing off the man's left cheek-bone, but the look in those steel-gray eyes more than made up for his bad aim. Somewhere from the machines that hung over his head and surrounded him, a tiny alarm began to beep.

It was a very annoying sound.

"Bullshit."

"Mr. Berlander, please try not to get excited."

Dammit, he *wanted* to get excited—he wanted to do more than get excited, he wanted to call the wind and tear the whole damn place apart, starting with Dr. Steel-eyes. But the warmth just kept making everything so soft and blurry.

"Why didn't yah just let me die—yah a'ready had mah land."

"I don't know anything about your land, Mr. Berlander," the doctor said, setting the cup of ice down on a small cart, "but I'm a doctor, and it's my job to keep people from dying."

"Even me?"

The doctor ignored the question and looked at his watch. "It's a little too late right now, but I'll make sure to call your granddaughter. She's very concerned about you."

"Ah'm sure she is. So tell me, Doc . . . how much is she cuttin' yah in for? Ah mean, that's gotta be the reason yer keepin' a dyin' man alive, ain't it?"

A little of the light faded from the man's eyes, and that's how Gideon knew the man was just another Sun Country machine. He shook his head a little too far to the right, and that's when he saw it: the yel-lowy stain that was seeping through the thick wad of bandages on his shoulder.

On where his shoulder had been.

The doctor reached down and tossed the sheet over it.

"That's just normal postoperative seepage, Mr. Berlander," he said, "it's nothing to worry about. A nurse will be in directly to change the dressing."

Gideon looked up at the man and grinned. "Wouldn't yah rather just lap it up?"

Sam Reynolds looked down at what had to be every adolescent male's dream date—a beautiful, unconscious woman sprawled helpless and half naked on a bed in front of him. He could do whatever he wanted and she'd never know. A quick hit-'n'-git and leave her to wake up in the morning to wonder, through her blinding hangover, just what happened.

Could be fun—had been fun back in college when he and a couple dozen of his dorm buddies had gotten a cute little froshie drunk and spent the better part of the night pulling a train with her as caboose. The sex hadn't been *that* good, and only got sloppier as more guys joined the party, but it had been fun and more than a little dangerous—you never could tell, at least not back then, when a girl was really drunk or faking it and would suddenly decide enough was enough and yell rape.

The froshie hadn't yelled rape. She'd been really drunk, and according to the guy whose room she'd originally passed out in, and subsequently woke up in, she was still drunk when she pulled up her panties and staggered back to her own dorm.

None of the guys ever bothered looking her up again—any girl who would purposely get drunk enough to pass out in a strange guy's room and get used like that was just not the sort of meat any self-respecting jock wanted to date—but Sam never forgot the thrill of danger she'd provided.

He rubbed a knuckle against the scar on his forehead as he looked down at the body on the bed. Fucking her now would be about as dangerous as falling asleep in front of the TV. And probably even less exciting.

Sam lifted one side of the heavy bedspread and tossed it over her. She sighed, sounding happy. He decided that was how he wanted to remember her—half naked and happy-sounding.

"Sleep tight," he said, and bent down to give her one last kiss . . . until he smelled the vomit on her breath. He pulled back as if he were about to be snake-bit. "Maybe next time."

She moaned a little when he closed the door—at least he thought he did; it could just as easily have been the wind. It had started gusting a few minutes after he'd scraped Sky off the restaurant's grand marble entrance, and been building in intensity ever since. A couple of times coming through an intersection, the wind buffeted the truck hard enough to push it into oncoming traffic.

He'd driven the five miles to Sky's apartment hunched over the steering wheel and cursing the wind under his breath.

God, he hated the wind, and it wasn't until that moment that he remembered how much he hated it. From as far back as he could remember. When he was just a kid and the other boys and girls in his neighborhood would rush out into the first windstorm of the season with their brightly colored kites, he'd be inside, sensibly watching Saturday-morning cartoons. When he got older, wind just meant having to use more styling gel to keep his hair in place.

By the time he'd pulled up to the curb in front of the apartment complex, Sam had pretty much decided he no longer cared about living up on the old man's ridge—exclusive neighbors and Mackay's five-star eatery notwithstanding. Having a breathtaking view was nice, but he sure as hell didn't want one that could actually suck the breath out of his lungs whenever it got to blowing.

Nope, he'd had the desert and its mystery—it was just about time to pack up the ol' truck and go west, young man, before he got any older.

Yeah, that was the ticket. He'd head west and maybe start his own little real-estate empire. "Reynolds' California Classics"—that definitely had a ring to it.

Whistling the theme from a current beer commercial softly between his teeth, Sam closed the bedroom door and pulled a small notebook out of his pocket. He couldn't just leave without saying good-bye.

Dear Sky,
Hope you feel better.
Have a good life—
Sam

Short, and sweet, and direct enough to forestall any emotionally charged phone calls to ask what he meant. It was obvious what he meant, and he knew her well enough to know she'd understand it immediately.

He didn't even think she'd mind all that much, really. They'd been drifting apart since her grandfather's "accident," and this way she'd have a lot more time to spend with the old bastard before he finally shuffled off this mortal coil.

He was doing her a favor, really, and one day she might even thank him for it.

"Yup," Sam said as he picked his way through the living-room clutter to the coffee table, "I'm a regular saint."

It took him a minute to decide where to put the note so she'd see it—that was another thing he didn't like about her, she was a bit of a slob—then stuck it under the yellow whistle. If she looked for it, she'd see it—if she didn't and called, he'd tell her where it was and hang up.

Quick and fast, like pulling off a bandage.

Sam turned around when he got to the front door to give the apartment one last look—*it really is a dump*—then turned off the lights and stepped into the howling night.

The wind slapped him across the face and tore at his clothes all the way to the truck.

God, he hated the wind.

Cielo.

Sky rolled over. Something prickly brushed against her cheek as the scent of Pine-Sol and pencils filled the air. She pulled the blanket tighter over her shoulder and buried her face in the smell of fresh antistatic dryer sheets. Ah.

Cielo . . . wake up.

Sky tried to stop her eyelids from twitching, without success, but managed to keep them closed.

"Sam? God, what time is it?"

Open your eyes, Cielo. We have to talk.

He sounded different. "Sam?"

Sky opened her eyes and gasped. She was lying on a bed of green pine and cedar boughs, wrapped in her bedspread. A small juniper fire burned in a circle of stones a foot in front of her, its banked light dancing off the walls of solid rock that surrounded her. A cave—she was in a cave.

How the hell did that happen? She remembered drinking too much and passing out, and Sam helping her stumble up the stairs to her apartment and . . . passing out. God, was this his idea of a joke just because she *may* have gotten sick all over his very expensive pair of black python Tony Lamas?

"SAM!"

A quick check under the spread showed that he still had some sense of charity left . . . but it wasn't much charity. He'd taken her shoes and knew she wouldn't be walking back to town in only a bra and panties and bedspread.

However far away town was.

"GodDAMMIT, Sam!"

. . . sam . . . sam . . . sam . . .

The cave extended far beyond the firelight. Sky counted sixteen echoes before they stopped.

"Sam?"

Something moved just beyond the light, something pale and slow, coming toward her out of the darkness. It had to be Sam—who else could it be?

"Hello, Cielo."

"Joseph?" Sky pulled the spread tighter over her shoulders and legs. "What's going on? Where are we? Did you bring me here?"

Joseph squatted down on the opposite side of the fire and sprinkled a handful of twigs into the flames. The fire popped and sizzled, growing larger as the air filled with a sweet pungent smoke that made her head feel too big for her skin. She could see the walls of the cave better now, they were covered with petroglyphs, some familiar like animals and handprints, some depicting fantastic beings rising from clouds of dust.

Sky rubbed her eyes and scooted back from the fire. "Joseph, please, what's going on?"

"We have to talk, Cielo."

"You . . . brought me here to talk? Joseph, I don't understand—"

Joseph raised his hand, signaling for her to be quiet. "This is where Gideon and I first met, right here—by the fire my father and grandfather and uncles had built. I had never been inside this cave until that day, so I had no idea how big it was or that it had another entrance. I don't think anyone knew that, but that's how he got in, Gideon—he was so scrawny and pale that when I saw him I thought he was a ghost. I think I yelled in fear.

"But not him—he was never afraid. Not even now."

Joseph tossed another handful of twigs into the fire and the flames shot up toward the shadowed roof. Sky could feel the heat against her face and the front of the spread, but she could also feel the coldness seeping up through the layer of boughs beneath her. She shivered, but inched away from the fire.

237

"I know you don't believe what I told you this afternoon, Cielo, but it's true."

True? What's he talking about, nothing happened this afternoon? I had a dream . . . but that's all it was, a dream.

"Yaponcha created you from Gideon's blood and from mine, to mend what was accidentally torn in two. You are the Chosen One, Cielo."

It's a dream.

"Accept your birthright."

Only a dream.

"Cielo, listen to me."

"NO!" Sky squeezed her eyes shut and pressed the spread against her ears. A reverse-color image of the fire danced against her closed lids. "NO! THIS IS JUST ANOTHER DREAM!"

"Of course it is. Open your eyes, Cielo."

Even though it was a dream and she knew it was a dream, she couldn't disobey the old man. Joseph smiled at her and nodded, the firelight deepening the hollows below his eyes.

"Your fear is from me, Cielo," he said, reaching his hand over the flames toward her. "You must fight it. Don't let it rob you of the power I so foolishly gave up. Accept it and use it for the good of your people."

Sky saw the sleeve of his shirt begin to smolder and the hairs on the back of his hand blacken, but Joseph didn't seem to notice. He kept his hand over the flames, waiting for her to take it.

"For both your people, Chosen One, the red and white. Accept this. Please."

The bedspread slipped from one shoulder as Sky reached out and took his hand. And for a moment, it was his hand—warm and solid, the palm and fingers callused, the flesh like tanned doeskin—then the living flesh melted into the fire.

The spread fell as the corpse-gray hand tightened around hers and pulled her to her feet.

The old man was naked, the color of smoke, his long hair twisted about his head like snakes trapped in a flood. He was only half a man—the lower half was a dust devil.

Yaponcha.

I AM PLEASED, CHOSEN ONE. COME.

Cold air took her breath away, and she looked down. They were far above the earth, sailing over the mountains toward the desert. The city passed below them in a series of twinkling lights, the cars, ant-sized, coming and going along roads no bigger than pencil lines. *So small, it looks so small from up here.* Canyons and dead rivers replacing the pencil roads, and still the wind carried them.

YOU HAVE CHOSEN WELL . . . WELCOME, WIND CALLER.

Yaponcha smiled and let go of her hand.

Sky fell back to the earth screaming, but had somehow managed to soften it to a whimper when the phone woke her up.

She was in bed, her own bed, covered with the same bedspread as in the dream, and she was alone. Soft, pale light was coming in under the drapes. And she was alone.

"Sam? Ow." Her head felt five times its normal size and filled with porcupine quills, all of which were sticking into her brain.

Sky closed her eyes and forgot all about the phone

until it rang again. And startled her and the hangover into full, shocking consciousness.

Head and heart pounding in unison, Sky suffered through two more mind-splitting rings before she inched her way far enough across the mattress to grab the phone off the bedside table.

"'Lo?"

"Ms. Berlander? This is Memorial Hospital."

Joseph was proud of his grandsons.

They hadn't complained about getting up early or missing their favorite Saturday-morning cartoon shows so they could drive out to the cottonwoods and be back before anyone noticed they were gone.

Well, they hadn't complained *too* much, which was why Joseph pretended not to notice the bandages on the boys' hands as they piled into the Chevy halfton next to him.

Joey had a bandage on his left index finger; Andrew had two: one across the web of his right hand and the other across his left palm. It had been the same for their father and uncle when they first got the pocketknives—the lure of the blade was just too strong for promises.

"Did you remember to bring the knives?"

Joseph had to shout over the sounds of the pickup's overly rebuilt engine and squalling shocks, but both boys heard him and nodded.

"Good. Do you know if they're sharp?"

Joseph could see the exchange of glances from the corner of his eye. "Yes, Grandfather, they're sharp."

"I thought they would be," Joseph said. "Have your

father show you his scar when we get back—he almost cut off his finger the first time."

He could hear them giggling even over the engine, and it was a good sound, a strong sound, but even the sound of their laughter wasn't enough to ease the pain when he saw the first billboard:

SUN COUNTRY HOMES' NEWEST COMMUNITY—COMING SOON PIONEER RIDGE
Executive View Homes

Joseph felt his stomach lurch toward his throat as he turned off the small access road and onto the paved blacktop. The homes that lined the wide street were still dark, the plastic-sheathed newspapers still gathering dew in driveways and manicured lawns. A few of those lawns had decorative lawn ornaments more suited for Mediterranean villas or fairy-tale castles. There was no feeling of community or place, just houses and lawns and two cars in each security-alarmed garage.

Joseph could remember when the land had been covered with scrub oak and creosote bushes. He nodded to the crested jay sitting on the yellow No Trespassing sign as he dropped the truck into low gear and began climbing the steep dirt grade. They'd have to widen the road and level it out before the rich white executives would feel comfortable driving their expensive cars up here.

"Grandfather, this isn't the right way . . . is it?"

Joseph glanced to the side just quickly enough to

let him know both boys were staring at him. Gideon's road seemed more treacherous than the last time he'd come to the ridge . . . and then he remembered he hadn't driven. The last time he had come to the ridge in solid form, as a man, was the day Thomas had been butchered.

"No, this isn't the way, but I know the man who lived up here and just want to see the land again before they start building. Do you mind? It will only take a moment."

"Nope. Sure, yeah, it's okay."

"Thank you," he said, and tried to ignore the smell of blood inside his head as he'd ignored the bandages and No Trespassing sign. "It won't be long, I promise."

Sky pushed herself up through a half-dozen waves of intense nausea as she gripped the phone. It was only after her back was firmly against the headboard that she realized she was shivering, and the involuntary spasms were shaking the bed against the wall.

"Is it about my grandfather?" she asked.

And was told, "Yes, it is. Hold for Dr. Winegardt, please."

Joseph motioned the boys to stay inside the truck as he walked across the graded patch of ground where he thought the graves of Gideon's wife and daughter, Sky's mother, once lay. It was impossible to tell for sure. The bulldozers and backhoes gleaming in the early-morning sun had done too good a job of destroying every trace of the man . . . of the family that once lived there.

Only a few fragments of the cabin remained, burnt black and scattered on the ground next to a large metal Dumpster like just so many dog turds.

"Forgive me," he told the desecrated ground, "I should have thought to bring blue corn as an offering, but I didn't know I was going to come here. I'm sorry—I didn't think it would be this bad."

"Hey, Tonto!"

Joseph stepped back as a man in a thick parka and hard hat stepped out of the single-wide trailer next to a row of Porta Pottis. The wind sang through the toilet's screened ventilation slots as it had once sung through the branches of trees. It didn't seem to care or notice the difference.

The man's shadow stopped within inches of touching Joseph's.

"Yo, Chief, this is *posted* private land—didn't you see the sign?"

"I saw it," Joseph said, backing up until there was a foot of sunlight between them. "I made a mistake coming here."

"Yeah, well, see to it that you don't make the same mistake again—you got me, kemosabe?"

"Yes, I got you." Joseph nodded to show that he did understand, then pointed to the ground where he thought the graves had been. "What did you do with the bodies?"

The man's hands folded into fists. "The what?"

"The bodies," Joseph answered. "There were two graves there."

"You trying to tell me this was Indian burial ground?" The man shook his head and grinned. The grin was as tight as his fists. "Sorry, Chief, but you're

243

going to have to come up with a better story than
that. Company always runs a title search, and this
hasn't been Indian land for a long time. You got a
problem, you contact Jennet Mackay and talk to him
about it."

"No, I don't have a problem."

"Then why don't you take your papooses and get
back to the reservation. My crew's gonna show up
any minute now, and you're blocking the road."

Joseph felt the wind at his back as he turned and
walked back to the truck. The boys had lost interest
in the construction site and were jostling each other
hard enough to make the truck rock on its axles. He
rapped on the driver's-side window and they stopped.

"Sit still now," Joseph said when he opened the
door, then looked back at the man. "The graves belonged to Gideon Berlander's wife and daughter."

The man shrugged. "We didn't dig up any bones
that I know of, Chief, and I never heard of this
Berlander. This land belongs to Jennet Mackay and
SC Industries, and you're smack dab in the way of
my crew. Now, pull that hunk of junk up so they can
get in, and then . . . get out."

Joseph did as he was told and watched three pick-
ups and two jeeps drive across the level, empty
ground before swinging the truck around and leaving
the ridge for the last time.

He would never come back, and part of him was
glad.

Sky exhaled slowly when she realized it was only
causing the blood to pound louder in her ears. There

wasn't even banal "hold music" she could concentrate on, just a silent auditory blackboard she could keep scribbling on.

Please hold for Dr. Winegardt. Yes, it is. Please hold for Dr. Winegardt.

He's dead. He died last night. I'm sorry, your grandfather's dead.

You never get put on hold for good news.

He's dead.

Sky crossed her fingers as the silence clicked off.

"Ms. Berlander? Hi, this is Dr. Winegardt."

"Yes. Hello, Doctor."

"Well, your grandfather went into respiratory arrest last night"—*He died last night*—"but we got him stabilized on a breathing tube, and this morning he's breathing on his own and in relatively good shape—all things considered. We're going to monitor him for another couple of hours, and then, if he continues to improve, we may even move him out of ICU and into the extended-care wing."

"He's . . ." Sky took a deep breath. "He's better?"

"Well, he's not going to get well, Ms. Berlander, but he's out of danger for the moment. But, like I said, we want to monitor him for a while. You can stop by this evening, if you like."

"He's okay?"

"For the moment, yes."

Sky hung up without saying thank you. She'd have to apologize to the doctor when she saw him.

He's okay. Gideon's still alive.

She should get up and get some aspirin. She should take a shower. She should call Sam and thank him for getting her back to the apartment in one piece. She should do something besides slide back under the covers and pull them over her head.

She should, but she didn't.

Gideon was alive.

And she'd never been sorrier about anything in her entire life.

CHAPTER 15

"We're going to move you now, Mr. Berlander. Are you ready?"

Gideon opened his eyes to a silvery-looking haze that surrounded the ugliest face God had ever put upon the earth.

"Goin'? T'hell?"

The sudden wide smile didn't improve the face. "No . . . only down to extended care. Don't worry."

"Wasn't worried," Gideon said, closing his eyes. "A'ready been t'hell once, and it wasn't that bad."

"Okay, here we go. Are you ready?"

"Yah ready, Giddy? C'mon, yah ready t'go or not?"

Gideon glared up at his best friend in the whole world—at least for the summer, so far—and thought again how unfair things were sometimes. Jake, the snake, was a full year younger than he was and already half a head taller, and could lift a whole lot more weight.

"What'cher hurry? It ain't gonna go noplace."

It was a small cave they'd found set low in the side of a rocky outcropping—that *Jake* had found while looking for a new pet snake to replace the one his dog ate.

Jake's face, never what anyone outside those related to him would call appealing, suddenly twisted into a mocking sneer.

"Yer scared, ain'tcha?" the younger, but taller, boy said without a trace of question in his tone. "That's why yah don't wanna go. Yer scared like one a mah maw's cookin' rab—"

Jake might have been bigger and stronger and a hell of a lot uglier, but he was, and always had been, a sucker for a straight-on nose punch. Which was probably the only reason, Gideon thought as he watched the boy hop from foot to foot, holding his nose and hollering, that they were still friends.

"Yah broke it!" Jake moved his hands away from his nose and yelped when he saw the amount of blood that covered them. "Lookid! Ah'm bleedin'!"

Gideon's right hand and knuckles throbbed in pain, but he wasn't about to let his best friend know that, so he folded his arms across his chest and snorted like he saw his daddy do after a good shot of whiskey.

"Ah seen worse," he said, "and Ah don't think it's broke . . . but it is swellin' like a drowned pig."

Jake grabbed his nose without thinking and hollered again.

"Hail Columbia, Jake!" Gideon laughed. "Yah scream like a girl!"

Which instantly shut Jake up. But not for long. "Well, Ah may scream like one, but yah ACT like one!"

Gideon unfolded his arms and didn't even mind the pain when he balled his hands into fists.

"Yah want a black eye t'go with yer broken nose?"

Jake wiped his hands off on the back of his dungarees and snuffled long and hard. The wet, slurpy sound made Gideon's belly quiver.

"Ah a'ready know yah can hit, Giddy . . . but yah still act like a girl."

Gideon took a menacing step forward, but Jake didn't back down. He just stood there, looking big and strong, and pointed to the little crack of dark in the side of the mountain.

"So prove yah ain't."

Gideon's belly began going all aquiver again when he looked at the cave. His daddy was all the time telling him not to go wandering into caves, especially in late spring, like it was now, when mama pumas and other hungry things were just looking for an easy kill.

And Lord knows, he'd be easy.

"All right, Ah will."

Turning toward the cave, Gideon took a good long breath and aimed himself at the cave as if his life, and not just his self-respect as a boy, depended on it. He could hear Jake's stumbling tread right behind, and that made him hold his head up a little higher and walk a little faster. As long as Jake was going to be in the cave with him, there was nothing he had to worry about.

Until they got to the entrance and Jake planted his slat-flat tail on a big mossy rock.

Gideon was so close to the cave, he could have reached out and slid his hand into the darkness if he wanted to. Which he didn't.

"Ain't'cha comin' in with me?"

And Jake, the rotten snake that he was, suddenly began to laugh and laugh like he was about to pitch a fit of some kind.

"Haw, haw! Ah knew it," the boy finally said when he caught his breath, "Ah knew yah wouldn't go in there by yerself! Yer a girl, Giddy Berlander, and Ah'm gonna tell all the guys. Haw, hee, haw!"

When he trod down on Jake's foot, Gideon was sorry he had decided to wear the tenner shoes that morning and not his hard leather-soled school and church shoes, but the sudden bellow of pain was better than nothing.

"Damn yah, Gideon Berlander! Ah'm gonna tell!"

"Yeah, 'cause tellin's all yer good for. Well, tell 'em all this while yer at it!"

Shucking off his coat only because his maw told him she'd skin his hide down to the marrow if he got it dirty, and he knew caves usually were, Gideon threw it on the ground next to his friend and marched, square-shouldered, back toward the entrance.

And almost passed out from sheer happiness when Jake said, "Yah know yah don't have t'do this. Ah mean, there ain't no one gonna know if yah back out right now.

" 'Cept me, a'course.

"Haw. Haw."

Gideon didn't look back or stop moving until he reached the entrance and felt the darkness settle down around him. The cave was warmer than the outside air and smelled like the vegetable bins out in the springhouse—moist and sweet and just a little musty. But it wasn't rank, and that was good—if it had been, he didn't think his wobbling belly would have stood it for long.

There was even a breeze of sorts that brushed against his face as soft as spider silk. All and all, it was a right fine cave—bigger than he thought, too. The entrance hadn't been more than a narrow crack in the side of the mountain, but a yard into it, the cave opened up enough that he could swing his arms straight out at the side and still not touch the ceiling even when he jumped.

It was a good cave.

"Giddy?" Jake's voice sounded like it was buried under a dozen quilts.

Gideon turned around and almost stumbled. It hadn't felt like he'd gone that far, but the pale gray light that marked the entrance was only just a little sliver.

"Jake?"

"Giddy? Hey, Giddy, c'mon out. . . . Ah was only foolin' yah . . . yah ain't no girl!"

"Jake? Hey, Jake, why don't'cha come on in?"

"Giddy? Giddy!"

Gideon liked the scaredy sound in his friend's voice. "Now who's the girl, Jake? Haw, haw, Jake."

"Giddy? Come out or Ah'm tellin'!"

"Haw, haw," Gideon shouted. "I'M GID-E-ON-BER-LAN-DER and Ah ain't no girl!"

"Gid-e-on. Ber-lan-der."

It wasn't an echo. The voice, though weak and shivery-sounding, was real and close. Very close. Closer than Jake, standing out in the sunlight just a dozen or so feet away. Closer than walls, and a lot closer than the ceiling. Maybe even close enough to—

Gideon screeched like his soul was on fire when a thin hand latched onto his leg and pulled him down into a pile of furs and skins. *Injin ghosts!* He'd wandered into a cave full of Injin ghosts. As a thin pair of legs wrapped around his, he wondered why his daddy had warned him only about pumas and not ghosts!

Ghost or not, it felt pretty solid when he jabbed his elbow into what he hoped was a belly.

"JAKE!"

A second hand slithered across his face and clamped his mouth shut. Gideon tasted dust and tallow.

"Shh! Don't speak." It was the same voice. "We have to be quiet."

Gideon tried to struggle free, but this time the *ghost* was ready for him. It clung to him like a second skin.

"Please . . . promise you'll be quiet and I'll let you go. Please—he'll hear."

"Who?"

A sound filled the cave before the ghost could answer—soft at first, but building until the rocks beneath the pile of furs began to shake.

"It's too late," the ghost said. "He's here."

Anything else Gideon may have wanted to ask, or scream, was drowned out by a river of wind that suddenly filled the cave. A light came with the wind, gray and thick like dust—blinding, painful after the darkness—but Gideon forced himself to keep his eyes open and look at the thing holding him.

It wasn't a ghost, it was a boy, not much older or bigger than himself. An Injin boy from the reservation. An Injin boy that looked as frightened as Gideon felt—a feeling that only got stronger when a low, ululating moan rippled through the swirling air above them.

"It's too late," the boy repeated. "He's here."

Gideon didn't mind the boy grabbing him this time, and did a little grabbing himself when the moan elongated into a howl and kept right on climbing until he was sure the sound would burst his eardrums.

He was surprised when he could still hear the Injin boy whimpering.

"S'okay . . . that—that's probably just Jake. He's only tryin' t'scare me 'cause Ah said he was a girl." Gideon took a deep breath and tried to outshout the wind. "Better stop it! Ah'm gonna tell yer maw, Jake!"

Something much larger than Jake swept into the cave and hovered above them.

He never asked what Joseph saw that day, but in Gideon's mind it was only a dust devil . . . a big one—big enough to swallow the gray man who sang to him and told him all sorts of wonderful stories.

But it was only a dust devil, and he'd never been afraid of those.

Never had.
Never would be.

"Haw, haw."

"Well, there you go, Mr. Berlander. It's so good to hear someone in your condition laugh. I'm proud of you. Okay, here we are, your brand-new room."

Gideon waited until the ugly nurse and two others hefted him from one bed and dumped him onto another like a sack of late-season potatoes, real gingerly, like they expected him to burst through his skin or something, before trying to work up enough spit to let fly.

Nothing—he was as dry as bone.

"Dammit."

The ugly nurse leaned down, close to his face. "Is something wrong, Mr. Berlander? Can I get you something?"

Gideon looked up at her and smiled. "Spit."

She didn't understand. "Oh, of course. I'll get you some ice chips."

He wished his voice were stronger, but he did the best he could.

"Haw, haw."

Joseph expected an argument when he told the boys their carving lesson would have to wait until he got back from the city, and he spent the drive back from the cottonwoods working on his explanation. They would be disappointed, and that tore at his heart almost as much as confronting Gideon tore at his courage.

But both had to be done.

By the time Joseph pulled Daniel's truck into the drive, he'd whittled the excuse down to a simple statement of fact: He needed to buy paints for the Kachinas.

Simple and true.

And barely heard.

Joey and Andrew had been out of the cab and clambering into the back of the pickup before Joseph set the hand brake. He'd told them, while they gathered the dozen or so pieces of fallen cottonwood, that each piece would have to be *carefully* stripped of its bark.

They'd been so overwhelmed with the thought of actually using their knives for *real* that neither boy looked up, or turned around, or noticed him leave.

He smiled, thinking about that, and tucked the Wal-Mart bag tighter under his arm. Inside were two sets of poster paints and a package of brushes, and two packs of bubble gum—just in case his grandsons had looked up to discover he'd left them.

A pack of gum each would be enough to bribe his way back into their good graces.

Joseph's stomach lurched as the elevator stopped. He hadn't even thought about bringing some kind of token to Gideon. A man doesn't visit his (dying) brother in the hospital without bringing a token.

Old One, how could you have let me forget?

But there was no answer but the soft whoosh of the elevator doors opening and the muffled concerns from the other passengers as they filed past him trailing strings of brightly colored helium balloons and boutiques of gift-shop flowers.

Joseph transferred the bag from under his arm to

his hand and let it swing visibly. Maybe the young nurse at the reception desk would think it was a gift even if Gideon wouldn't.

She was already smiling when he stopped in front of her.

"Good morning, sir, may I help you?"

"Yes," Joseph said, lifting the bag so she could see it, "could you please tell me which room Gideon Berlander is in?"

"Berlander?"

"Yes, he was in the ICU, but they told me he'd been moved here. Gideon. Berlander. I'm . . . an old friend."

While the nurse looked down at a chart, Joseph touched the medicine pouch at his throat and prayed. He had to see Gideon this one last time, before it was too late.

The nurse was still smiling when she looked up.

"Yes, sir. Mr. Berlander is in room eight-nineteen. Go down this hall and then turn left. It will be the fifth room on the left."

Joseph let his hand drop from the medicine pouch and thanked the Old One.

"May I ask how he's doing? The nurse in the ICU didn't say much, just that he'd been moved. Is he all right?"

"This is extended care, sir," she said, as if that answered his question. So he thanked her as if it had.

Gideon felt him standing next to the bed before his spirit had fully returned to him.

"Come t'gloat, Joseph?" he asked as he opened his eyes to the room's artificial twilight. The nurse who'd made sure he was trussed up good and proper, making sure all the needles were in place and the bedrails up like he was some helpless baby, had asked if he wanted the curtains open and he told her . . .

. . . something, he couldn't remember what exactly, but she'd kept the curtains closed, so maybe that's what he'd told her to do.

But the room was still bright enough for him to see where Joseph was staring.

"Yah should'a been here before they changed the dressing," he said, "it was a real mess. And painful as all get-out. 'Course, if the old stories are true, yah probably felt some o'that, didn't yah?"

Gideon chuckled when the old man touched his right shoulder. A plastic shopping bag dangled from his wrist.

"Yeah, thought so. Well, sorry t'put yah through all that, but Ah didn't have much say in the matter. What's in the bag? Yah bring me some cookies?"

Joseph lowered the bag quickly. "No, it's just something for my grandsons. . . . I didn't bring you anything. I'm sorry, brother."

"Save yer apologies, *brother*. It ain't like Ah'll be needin' nothin' where Ah'm goin.'"

"You know, then?"

"That Ah'm dyin'. All men die, brother, yah know that."

"Yes, I know," he said, "but you and I are not like other men, little brother. When you die, I will follow—I know that."

Gideon smiled, but only until the air coming through the tubes in his nose had filled his lungs enough to laugh.

"And yer scared. Dammit, boy, ain't yah lived long enough?"

Whatever the old Indian was thinking, he didn't let it show on his face.

"However weak you think me, Gideon, I am not afraid of death."

"Well, good t'see yah finally got a little backbone. Yah sure looked scared t'me when that rapin' bastard o'yers died. Ah saw death look yah in the eye that day, boy, and yah didn't look back."

"Stop it."

Gideon's lungs were burning from the friction his last bout of laughter caused, but he managed what he thought was a pretty convincing snicker all the same.

"Why, what'cha gonna do?"

Joseph's hand closed around the front of his collar. "I didn't come here to fight, brother."

"Good thing for you."

"Gideon, listen to me. . . . Our time is almost over. We have to hand over the power to the new Chosen One before it's too late."

Gideon shook his head. "Too late for what, little brother?"

Joseph jerked back as the wind smashed into the window hidden behind the drape.

"Ah ain't ready t'give nothin' up. Not until those who stole mah land pay for what they done." He smiled, and the wind screamed in pain. "But don't'cha worry, brother, Ah'll let yah know when Ah am ready. 'Fact, yah'll probably be one o'the first Ah tell."

As much as he enjoyed watching the old Hopi squirm, Gideon was finding it hard to concentrate.

He closed his eyes, and the wind sounds died. *Damn, didn't mean t'do that.*

What was Ah doin'?

Gideon kept his eyes closed because it felt good. "Go back t'the reservation, Joseph, and let me be. Ah'm tired."

"You're dying, Gideon."

Gideon opened his eyes, but the wind was still quiet.

"These are your last moments. Give me your powers and I'll give them to Cielo."

"So that's yer plan, is it?" He forgot and started to laugh, then couldn't stop himself until the blood stopped it for him. "Yer gonna take 'er all for yerself . . . and that ain't 'er name. Stupid name, a'ways thought so. Sky, hell . . . maybe Ah knew it even then."

"Knew what?"

Gideon swallowed and wrinkled his nose at the taste.

"Brother?"

"That she was more yer blood than mine. Ah tried t'teach 'er once, back when she was just little and she ran—just like yah tried t'run when the Old One came sweepin' down on us. . . . remember? Yah remember how yah tried t'run, Joseph?"

"So that was why."

"What'cha talkin' about?"

"Nothing. Gideon, please." The room began to get darker, shrinking into night as Joseph held out his hand. "Release her to me."

"Hell no. She's mah granddaughter, too."

"I didn't mean Cielo."

"That ain't her name. . . . Glory shoulda gotten rid o'it before it killed 'er, but she was weak, like her brat. Ah tried t'show 'er, and she ran. Mah arm hurts, Joseph."

Gideon thought he saw the old man nod, but wasn't sure. It was so dark in the room now, even Joseph looked white.

"I know, Gideon. Please . . . please."

"Joseph, open the window, will yah? Ah can't breathe in this room."

One of the machines attached to him suddenly buzzed like an angry hornet. Didn't scare him, though—and neither did the look on Joseph's face when something white and hazy, like a cloud, came spewing out of him on a fountain of blood. 'Fact, the look on Joseph's face was mighty funny—it was the look of a man who knew he'd just lost everything that ever mattered.

"*Gideon!*"

He sounded funny, too—far away and left behind.

"*No, Gideon . . . you can't let go. Gideon?*"

Another voice, just as distant and insignificant, suddenly fluttered in his ear.

"*Mr. Berlander?*"

"*Help him, nurse. Please, he has to wake up.*"

"*We'll do everything we can. Now step back, sir, please. Mr. Berlander?*"

"*Gideon . . . don't do this. Wake up!*"

"*Move back, sir! Mr. Berlander? Mr. Berlander.*"

"*Gideon!*"

"*Code Blue . . . get the crash cart in here. . . . Mr. Berlander?*"

"*GIDEON!*"

It was all so funny, Gideon laughed until he thought he was going to split a gut and kept right on laughing even after he did. But it didn't hurt, and neither did his arm now—hell, nothing hurt no more.

Gideon? Mr. Berlander? You can't do this, Gideon. He's gone. No. Call it. Gideon! Time of death—9:54. NO!

WELCOME, WIND CALLER.

The Old One nodded and reached out his hand.

Well, hell, Gideon thought as he died, *this is gonna be fun.*

CHAPTER 16

Sky leaned back against the elevator's copper-tinted mirror tiles and watched the floor-indicator panel above the door while a little girl, no more than six, provided the audio.

"Three. Four. Five . . . uh-oh, we're stopping. Gotta step aside, Mommy, this man wants out. Bye-bye, man. Yeah! We're going again. Six! Six! Is this where Grammy is, Daddy? Yea! Come on, doors . . . open, open, open. YIPPEE! GRAMMY, WE'RE Here!"

"Poor Grammy," someone said as the doors closed, and Sky smiled.

She still didn't trust her head enough to actually laugh out loud. One prolonged shower, three cups of black (*ugh*) coffee, four hours of sleep after the hospital's much-too-early good news, and two migraine-strength Excedrin hadn't helped as much as she'd hoped. Sky could still feel the hangover behind her eyeballs, just waiting to attack.

If the little girl hadn't gotten off when she had, Sky would have gotten out and taken her chances walking up the last two flights.

And was just as happy it hadn't come to that.

When the doors opened on EIGHT, Sky followed another passenger out of the car and up to the nurses' station, stopping as far back as she would have if they'd been in line for an ATM. The man's departure and a smile from the nurse on duty, and Sky stepped up to the desk.

"My grandfather was transferred up here this morning. Gideon Berlander?"

"Oh. Yes. One minute, please, Ms. Berlander."

The phantom hangover nudged the back of her eyes hard enough to make her belly cramp, and Sky found herself bracing herself against the front of the desk as the nurse paged Dr. Winegardt.

"Wait a minute," she said to get the nurse's attention. "I got a call this morning saying he was all right . . . and that was just a couple of hours ago."

The nurse nodded, but her gaze never quite reached Sky's face.

"I know. But this *is* extended care, and sometimes these things can— Oh, here's the doctor now."

Sky had never seen anyone so eager to hand off a problem—or a man less happy to receive one. Though still the bright-eyed young man she'd met before, there was a thinness to his lips that made him look just a bit older and wiser.

It was a slight, but only slight, improvement.

"Ms. Berlander," he said by way of a greeting, "I don't know what to tell you."

"He's dead?"

The doctor wasn't having any more luck at meeting her gaze than the nurse had, but his head nodded once, very slightly. Sky exhaled slowly and let go of the desk. It was very strange, but she suddenly felt fine. Better than fine, she felt reborn.

It was all she could do to keep from smiling. "How did it happen?"

"Here," Dr. Winegardt took her arm and led her to a small, glass-enclosed waiting room. It was smaller than the one on the ICU floor, almost cozy in a somber sort of way, just the right size for a family of four to grieve in—undisturbed and isolated, but always just a glance away from an entire bank of health care professionals. "This is more comfortable."

Sky sat down on the sand-colored sofa and folded her hands in her lap. "He's dead."

The corner of the doctor's left eye twitched when he sat next to her. "Yes, I'm so sorry, Ms. Berlander. We did the best we could, but given the trauma he suffered and his preexisting condition . . . it was just too much for his body to handle. I'm sorry. But if it's any consolation at all, he didn't suffer. We're reasonably sure he slipped into a coma right before the end. I don't think he knew what was happening."

Sky nodded, afraid to open her mouth for fear of what she might say. Or not say.

The moment of silence stretched uncomfortably long between them.

"Well." Dr. Winegardt smiled, nodded, and

checked his watch as he stood up. "I have a consultation at eleven, but please feel free to stay here as long as you like until you feel . . . settled."

"I'm fine, Doctor," Sky said, and surprised herself when she got to her feet. "May I see him?"

"Let me check, okay?" He was halfway through the glass door when he stopped and turned around. "Would you like to talk to someone? We have a very good grief-counseling program here, and I could have one of the counselors come by—either here or whenever it would be convenient for you."

Sky shook her head. "No, that's all right. I'll be fine. I'd just like to see him now."

"Sure. Let me find out."

Sky took his place at the open door and found herself caught between the silence of the glass room and the muffled hospital sounds.

"It's as quiet as a grave," she whispered as the smiling nurse signaled for her. "He was probably glad to get out of here."

The Old One had gone, but Gideon decided to stay and watch the fun.

And Lordy Lord, it was that—'cept he didn't particularly care for the way they were treating his body. He might not be using it anymore, but dammit, it had been his and they should be showing it a hell of a lot more respect, instead of tossing it around like it was nothing more than a chunk of meat.

Even if that's what it was.

Gideon moved closer to the bed without actually moving and found he mightily enjoyed the feeling. It had the feel of drunkenness about it, but it was a hundred times better—he knew he wasn't going to have to wake up to a day's worth of misery.

Hell, he wasn't going to wake up at all!

"Hah!" The laughter just sort of escaped him, and he had to stop himself from laughing on purpose when a burly-bag of a nurse suddenly stopped messing with his body and looked up.

She heard him. He might be dead, but he'd make damned sure he wasn't going to be forgotten.

"Did you say something?" the nurse asked the woman standing in the doorway.

The woman folded her arms across her chest and braced herself as if she expected to be dragged into the room against her will. It was the same thing she used to do when she was little and didn't want to take her Saturday-night bath.

Sky.

Well, well, Gideon thought, *mah precious little granddaughter come to visit.*

"No, I didn't say anything. The doctor said it was quick, that he probably didn't feel anything."

That's what yah think, is it, 'breed?

"I'm sure he didn't."

The nurse was smiling now while she tucked the clean white sheet in around his body like a shroud. Gideon could almost feel the starchy material against the raw nub of his shoulder, and he lifted an invisible hand toward the remembered sensation. Being dead was a wonder.

"We had him on monitors right up until the end, and I can tell you there were not significant changes in respiration or heart rate." The nurse gave his empty chest a solid thump and backed away from the bed. "He might have dreamed a little at the end, but that's all. Stay as long as you like. We'll have the release papers at the desk for you when you're ready to leave. Do you have a funeral home you'd like us to contact?"

"I . . . I don't know. Does the hospital . . . have referrals?"

What the hell? Yah can't be bothered lookin' for a gravedigger yerself?

The nurse nodded and gave Sky a gentle touch as she left. "I'll print out the names of a few. They'll be at the desk with the other papers. When you're ready."

"Thank you."

Gideon drifted closer until he was right in front of her and hovered there. He was close enough to see the coffee-brown rings of her eyes tighten down a little, as if he still had substance.

A moment later, she walked straight through him without so much as a shiver.

"What am I going to do with you?" she asked his body. Gideon drifted on over, just in case his body wasn't as dead as everyone, including himself, thought it was and had an answer for her.

It didn't.

Sky looked over her shoulder quick, like she was worried someone was watching, then reached out and touched what had been his left cheek.

"Rest in peace, old man," she said as she tugged the stiff white sheet loose and tossed it over his face. "Not that you deserve it. And give my regards to the red-dirt man when you see him . . . you bastard."

Red-dirt man . . . what the hell is she talkin' about?

267

"*Sky!*"

She heard him, he knew she heard him, but she turned and walked away like he was nothing but some roadkill left by the side of the road.

"*SKY! Yah come back here! Yah listen t'me, gal—ah'm yer granddaddy!*"

But not the only one.

Damn, he'd been so busy dying, he'd almost forgotten all about Joseph.

"*Yah come here and try t'steal what the Old One gave t'me? Tellin' me the power's gotta be passed on t'the next Chosen One. Well, Ah tell yah this, brother . . . there ain't gonna be a next Chosen One, 'cause Ah ain't done yet.*

"*And Ah'll prove it.*"

Gideon gave the sheet-draped object on the bed one last look and moved over to the window. The drapes fluttered a little when he passed through them, but not so much as anyone who might have looked in would notice. He didn't want to tip his hand just yet.

Soon, but not yet.

The window offered no more resistance than the curtains had, and Gideon's upper body slipped through the reinforced glass like a shadow. He saw her in the parking lot, eight floors below, playing with an empty soda can . . . rolling it first one way and then the other, mindless as a child with a toy.

"*Well,*" he said, shaking his head, "*that's about t'change.*" And he called her.

The empty soda can glinted in the morning sun, tumbling through the air as she raced toward him. Gideon stretched out his left hand and would have breathed a sigh of relief if he'd still been able. He'd been worried that Joseph was right about the power needing to be passed on.

"Damn old man. Yah a'most had me believin' it . . . yah only knew the stories, little brother—and stories ain't nothin' like real life. And Ah'll be by directly t'show yah.

"But Ah got a few things t'clean up first."

The stump of Gideon's right arm twitched in envy when he raised its remaining twin over his head and leaped out onto the wind's back. She bucked and tossed and tried to throw him like she had the Old One when he rode her.

But he hung on tight, and the tighter he held her, the more of him was blown away—piece by piece by piece until every part of him that remembered what it was like to be a man was blown away.

Almost.

It sounded like a small sonic blast going off right behind her.

"What was that?" Sky said, maybe a little too loud for the otherwise hushed tones of the ward, but neither the nurse nor grief counselor seemed to mind. Both women jumped just as high as she had.

"A terrorist attack!"

The nurse had said the words with all the conviction of a woman who still hadn't gotten over the trauma of the 9/11 tragedy, and the grief counselor had simply looked at her as another potential client.

"No, I don't think so," the woman said, looking at Sky. "Try to stay calm."

Sky bristled at the nonverbal insinuation that she

was anything less than calm and would have said so—if the next words out of the woman's mouth hadn't stopped her like a deer caught in a semi's headlights.

"We're fine," the counselor said. "It was only the wind."

A moment before Joseph heard the wind, he felt his heart seize in midbeat. The same thing happened when Gideon died, but this time the momentary death was accompanied by a pain in his belly and right shoulder. He barely managed to pull onto the shoulder of the road and hit the brakes before the wind slammed into the pickup.

His head whipped backward against the seat rest and the new pain joined the others.

The windstorm lasted only a moment or two—what the well-dressed meteorologists on the Weather Channel called a "microburst"—but it lasted long enough to sandblast the back bumper and break both taillights.

Rubbing the back of his neck, Joseph leaned forward over the steering wheel and watched the wind twist itself into a dust devil the size of a three-story building.

"You don't have the right to do this," he said. "Our time is over. Stop it."

The dust devil swayed like a cobra in front of the truck, then suddenly spun away, plowing through a stand of mesquite trees. A field sparrow darted from the tangle only to find itself swallowed by the column of air. It fell to the ground a moment later, a small, twisted mass of bloodied feathers and broken bones.

Gideon had never liked sparrows.

"You still like to torture helpless animals, don't you, little brother?"

A rock smashed into the driver's-side window, directly opposite Joseph's head, as the dust devil spun itself out.

The grief counselor smiled and touched Sky's arm. It was a light touch that lingered against the sweater's nap only long enough to convey a sense of understanding and sympathy, without leaving any sort of warmth behind.

Sky wondered if that was taught as part of the training or if the woman had perfected the move on her own. Either way, it was effective—it brought her back to reality.

"Are you *sure* you're all right?" the woman asked. "I have some time, if you'd like to talk about anything."

"Thanks, but I'll be okay." Sky smiled, hoping that would prove her point as the nurse handed her the plastic bag containing Gideon's personal effects: a comb; a wallet with seven one-dollar bills and fifty-three cents in change; a stained, possibly red bandanna; a folding knife; the stub of a pencil, No. 2; and a watch fob, minus the watch, made of braided hair, blond.

And a willow whistle.

Sky closed the bag and tucked it under her arm. "Really, I'll be fine now."

* * *

Gideon stretched out his arm and a row of early field corn collapsed in on itself. He nodded at a herd of docile Navaho sheep and laughed as they stampeded over a cliff.

Damn. If he'd only known, he would have given up and died a long time back.

Maybe even the day his Glory died giving birth to that ungrateful half-breed bitch.

"Hell, Joseph . . . yah was wrong about this and yer just as wrong about her. The Old One didn't have no hand in her birthin'—it was that son o' yours come sniffin' my daughter, that's all. Sky . . . hell, yah shoulda let her die the day she was born. She got yer fear, right enough . . . nothin' o' mine—and Ah'm gonna keep it that way."

He turned hard and gave the wind her head, let her race fast up over the foothills and onto the ridge before he pulled her back. She bucked a little, kicking up clouds of dust, and that was fine by him. He wanted as much dust and devilment as she had in her.

Right here.

Right now.

"Mah land."

If he hadn't known the lay of the surrounding hills by heart, he might have thought he'd come to the wrong spot.

It was even worse than his fevered nightmare had envisioned. The only thing missing was the army of silver-headed men in blue overalls.

The land that had held his home, his garden, the graves of his wife and daughter, had been scraped clean, flayed and stretched out, pockmarked with wooden stakes that flew tiny yellow or red flags. A line of blue flags led toward a small white trailer and the two portable outhouses over where the spring-house had been.

Gideon moved across the smooth ground until he came to the bright yellow and blue COMING SOON FROM SUN COUNTRY HOMES: PIO-NEER RIDGE billboard. It was a flimsy thing—stuck up on two one-by-threes and planted a foot into the rocky soil where Glory'd had her little playhouse, tall as a man standing on tippy-toe—hardly worth the ef-fort it would take to blow it to hell.

But he did anyway.

At the first gust, the sign snapped in half. COM-ING SOON FROM SUN COUNTRY HO caught the updraft and did a full loopidy-loop before crash-ing into the cab of a backhoe. MES: PIONEER RIDGE, still attached to the wooden uprights, sacri-ficed showmanship for accuracy: It broke one of the trailer's windows and almost impaled the man who was stepping out of it at the time.

"Jesus Christ!"

Gideon would have applauded if he'd had two hands, but since he didn't he let the wind show his appreciation.

She came in fast, snaking toward the dump trucks and graders at knee level. The machines didn't no-tice, but a few of the construction workers were knocked down and dragged a couple of yards. Dou-bling back, she mowed down a wide swath of the lit-tle red and yellow and blue flags and drove a half-dozen into the side of one of the outhouses. The man inside wasn't at all pleased and didn't have one nice word to say for himself when he came barreling out with his pants down around his ankles and the wind hit his Johnny Snake.

"SHIT!"

"Looks like you still are, Henry."

"FUCK YOU!"

"No, thanks."

"SHUT THE FUCK UP, ALL OF YOU!"

All eyes, including Gideon's, turned to watch the man who'd almost gotten himself impaled by the trailer struggling against the wind as he tried to cross what had once been the cabin's front porch. Poor man wasn't making much progress. For every step forward, the wind pushed him back an inch; it was just so pitiful, Gideon decided to help.

Only a couple of the men were smart enough to keep their mouths shut when the wind suddenly died and their boss hit the ground like a sack of condensed shit.

"FUCKING WIND!" The man shouted even though he didn't have to. It was quiet on the ridge again, with only a tiny stirring of air—just enough to flick a handful of dust in the man's eyes as he was getting back to his feet. "SHIT, I told Mackay this would happen if we took down the windbreaks. Whadda yah all looking at? Get your thumbs out of your asses and get back to work. Henry, pull up your goddamned pants and start putting those survey stakes back. Leo, you and Dave—"

Gideon nodded, and a tiny dust devil grabbed one of the stakes and hurled it at the lead man's hard hat. It made a lovely pinging sound.

The other men ducked for cover when another dozen or so came flying their way.

"God DAMN! Okay, that's it." The lead man was shouting again, but this time he had reason. "We're done for the fucking day! Store everything that's not nailed down in the trailer and lock up the machines. Mackay's not paying us for hazardous duty. Now, MOVE IT!"

Gideon kept the wind blowing hard and steady, but let the men go. None of their faces was familiar, and he'd never been one to take his anger out on an innocent—especially when there were others who were more deserving.

The men who stole his land. The doctor who took his arm.

Joseph.

Sky.

Yup, more than enough to keep him busy . . . to keep *them* busy for quite a while to come.

"But first things first."

By the time Gideon had swept the ridge clean, the sun was low in the western sky and the first lights were beginning to show themselves—both in the sky and down along the valley floor.

The town didn't look half bad tonight—inviting, almost.

Gideon called, and the wind swept him into her arms.

He'd never been one to say no to an invitation.

CHAPTER 17

It was just after five when Sam kicked the front door shut behind him and hit the switch for the living-room lights with his elbow. *Thump, click.* The two sounds, coming only a second apart, echoed through the otherwise quiet condo and only helped amplify the Saturday-night sounds that surrounded his two-bed/one-and-a-half-bath Fortress of Solitude. Music, laughter, the steady hum from the hot water pipes in the walls, and televised voices competing with real ones.

The sounds of Home, Sweet Home.

Damn. He needed to get out, and fast.

He may have once been momentarily blinded by images of hot tubs and sweeping vistas . . . and standing tall against the sky—but the realization that he still would have been only one more medium-sized fish in a relatively small pond left a bad taste on the back of his tongue.

And a twinge along the scar on his forehead.

The only souvenir he'd be taking with him from lovely Richland, Arizona.

"Yes, sir, Cali-fuck-ya here I come."

Sam whistled the tune as he walked into the kitchen to relieve the side-by-side of its burden of beer by one can, then used the open door as an arm-rest while he washed away the bad taste and perused the interior for dinner.

"Let's see . . . what looks good."

Sam took a couple of sips while he contemplated his choices. He'd done his full Saturday regime of carb-destroying activities—weights, treadmill, ten laps in the gym's Olympic-sized pool, another two laps in the gym's Olympic-class aerobics instructress, more weights, more laps, sauna—and rewarded himself by reaching over the protein drinks and relatively fresh organic fruits and vegetables for the plastic-wrapped container of week-old chili.

"Yum."

The chili had coagulated to aged perfection during its residency. Amber pools of fat lapped leisurely against the chunks of pork and jalapeño peppers as he carried it to the microwave. His mouth began watering the moment the spicy scent breached the oven's magnetic seal.

Sam finished the first beer and was reaching for a second when the timer went off.

"Those poor health Nazis don't know what they're missing," he said, sliding a pot holder carefully under the bowl before he attempted to pull off the melted plastic wrap. He'd learned the hard way that being careless around steaming chili was akin to walking up to someone trying to disarm a bomb and popping a balloon.

Not a good idea.

Three drops of Tabasco, some grated sharp cheddar spooned on top, and another beer, and Sam settled down into his recliner to watch the evening roll in.

He had a TV in the bedroom—for sports and the Playboy Channel—but preferred to watch the real dramas that were going on in the apartments he could see from his front window. Fifteen different opportunities to indulge in a little healthy voyeurism.

Who needed television when a man had all that?

Sam smiled around a particularly chewy piece of what he hoped was pork when the apartment directly across from his became a virtual fortress of light. That could only mean one thing: The carrot-topped three-year-old had finally gotten tall enough to reach the hall switches. She raced past the living-room picture window a moment later, trailing a blanket over one shoulder like a pint-sized Amazon.

She was a doll, and she made Sam glad he'd decided long ago never to have kids.

"That's it, baby," he said, toasting her with the beer can, "keep your folks on their toes. Now, let's see how the lovebirds are doing."

The window one floor down and two over was still dark. Pity. The lovebirds—young, dual-incomes, Jeep Wrangler for him, VW Nab for her—had had a fight that morning. Red faces, wild eyes, clenched fists, a few tears, a lot of shouting, the whole works short of actual physical confrontation—and he'd watched every glorious moment over coffee and a raspberry Pop-Tart.

Sam gave the window another five seconds—still dark—and moved to the middle-aged couple: three right, two up. He worked, she stayed home. They were both hitting the downside of fifty, getting a little paunchy in places, and were generally kind to each other. There was nothing extraordinary about them except for the fact that they were closet nudists who didn't always remember to close their drapes all the way. They were one of Sam's favorite couples, next to the sparring lovebirds and the pair of lesbian physical therapists—bottom floor, across from the laundry room—but he had to be careful as to when he watched. On weekends, the only safe viewing time was at night: Every Saturday and Sunday, rain or shine, Mr. Nudie liked to cook bacon without wearing an apron.

It made Sam tremble just to think of it.

More apartments lit up and curtains were drawn, TVs went on, and dinners were getting under way, but the lovebirds' apartment stayed dark. *Oh well, can't have everything*, he thought, and waved at the little redhead when she appeared in the window, "blankie" in hand, nose and forehead pressed to the window. She didn't see him; all her attention was focused down, toward the landscaped atrium, as the security lights came on. Shadows suddenly graffitied the lower floors and reached for her.

Sam chuckled when she just as suddenly turned tail and ran. God, he could remember doing that— scaring himself silly just for the fun of it.

"Boogeyman'll get ya if you don't watch out."

The lesbians' light came on just as one of the shadows broke away from the others and began moving slowly down the path. Somebody was out for an early-evening walk.

Sam spooned another mound of chili into his mouth and chased it down with a heathy swig of beer as he got to his feet. He might never know the joy of looking down on people from the old man's ridge, but he sure as hell could make up for it now.

A belch caught him by surprise and singed the back of his throat as he watched the solitary figure move slowly through the pools of light. The wind had come up, kicking up the shadows and tearing at the person's clothes. Sam couldn't tell if it was a man or a woman, but he noticed there was something wrong in the way the person moved, lurching from side to side, but not like a drunk would move. . . . It almost looked like . . .

Shit. It almost looked like the person was floating above the ground.

"Trick of the light, or maybe it *is* the boogeyman."

The minute the words left his mouth, Sam's inner child almost pooped his britches, and his adult self wasn't faring much better with the chili.

"You asshole," he told both selves, deciding at that instant that the figure was (1) male and (2) totally and completely shit-faced drunk. "Just look at him. Hell, can't walk straight and he's swinging his arms like he's conducting some kind of fucking orchestra."

No, not both arms, just the right one—swinging it high over his head one minute and then twisting it out and down the next.

"Drunk and crazy," Sam said, and was beginning to

feel like the asshole he'd called himself when the man stopped directly below his window.

Gideon Berlander's empty right sleeve waved at Sam as he looked up.

And smiled.

"I'm really sorry about your friend, Dad."

Joseph wiped off a drop of wood glue from Nataska, the Black Ogre, which Joey was carving, and looked up. Daniel was standing just inside the kitchen door, thumbs hooked into the front pockets of his jeans, shoulders slumped.

He'd been apologizing all evening for the way he'd acted when he saw the damage to his truck.

"And I'm sorry about what I said this morning." Daniel shrugged and looked east, toward the rising moon. "It wasn't your fault, I know that. Shit . . . I mean, shoot, a sudden gust of wind like that." He shrugged again. "It happens. In fact, I heard the same thing happened to Jimmy Bunzel this morning. You know he's part of the crew working on that new housing development up on the ridge? Well, he said it got so windy up there the supervisor called a shutdown. Jimmy said he never saw it so windy before.

"Wind stirs things up, you know?"

"I know," Joseph said, and set the rough-shaped Kachina down next to the cottonwood limb Andy had stripped of bark and then gotten bored with. The bag of paints was still on the kitchen table. Unnoticed. "The wind does that. Makes people edgy. Daniel, do you remember your brother at all?"

Daniel's silhouette softened, allowing more of the light to escape into the night.

"Yeah, a little, I guess. I remember him being tall."

Joseph smiled and pulled his coat tighter over his shoulders. The gardening shed wasn't insulated and the wind had found every chink and fissure.

"You're taller."

"Really? Cool."

It seemed to Joseph that Daniel was going to say something else when there was a muffled thump, followed by a piercing screech, and the moment was lost.

Daniel shook his head and stepped back into the kitchen. "ANDY! JOEY! Knock it off, right now."

There was one more thump. "Boys! Did you hear your father?"

The wind had stirred up Estralita's mood as well.

"I'd better get in there and help with supper, or we might not get any," Daniel said. "I'm sorry about this morning, Dad. I shouldn't have gone on like that."

"Do you really mean that?"

"Of course I do."

"Then prove it." Joseph could feel his son's eyes on him as he walked to the door and held out the wad of crumpled bills. "Here, there should be enough here for a motel room in town."

Daniel backed away from the money as if it were a sidewinder. "What are you talking about?"

"There should be enough here for a nice dinner and movie, too. Maybe there's a Western playing somewhere." Joseph smiled. "I used to like Westerns, even though we always lost. Please, Daniel, take the money and do this for me."

"Why?"

"Because . . ." The wind snapped at him, warning him to be quiet. Joseph brushed her aside and pressed the bills into his son's hand. "Because I'm a foolish old man who watched another foolish old man die. Please, do this for me?"

Daniel's fingers closed around the money, but still he shook his head. "I don't like taking your money, Dad. You need it."

Joseph touched his son's chest with the flat of his hand and smiled. "I need this more. But one more thing: Tell Little Star this is your idea, a surprise before the baby comes. Okay?"

Daniel looked down at the bills, then stuffed them into his pocket. "Okay, but she might ask you to babysit."

"No, you have to take the boys." Joseph turned and walked back to the shed. "I'm going to be busy tonight."

"I'll try, Dad, but she might not feel like doing anything. The baby's been really active today."

"You have to convince her to go, Thomas."

"What?"

"Daniel," Joseph corrected quickly. "You have to convince her to go . . . to enjoy herself and the sons she already has."

Daniel sighed and disappeared into the house. "I'll try."

Joseph heard Estralita's answer almost immediately—"*What? But I have dinner on the stove.*"—and his grandson's pleading shouts—"*Oh, please, Mom. Please, Mom.*"—and silently thanked the Kachinas that Daniel hadn't waited until he was alone with his wife before making the suggestion.

The next voice he heard was Joey's, calling from the kitchen door. "Grandfather? Dad's taking us to town for the night, and Mom wants to know if you want her to warm up some stew from last night or if you want her to make something different."

Joseph reached down and picked up the willow whistle he'd began working on when the boys had grown tired of carving and gone into the house to their video games and cartoon shows.

The whistle was still pale white, the color of bone.

Joseph slipped it into his coat pocket as he walked back to the house. "Tell your mother stew would be fine."

The wind moaned as it passed him . . .

. . . rattling the window glass as Sam looked down.

"What the hell?"

The old man looked up at him, grinning like he'd lost his mind. And maybe he had, maybe his mind had gone on to its reward before his body. That was the closest thing to a rational explanation Sam could come up with for why a man who'd been dying only a few hours before was standing out in the cold evening air in his bare feet, wearing nothing but a hospital gown, the empty right sleeve whipping back and forth in the wind.

"You're nuts, old man," he said, and accidently tapped the window with the edge of the bowl. The sound was surprisingly loud. "Shit."

Sam hated using his cell phone for non-business-related calls, but the only other phone was sitting next to the couch a couple yards away and he didn't want to take his eyes off the crazy old coot any longer than he had to.

Setting the bowl and can down on the window

ledge, Sam nodded down at the crazy old man and fished the cell phone out of his pants. Gideon Berlander nodded back.

"Oh, that's right, you just keep on nodding and grinning, old man," Sam said as the phone's memory chip speed-dialed the hospital, glad that he hadn't gotten around to erasing it . . . or Sky's. Unless he missed his guess and the hospital had simply kicked the old man out, they'd be financially grateful to get his call.

If they weren't, he'd call Sky and tell her to come fetch her poor, befuddled granddad.

"And if she doesn't want you, I know a couple good nuthouses that will be more than happy to—"

"Memorial Hospital. How may I direct your call?"

Sam winked at the old man. "Department of missing patients, please."

"What?"

"Sorry. I need to talk to someone about a patient of yours—Gideon Berlander."

The woman said, "Thank you. I'll transfer you. One moment, please."

Sam placed his free arm across his chest and listened to the wind hiss through the phone line. Berlander might not think so, if he was still able to think, but Sam was doing him a real favor. No man, not even a bad-tempered old idiot like himself, deserved to die out in the cold.

"Yes, sir," Sam said as the static ended and someone picked up the phone. "I'm a regular saint."

"Morgue," a man's voice said.

The cell phone knocked against the scar on his forehead when he stepped back from the window.

Sometimes the outside noises made it through the double panes. "What?"

"Um, this is the hospital morgue. Can I help you?"

"No, sorry . . . they connected me to the wrong department. I was just checking on a patient."

"Oh. What was the name?"

Was? "Okay, maybe *you* can transfer me to the right department. The patient *is* Gideon Berlander."

Sam could hear the soft rustle of paper in the background.

"Yeah, Berlander, Gideon, NMI. He died this morning at—"

The old man was gone when Sam leaned his head against the cold window glass and looked down.

Gideon laughed, and the wind echoed it.

He held out his hand and the wind turned.

The city lay below them.

Like a spring lamb.

Ready for the slaughter.

And he was starving.

CHAPTER 18

Josh farted when he came.

He couldn't help himself—he *always* farted when he came. His doctor suggested cutting back on gas-producing food items, like beans and beer. Josh stopped eating Mexican food and switched from beer to wine without any noticeable results. His lower GI didn't seem to care.

Fortunately, his newest hump was a screamer and into scented candles.

Josh farted two more times before the muscles along his spine relaxed. He gave her a kiss and felt her sigh against his cheek as he rolled off.

"Oh, man, that was really good." She looked at him with honey-colored eyes and licked her lips. "You're even better than Mr. Hallen."

Josh lifted himself onto one elbow and glared at

her through the glow of the *Save the Whales* desk lamp. "Who?"

She giggled, and the sound reminded him of just how young she was. Thelma Nadine Parks: nineteen, blond, Perfect Ms. Cheerleader on the outside, and whore on the inside. She was the closest thing to Heaven Josh knew he'd ever get.

And he got her as often as possible.

"Hey, I'm not joking," he said, pinching her right nipple to let her know that. "Who is this Hallen jerk?"

Thelma pouted but didn't move her breast out of harm's way. Sometimes she liked it rough.

"Don't be jealous," she said, "he's just a teacher."

"You screwing teachers now, are you?"

"Only the ones who threaten to give me F's. Besides, I lied about Mr. Hallen." She kept a straight face for two beats and then quickly rolled off the four-poster in the opposite direction. "He was better."

Josh aimed an open-handed swat at her pink ass and missed by a mile and a half.

"Bitch."

"Bastard."

"Ballbreaker."

"Spurious panderer."

"What?"

Thelma grabbed the left post at the foot of her bed and swung around it with a stripper's grace. Josh just loved watching her move, but he couldn't let her know that. She was already getting too big a head instead of giving it.

"It's what Mr. Hallen called himself while I sucked

him off in his office. I dunno what it means, but it sounds way cool, don't you think?" Her wicked little smile suddenly turned into an equally wicked grimace. "Eeeoou, what's that smell?"

"Testosterone," Josh said quickly. "You mean you really went down on him just because he was going to give you a lousy F?"

She seemed genuinely shocked that he had to ask. "I have to keep up my GPA if I want to get into Harvard Business School. Geez, I don't know why you're making such a big deal about it. It wasn't like he was good-looking or anything."

Having said her piece, Thelma flopped down on the bed and began picking lint balls off her pink-and-white flannel sheets. She was pouting again, and the combination of that and her studied concentration of lint removal made Josh hard all over again. She might be a round-heeled little bitch, but she was his round-heeled little bitch.

At least until she went away to Harvard.

As if that was ever going to happen.

Much as he liked fooling around with her, he'd seen too many like her fall off their high horse right into a mid-income, not-so-happily-ever-after life of "settling fors." "Settling for" a husband and kids instead of a career. "Settling for" a minivan instead of a Corvette. "Settling for" three days a week at an air-conditioned gym instead of trekking through the Himalayas.

Josh had seen his mother settle and was just as glad. Women needed to be settled, otherwise they got into trouble.

He reached over and slapped Thelma hard on the ass.

"OW! What was that for?"

"Four score and seven years ago." Smiling, Josh grabbed her shoulders and pulled her on top of him as he rolled onto his back. "Our forefathers brought forth a great nation. . . . Now, you climb on up here and bring forth me."

Thelma looked at his erection as she got to her knees and sighed dramatically.

"Jesus, are you on Viagra? I'm going to be all sore in the morning, and I'm supposed to play tennis with the gang."

Josh was going to comment that tennis had better be the *only* thing she'd be playing, but got distracted the moment her tight little pussy settled down over him.

"Oh yeah, baby," he purred, eyes closing as she got into a steady up-and-down and up-and-down and—

She suddenly clenched up hard enough to pop Josh's eyes wide open.

"SHIT! Jesus, what are you trying to do, snap it off?"

Thelma's eyes were almost as wide as his. "SHH! I heard something."

Josh felt himself deflate as he pushed her off. She fell to the mattress like a mannequin—stiff and unyielding. He'd never seen her like this before and, given that he'd just heard something moving around the living room, decided he'd probably never have to see it again.

"I thought you said your father'd be gone for another couple of hours."

He was up and pulling on his jeans before she'd even found her robe.

"He was supposed to be. Fuck, he never comes home this early unless he's—" The robe slipped off the one shoulder it was covering as Thelma tiptoed to her bedroom. The sounds from the living room were getting louder. "Shit, he's drunk."

Josh had just finished buttoning his shirt when she turned around, as calm and collected as a naked teen could be.

"Okay, here's the plan," she whispered while she pulled the robe around her and tied it shut with a big, floppy bow. Josh knew just how the bow felt. "You wait until I get him into his room and then beat it. I'll call you in the morning."

"What about the car?" Josh said, finding and stuffing his Jockey shorts into his back pocket. "I left it out in front."

Thelma shrugged. "Listen to him—he's so drunk he can hardly walk. I don't even think he'll notice your car, but if he does, I'll say 'what car?' Believe me, it won't be the first time."

Josh would have liked a little more explanation about that last remark, but Thelma was already gone. He could hear her soft voice—"Daddy? Daddy, are you okay?"—echo down the hall and then there was nothing but the thumps and bumps and shuffling sounds.

"Shit."

A minute passed. Two. Josh grabbed his jacket and was heading for the window when the door slammed open.

"FUCK!"

Thelma held on to the door frame and leaned into the room, giggling like a lunatic.

"Did I scare you?" She batted her eyelashes at him. "You don't have to worry—I knew it was *way* too early for it to be him. Get back into bed. I'm just gonna take a quick shower. Here, catch."

Josh caught her robe when she threw it and felt his heart bounce back up into his throat when there was another muffled thump from the living room.

"What is that?"

Thelma rolled her eyes at him. "It's only the wind, chicken. Be right back."

He let the robe slip out of his hands when he heard the shower hiss on. She always took a shower as soon as they'd made love, almost like she couldn't stand having his smell on her. Josh was wondering how many showers she normally took during the times he didn't see her when a tree branch banged against the side of the house. He jumped back so far it almost made him laugh.

Might have, if he suddenly hadn't thought about Will. And what happened to him up on that damn ridge. Shit, he hadn't thought about it in almost a week—more or less, less as time went on—but the sound of the wind brought it all back. All of it. The sounds and sights and butcher-house smells of it.

Josh sat down on the edge of the sex-rumpled mattress and took a deep breath. He hadn't noticed any wind while they were fucking like bunnies, but then again, she hadn't noticed his farts, either.

"Knock it off," he told himself, even though he knew he wouldn't listen. "It's only the wind, asshole. What happened to Will was a freak accident. God."

And God answered.

Josh heard a crack like a giant ripping a circus tent in half, and a minute later something large and heavy crashed into the house. A tree had gone down somewhere, and he just hoped it wasn't on his car.

"Thelma?" He was opening the bedroom door when the second half of the giant cottonwood next to the house came crashing down through the ceiling. Windblown fragments of tree bark and needle-sharp twigs swarmed around his face and hands and tore at his clothes.

Just like Will.

The wind shifted the tree just as he got the door open. If he'd been a second slower, it would have crushed him against the wood like a bug. *Like Will . . . the wind is trying to kill me just like it did Will.*

The door slammed in his face.

"THELMA! Come on, we have to get out of here!" Josh pounded his fist against the bathroom door. "A tree fell on your house—didn't you hear it?"

She must not have. He could hear her whistling above the sound of running water. Josh twisted the doorknob and found it locked. She'd locked it to keep him out.

"Bitch! Come on, open the door. We have to get out of here."

The shower curtain rattled on its metal rings, but the water kept running and she kept whistling.

"FINE! Stay here, for all I care. The whole house can fall down on you for all I care. Did you hear THAT?"

The doorknob turned to the right beneath his fingers as the door opened.

"Well, that's more like it. I swear to God, Thelma, if you ever pull something like that again, I'll . . . Oh. My. Christ."

She was sprawled half in, half out of the shower stall, the striped shower curtain fluttering around her and the cottonwood limb that crushed her. The whistling he'd heard was coming from the broken shower rod above her head.

"I gotta go now," Josh told her as he backed out of the room. Her eyes, gold ringed with red, followed him as far as the door and went blank. "There's nothing I can do. You understand, don't you?"

The whistling stopped as the wind shifted, curled in behind him, and tickled the back of his neck.

"I'm sorry, baby."

No, a voice whispered, *but you will be.*

Josh spun around, expecting to see Thelma's father in a drunken rage—and found himself engulfed in a cloud of swirling debris. He couldn't tell if it was him screaming or the wind as it picked him up and hurled him backward into Thelma's room. Whoever or whatever made the sound, however, stopped abruptly when Josh hit the splintered cottonwood. His lungs deflated so quickly that tiny pin-bursts of color danced in front of his eyes until he was able to draw a breath.

It felt so good to be able to breathe again that Josh didn't notice until the buttons popped off his shirt and he realized his lungs were still filling and he wasn't the one doing it. The wind was filling him like a balloon.

Josh twisted his head to one side and felt his lips ripped away as the wind snapped his head around.

He screamed, but the sound never had a chance—it was pushed back down his throat on the crest of a wave of air. The last button on his shirt shot across the room, embedding itself in the wall next to Thelma's poster of Buffy, the Vampire Slayer, when Josh's lungs burst through his rib cage.

Ribbons of blood and tissue floated in the air like streamers at a going-away party.

His.

Gideon rubbed the empty socket where his right shoulder had been and stepped back, admiring the frayed corpse dangling from the cottonwood.

The Old One never once mentioned this part, and Gideon wasn't surprised. Yaponcha was an Indian, after all, and livin' and breathin', or immortal, one dirty red man was much like another—they kept all the good secrets t'themselves.

It wasn't fair, but life wasn't. Death, on the other hand, oh, death was a great equalizer. It evened things right up.

Gideon nodded, and the wind swirled in around him.

As much as he would have liked to stay and play with his kills, there were still a few things that needed evenin' up.

Sam took the corner too fast and almost slipped on the wet concrete walk. The sprinklers had come on at almost the same moment he'd slammed down the phone, cutting short the morgue attendant's suggestion that he might want to keep a little closer tabs on his hospitalized friends and/or relatives in the near future. *Fucking asshole.* If anyone needed to keep better tabs on their patients, it was the fucking hospital.

Of course, that was right before he'd looked away and the old man disappeared. A minute, that's all it was, one lousy minute.

The soles of Sam's cross-trainers left ripples in the standing water as he slowly jogged down the sidewalk. It was crazy—there was no place for the old man to hide, and he couldn't have made it to either the front or back entrance. No one, especially not some old man fresh from the terminal ward, could move that fast.

"Goddammit, old man, where are you?"

Sam's sweatpants and jacket were soaking wet by the time he completed the circuit around the atrium and ended up in the spot where the old man had been standing.

"Where the hell are you?"

He wasn't sure what made him look up at his apartment, but when he did he saw Gideon Berlander standing in the window. Smiling down at him.

"What the fuck?"

Joseph used a wooden box and stack of tires to shield the small fire to the north and east so old Mrs. Nampeyo or the Perez family wouldn't notice the flickering light and feel obligated to come over and see what was going on. He didn't want anyone to witness his suicide. There would have been too much to explain, too many questions to answer, and too much time had already slipped away.

Little Star had refused to leave until she'd warmed up a potful of stew and made enough cornbread to hold him until they got home. But even then she worried about leaving him alone and found every possible excuse to linger. Joseph finally demanded she get in the truck and stop being foolish—he was a man, not a child, and didn't need a mother hen pecking at him.

His words had hurt her and he was more sorry than she would ever know, but he would never apologize for them.

He wouldn't be able to.

The family would find him when they returned the next day, and Daniel would tell Little Star to stay in the truck with the boys. There would be some grieving, yes, and questions, but Joseph knew his son would think that he had killed himself out of depression over the death of Gideon Berlander.

Joseph held his hands up to the fire and felt the cold press against his spine. He was killing himself because of Gideon, but not from grief. He had to die to destroy him.

"If I can," he said to the crackling flames, "with your help, Old One. I know I've been weak . . . and the pain that my weakness has caused others. You gave me so many chances to prove my worth, and I have turned my back. Forgive me, Old One, I have squandered all that you have given me, and I am ashamed to come before you now to ask this . . . but hear me, Old One, and grant me this one last thing."

Joseph shivered again when he moved his hands away from the fire's warmth and looked up into the night sky.

"Grant me the strength to die well."

The air stirred around him, soft and warm.

"Thank you, Old One."

Joseph pulled the air deep into his lungs as he began rocking slowly back and forth in front of the fire. When he exhaled, the song began—an old song, without words, a song passed on from one generation to another, unchanged since the beginning. A song of cadence and control, sung in time to the gentle sway of the body. A song of the earth and sky. A song of strength and power.

And command.

As he sang, Joseph opened the medicine sack around his neck and emptied the contents into his left hand. He wouldn't need the sack or medicine it contained after tonight. Sky would have to make her own.

"Convince her," he said as he pulled the willow whistle from his pocket and held it over the fire. "I failed her, too, Old One. . . . I could have taken her the day I named her and brought her home. She is as much my blood as his. Let her understand and accept this legacy."

The breeze touched his cheek and sped away. There could be no promise. Yaponcha could only offer Sky the power; she was as free to choose what path her life would take as he had been.

Gods can only offer, not demand. Gideon never understood that.

Closing his eyes, Joseph rubbed the medicine herbs into the whistle and felt the breath of the Old One encircle him.

"Oh, Great Spirit, Whose voice I hear in the wind,
And whose breath gives life to all the world,

Hear me. I am small and weak,
I need your strength and wisdom.
Let me walk in Beauty and forever behold the red
and purple sunset.
Make my ears sharp to hear your voice
And my hands to respect the things which you
have made.
Let me see the lessons which you have hidden in
each leaf and rock.
Make me wise that I may understand the things
which you have taught my people.
I seek wisdom, not to be greater than my
brother—"

Joseph had to swallowed hard to push down the
sudden tightness in his throat.

"But to overcome my greatest enemy, myself.
Let me walk a straight path with clean hands,
So that when life fades, like the fading sunset,
My spirit may return to you without shame."

The prayer to the Great Spirit said, Joseph opened
his eyes and felt his heart flutter against the cage of
his ribs like a frightened bird. The whistle was the
color of a storm cloud, gray, the color of the world
beneath, the world opposite the Land of the Sky
People.

Joseph tossed the whistle into the fire and sat back
on his heels, watching it burn.

The Old One had made his decision: Joseph could
fight Gideon, but only as a man of the earth.

A man of flesh and blood against one of wind.

"It will make a good story," he said, and scooped dirt onto the fire when he heard the familiar squeal-rumble of Daniel's truck pulling into the drive. "No, Old One . . . not them. Please."

Andrew was the first out of the back of the truck, kicking free of the quilt Estralita had wrapped around both boys and leaving his brother to struggle with the two plastic grocery bags.

"Hey, brat! Take one of these."

Andrew made a quick U-turn and snatched the smaller of the two bags out of his brother's hand without slowing down.

"What are you doing, Grandfather? Are you roasting marshmallows? Can I have some?"

"No, nothing. I wasn't doing anything." Joseph took the bag and walked the child back to the truck. There had to be a mistake; they weren't supposed to be back yet. "What's wrong? Why did you come back?"

Daniel was holding a large grease-stained bag, which he handed back to Estralita when she finally inched her way out of the cab.

"Dinner," she said, smiling. "That stew and corn bread wasn't enough and we know how much you love sesame chicken. Come on, hurry so it doesn't get cold. Boys—come inside and wash."

Daniel met Joseph's stare and shrugged. "She was worried about you not having enough to eat, so we stopped over at the Happy Chinaman's and got the works. I think there's even some litchi puffs or something—'Lita thought they sounded good, but I think that's just the pregnancy talking."

A small frown creased the skin between his eyes when Joseph grabbed his arm.

"You were supposed to stay in town tonight. As a special treat."

"Hey, it's okay, Dad. We stopped on the way back and got videos. . . . we even got you an old John Wayne Western, how's that? Tonight'll be special, don't worry. Besides, there's a windstorm kicking up that you wouldn't believe."

Joseph glanced up at the clear desert sky. "Windstorm?"

"Yeah, must be kin to the freak wind that hit the ridge. It was fine until we got close to town, and then . . ." Daniel clapped his hands together hard enough to make Joseph start. "Visibility went down to practically nothing, and when the boys started coughing we turned around and came home . . . by way of the Chinaman's and video store. Which reminds me."

Daniel reached into his back pocket and pulled out almost as many bills as Joseph had given him. "I promise: Unless the baby comes early, we'll plan the stay-over for next Saturday. Okay?"

Joseph pocketed the money and nodded. Next Saturday would be too late. Tomorrow would be too late.

"Okay. Let's go eat sesame chicken and watch John Wayne rid the West of our ancestors."

Protect them, Old One.

CHAPTER 19

Sky topped off the "World's Greatest Teacher" mug she had gotten as a Christmas present her first year of teaching and pointedly ignored the foil-wrapped plates of cookies and casseroles that lined most of the kitchen counter space. They were from neighbors, having arrived on an average of one every half hour or so since ten o'clock that morning, when she innocently told her on-site landlady the truth about how her grandfather was doing.

Food and sympathy began making its way to her door soon after that.

But answering the door gave her something to do while she cleaned and sorted and bagged and dumped. Sam's note had been in the first bag of trash she'd taken down to the Dumpster.

"Are you sure I can't get you anything?" she asked the young man perched on the edge of her couch, trying to look professional as he clutched an obviously brand-new briefcase to his chest.

His name was Eugene, and he'd come in response to one of the calls she'd made after going through the "Funeral" listings.

The weekends, Sky found out after her third call, were peak burial times. The young man's company, a local firm that specialized in low-cost cremation without interment, was the first to have an actual human being answer the phone and not some recorded voice suggesting, in overly sympathetic tones, that she leave her name and number and reason for the call so a trained representative could contact her during regular business hours.

That had been enough of a recommendation for Sky, and she asked that they send over a representative as soon as possible.

Eight hours later. She'd have to remember not to die on a weekend.

"I have tea if you don't like coffee. Or soda."

There was another knock on the door before he could answer. He seemed almost relieved that he didn't have to make a decision.

"Excuse me."

Sky set the mug down on the coffee table next to the stack of "Current" mail and the small yellow whistle Joseph had left. She'd thought about throwing it out along with Sam's note and the other trash, had even picked it up a dozen times and held it over an open black garbage bag, only to put it back on the table. Not because she believed any of the mumbo jumbo Joseph had told her, but . . . because it was a gift.

From her grandfather.

Lose one, gain one—it all evens up in the long run. Like death.

Sky hoped her smile looked genuine when she opened the door. Mrs. Nakamura handed her a foil-covered paper plate and looked past Sky to the young man on the couch.

"I was baking brownies, which I know how much you like," Mrs. Nakamura said, giving Sky a quick glance. "And I was sorry to hear about your grandfather. If there's anything I can do . . ."

Sky promised the woman she'd let her know and closed the door.

"Sorry." Removing the foil, Sky placed the brownies in front of the young cremation specialist. "It's been like this all day. Please, help yourself."

"Thanks." He took the topmost brownie out of politeness. "I guess people always bring food, you know, in situations like this. Looks good."

Sky agreed that it did, indeed, look good.

"So, I guess . . . we should start."

Sky thought they should.

"Okay, then."

Laying the briefcase across his knees, Eugene opened it—one-handed—and set the brownie down on a Richland-area map as he pulled out a glossy brochure.

"This shows you a list of our pre-need prices and also gives you an idea of what you can be expected to pay for interment in some of the mortuaries we regularly deal with. Now, some of the mortuaries will pay a percentage of . . . our charges if you use their facilities to hold the memorial services. And whatever else you might require."

He cleared his throat when Sky took the brochure.

"Your prices seem very reasonable," she said, even though she had absolutely no idea what was reasonable when it came to cremation and interment.

"Oh, and just so you don't miss it." He reached over and turned the brochure. "We also offer a scattering service, if you'd rather go that way. It's cheaper . . . I mean, it's less expensive and allows you to scatter the departed's ashes wherever you think they would be the most happy."

The ridge, Sky thought. *The old bastard would be happiest back up on that ridge.*

"Sounds good," she said. "Let's do it."

Eugene's professional demeanor eased into a slump as he popped the brownie into his mouth and leaned forward to fill in the contract.

"When can your people pick up the body?"

Sky handed him the mug of coffee when he started to choke, eyeing the plate of brownies.

"Are you all right?"

His face was red and there were tears in his eyes, but he nodded once he'd washed down the brownie enough to speak.

"You mean the . . . departed is already dead?"

Sky handed him back the brochure. "Is that a problem?"

"No, no, really, it's okay. I'm just used to talking to people who are pre-need. This is at-need, but it's okay. I think I have the right forms. Can I use your phone?"

Sky pointed to the wall mount in the kitchen.

"Thanks." He had the receiver off and to his ear when his face went red again. "Um, where is the departed exactly?"

"Memorial Hospital, and you'll be asking for Gideon Berlander." Another knock on the front door saved Eugene any more embarrassment. "Excuse me."

The edge of the door caught her left shoulder when it swung open.

"Where is he?"

Sky heard the phone settle back against its cradle as she backed into the room.

"What are you talking about, Sam? Who?"

"Your fucking grandfather."

The empty soda can rolled across the parking lot and was crushed beneath the front left tire of a speeding ambulance. He didn't know if it was the same can he'd seen that morning—not that he particularly cared one way or the other—but he did like the way it flattened out all nice and shiny.

And sharp.

It'd do nicely.

The wind lifted the can off the blacktop as if it were nothing more than a piece of paper and spun it into the soft skin just under the ambulance driver's chin. The man went rigid as a board, then keeled over backward in a cloud of swirling red mist that splattered all those assembled—

—with the exception of the patient on the roll-away gurney. He was rolling away down the parking lot, bellowing like an unmilked cow.

Right before he met up with the front bumper of another speeding ambulance.

Gideon couldn't hear himself laugh as the windstorm engulfed the hospital, but that was all right—he remembered what he sounded like.

Hell, he remembered everything.

"Winegardt! Get up!"

He opened his eyes, but he was acutely aware that he still wasn't awake.

"Winegardt, did you hear me?"

A couple more synapses fired, enabling him to recognize the voice as belonging to Marvin the Martian, aka Dr. M. Marino, chief resident and his immediate superior.

"Yes, I heard you." Winegardt pushed himself into a semi-vertical position on the break room's narrow couch and tried to blink himself fully aware. "What did you say? Why is it so dark in here?"

Dr. Marino sneered at him through the odd gloom. "That's why I woke you up, Sleeping Beauty. Windstorm knocked out the main electrical system, so I want you to go help the other little residents make sure the patients remain calm."

"How bad is it?"

"How bad does it look, Winegardt? We have the backups going, but we're only running at eighty-seven percent. If we can't get the system up and running at full power, we're going to start losing people. Does that tell you how bad it is?"

Winegardt knew better than to say anything else. He nodded and quickly followed the chief resident out into the dimly lit corridor, where a very controlled chaos reigned. It was just his luck to still be on ICU rotation during a power outage. One of the overhead lights flickered and went out as he followed Marino past the nurses' station.

"Damn!" The head nurse slammed her fists against the top of the work desk and glared at the dead bulb. "As if the wind isn't doing enough damage by itself. I just got a call from the ER. We lost our ruptured appendix with possible peritonitis."

Winegardt had to do a quick sidestep to keep from running into the chief resident's back when the man stopped dead in front of him.

"DOA?"

"Beats me," she said, giving the offending light one last glower. "ER and Admin are going nuts, and I hate to think of what's happening in Peeds and Maternity. All I can say is knock wood we're doing o— Shit."

Every light on the patient call board suddenly blinked on.

"Now, that's just not right!" Winegardt leaned across the top of the workstation to watch her flip switches and finally bang the side of the panel with her hand when every one of the room call lights blinked back on. "I don't even have patients in four of these rooms."

"Bogies," Marino said with a note of authority Winegardt had come to both fear and admire. "That's what we called them in Desert Storm. Electronic blips. E-ghosts, if you will. Happens when there's a power surge. Winegardt, unplug the equipment in the empty rooms while you make rounds. I'll be up on nine."

"Better take the stairs," Winegardt said, and immediately regretted it when Marino stopped in front of the elevators. "You know, in case there's another glitch."

The chief resident pressed the call button and turned around to gave him a look that should have instantly turned him to stone.

"The elevators have their own backup generators," Marino said as the doors opened and he stepped down into thin air.

Winegardt couldn't tell if the scream that followed came from Marino or the nurse or if it was just the sound of the miniature tornado that suddenly exploded out of the empty shaft.

Patients' files, memos, pens and pencils, and every piece of equipment that wasn't fastened down, and even a few that were, were sucked into the vortex. The glass walls, designed to protect the critically ill from airborne infections, imploded. The razor-sharp fragments sounded like wind chimes as they slashed through everything in their paths.

The droplets of blood gave the whirlwinds a reddish glow.

Winegardt had seen enough.

Turning, he made one grab for the nurse's arm, but didn't try again when he missed. She was slumped across the top of the station, eyes fixed and staring, a ragged hole where her nose had once been.

"SHIT!"

The desk phone disconnected itself and caught Winegardt under the chin as it flew past. He felt a sharp pain in both knees as he went down, and was thinking, *I wonder if my insurance will cover all this*, when someone stepped out of the elevator and walked over to him.

It was almost impossible to see who it was through the flying debris, but Winegardt knew the man was old—and a patient, from the knee-length hospital gown that flapped around the knobby, blue-veined legs.

"Help me."

The voice was so soft and ragged, Winegardt wondered how he was able to hear it above the sound of the wind, but he had.

"Help me." The voice had lost a bit of its ragged edge. "Help . . . me. Help. Me."

Winegardt protected his face as best he could as he looked up. "Jesus."

The old man shook his head and grinned. The empty right sleeve of his gown snapped in the wind like a banner.

"Appreciate the thought, but Ah ain't no son o'God. Ah'm better'n that. Let me show yah."

Gideon Berlander, the old man he'd signed off on and promptly stopped thinking about, was still smiling when the wind engulfed him. Winegardt had no trouble figuring out where the screams were coming from now: They were all from him. The old man just kept on smiling, silent, while the wind stripped his flesh from his body.

Blood and tissue rained down on him as he tried to back away.

The nurse had been lucky. So had Marino. They had died fast. Not like him.

Winegardt knew the moment the tip of the funnel amputated his feet that his death was going to be slow and painful. And very, very messy.

He kept right on screaming until Gideon Berlander's frayed skeleton reached down through the wind and yanked his tongue out.

The last thing Winegardt heard, above the sound of his own gurgling, was the sound of bones rattling as the skeleton tried to laugh.

Gideon couldn't remember ever having so much fun in his life.

So he saw no reason to stop.

Sky braced herself against the door, glaring at him. "Are you drunk?"

"No, that's more your hobby." Sam pushed his way into the apartment but stopped when he saw the boy cowering in the kitchen. "Well, isn't this nice? We must be having a party. Oh, yeah, definitely—look at all the food and, oh, unless my eyes are deceiving me, you've cleaned up a bit. Much better for the recuperating patient. Come out here, old man!"

"Sam, stop it!"

He brushed her aside, moving like a storm cloud through the living room to the bedroom. Nothing. Same with the bathroom. Sky was holding the phone to her ear when he walked into the kitchen.

"Where is he?"

"Get out of here, Sam." She punched in a nine and a one. "Before I call the police."

Sam leaned against the wall next to the phone and smoothed down his mustache. He would have winked, but the scar was already itching like crazy.

"Good. I have a couple of things I'd like to talk to them about, too."

Her finger moved away from the dial.

"I'm serious, Sam—just leave. Okay?"

"Not until you call the police," he said, "or tell me where he is."

"Who, Sam? Who the hell are you talking about?"

"Who do you think I'm talking about, bitch? Your granddaddy."

It took two tries, but Sky finally managed to hang up the phone. "What?"

"Shit, save the big eyes for court. Now, I don't know where you're getting your information, but I had nothing to do with your grandfather's accident, and getting him to parade out in front of my home is not going to make me confess to something I didn't do. And you can tell him that, wherever he is."

"Sam . . ."

Sam covered her mouth just hard enough to press the imprint of her teeth against the inside of her top lip. He didn't want to hurt her—not really—but he did want her to know he was tired of all the bullshit.

"Shh. You tell him that the moment he stepped into my apartment he was trespassing, and you can also tell him that I will be pressing charges. Against both of you, since I don't think he was in any condition to have driven himself over to my place. What'd you do, drop him back at the hospital when you were done with him?"

Sam looked over Sky's shoulder and winked at the

young man. Mistake. The scar started itching again, but his biggest mistake was taking his eyes off her.

Sky stepped back and slapped him as hard as she could. The itching stopped.

"Get out of here, Sam."

"Without a good-bye kiss? Sorry, not until you call your grandfather and—"

"He'd dead. He died this morning."

Sam shook his head and listened to the muscles creak along the back of his neck. "No."

"I'm making arrangements for his cremation right now. He's dead, Sam."

The boy nodded when Sam looked at him.

"I just saw him."

"I don't know who you saw, Sam, but it wasn't my grandfather."

"No. Where is he?"

Sky took a deep breath and picked up the phone. "Fine, if this is the only way I can convince you."

"Who are you calling? You're calling him, aren't you?"

She didn't look at him. "I'm calling the hospital. Maybe they can convince you that— GOD!"

The handset knocked into the wall when Sky dropped it. Sam would have never thought it possible for a mixed-blood to go pale, but she accomplished it. In spades.

"It can't be."

Sam snatched up the phone and put it to his ear, cringing at the roar of static that filled the line. But there was another sound beneath the shrieking white noise . . . a voice . . . growing louder and more distinct as he listened.

"Ah'm waitin' for yah, company man. Ah'm waitin'. Best get on over here."

Sam hung the phone up and winked. The scar didn't even tingle.

Sky followed him halfway down the stairs. "Sam, he's dead. Please, if you ever cared anything about me, listen to me."

Sam blew her a kiss.

"What makes you think I ever did, baby?"

She didn't say another word after that, and Sam was glad.

His exit line had been perfect.

Sky had never fainted before, but she was pretty sure she was very close to doing exactly that. Intermediate flashes of light swirled in front of her eyes, and her heart was beating so quickly she couldn't take a deep breath.

She knew—logically—that the voice she'd heard through the static wasn't . . . *couldn't* have been Gideon's. He was dead. The hospital hadn't made a mistake; he was dead and she'd seen his body. It was hospital policy. She'd had to identify him . . . his body . . . before they could take him . . . it . . . down to the morgue.

He. Was. Dead.

Gideon Berlander was dead and had been dead for almost thirteen hours. Dead and on his way to cremation and whatever came after.

Sky tightened her grip on the balcony railing when a stray breeze brushed against her cheek. He was dead; Gideon Berlander, her grandfather, was dead. But that didn't seem to matter. It *was* his voice she'd heard.

"*Ah can smell him on yah, gal, but Ah got t'tell yah, that ol'man is just like the rest o'em . . . dirty red men— can't trust nothin' they tell yah. And yah'd better not . . . if yah don't want t'join yer mama.*"

Sky took a deep breath and almost jumped over the railing when a hand settled on her shoulder.

"Sorry!" Eugene looked pretty close to passing out himself when she turned around. "I'm sorry . . . I didn't mean to startle you."

"God! No—no, it's okay."

"Um, okay. Ah—about what that man said . . . about your grandfather, ah, still being alive and everything? Um . . . Maybe I should come back another time."

Sky shook her head and steered the young man back into the apartment. "No, he was mistaken—my grandfather is dead, and I want him cremated as soon as possible. Now, I know you have to call your company to set things up, but I have to make a quick phone call and then it's all yours, okay?"

Eugene's answering "okay" didn't sound convincing, but he returned to his place on the couch and began shuffling papers while Sky took the handset and stepped deeper into the kitchen.

She hadn't realized she'd been holding her breath until she heard the voice that answered.

"Hi . . . Joey? This is Sky Berlander. Can I speak to your grandfather, please?"

CHAPTER 20

Joseph could feel their eyes on him while he listened and nodded, pretending to answer a question that was never asked. Sky's voice was steady, but each word had a flint edge to it, as if waiting to crumble if she spoke them too loud.

"I know it couldn't have been him, Joseph." She hadn't called him Grandfather once, but it was a small thing between them now and he forgave her. "But it sounded . . . Oh God, Joseph, it was him, wasn't it?"

"Yes." Another nod and he could feel his family's attention drift back to the flickering images of John Wayne making the West safe from the likes of them. "It was him, Cielo."

Silence nestled against Joseph's ear while he waited. In the background, someone got shot and Andrew cheered.

"Joseph, things like this don't happen in real life."

"It's happening now, isn't it? Do you still have the . . . gift I left you?"

"The whistle? Come on, you can't honestly think I believe that stuff you told me?"

"You called me, Cielo, so a part of you has to believe it. I will do what I can here, but it won't be much and he knows it." Joseph glanced over his shoulder, making sure his family was engrossed in the black-and-white film, before turning back to the phone and lowering his voice. "You must go to the place he felt the most power and call him. He'll come. . . . He won't have a choice."

"God . . . then what? Jesus, what am I saying? He's dead!"

"And you're alive, and the Chosen One . . . that's what you have to show him. Cielo, I am so s—"

The phone and lights both went out as the wind rammed into the side of the house.

"Well, hey-ho-HI, there, fellow RichlanDERS. WOO! I hope all of you have found nice holes to crawl into, because man, oh Manischewitz, is it ever BLOWING IN THE WIND out there, and I'm not talking about Bob Dylan's 1962 hit song even, though I suspect I'll be playing that pretty soon unless we get a real change in the weather. Which doesn't seem too likely."

Sam hunched forward over the steering wheel and wiped the condensation off the corner of the windshield with the side of his hand. The blur was a distraction, and he was having enough trouble seeing through the windblown dust as it was. The DJ's voice was a distraction, too, but it managed to do an even better job at drowning out the sound of the storm than the moldy oldies the station played nonstop, twenty-four/seven.

But just to make sure, Sam punched up the volume another two decibels.

"At least that's what the Weather Guessers here at the station are telling us right now, and here I always thought March was supposed to come *in* as a lion and leave like a lamb. Well, if that's true, then this lamb is a big, hunking, mutant, Chernobyl kind of lamb. We're getting reports of funnel cloud sightings and wind gusts getting up to fifty miles per. Police and fire rescue already got their hands full, people, and have asked that if you don't need to go out tonight, don't do it. Remember that hole I mentioned earlier? Well, you may just want to take my suggestion and find one. Heck, that's what I'm going to do. I got me a pillow and blanket, and when my shift's over I'm going to crawl under a table in the break room and stay the night. You do the same—kick back, get comfortable for the best of the sensational sixties. And now, not Dylan, but how about a little Jim Morrison."

Sam leaned back, nodding in time to the opening strains of "Riders on the Storm." It was the perfect song for a night like this, and the storm agreed. The landscape suddenly blinked out and a thick scent of ozone filled the cab. The lightning strike was close enough to raise the hairs on the back of his neck and arms. A moment later, the thunder bounced the truck across two empty lanes of traffic and took away his hearing.

"Damn," Sam said, and kept saying it until he

could hear himself above the reverberating echo. "Damn."

If he hadn't seen the blue and white reflective off-ramp sign coming up on his right, he would have turned the damn truck around and let the wind push him all the way home.

RICHLAND MEMORIAL HOSPITAL
½ MILE

"About fucking time."

He was only going twenty, and he eased into the curve as carefully as an old lady driving to church, but still he almost broadsided the ambulance.

It was on its side at the top of the ramp, roof and side panel crushed in. The back doors were missing, and the wind plucked at the gurney that was still inside. Sam didn't see a body, but he was careful not to look too closely as he drove past. Besides, the hospital was close enough for a rescue team to be able to get to the injured in under ten minutes—they didn't need him poking around the wreck.

Another crack of lightning ripped the night apart just as Sam was coming around to the front of the ambulance, and in the flash he saw the driver, what was left of the driver, through the broken windshield.

And what was left grinned at him.

"Jesus."

"AW!"

The voices of his grandsons floated through the darkness like ghosts as Joseph hung up the phone. His son was more pragmatic.

"Well, looks like we're going to have to wait and see what happens in the morning."

"But Daaaaaad."

"But what? Storm's knocked everything out—what do you want me to do?" Joseph heard the sound of Daniel's work boots as he crossed the room. The darkness shifted to a pale blue when he opened the curtains. "I don't see any lights anywhere. Looks like we must have lost the main lines."

He yawned, and Joseph struggled not to join him. "Might as well call it a night, I guess."

"But it's still early."

Daniel squinted as he held his watch up to the lighter darkness beyond the window. "It's almost nine. Darn, it felt later than that."

"Even so, I think it's a wonderful idea," Estralita said, pushing herself to her feet. She'd changed into her flannel nightgown and bathrobe as soon as she'd made sure the men could actually open the containers of food and serve themselves, and began dozing halfway through the first video. "I'm going to bed."

"Are you feeling all right, Little Star?"

Her pale silhouette took a step toward him. "I'm f—" *Thump.* "OUCH!"

"Mom?"

"Honey?"

Joseph could just barely see her bend down to rub one of her legs. "I bumped into the table. Maybe you'd better get some flashlights and candles from the kitchen, Daniel."

"Good idea. Everyone stay put until I get back."

"Can I come, Dad?"

"Me, too?"

320

"Okay, Joey, you come with me. Andy, stay with your mother and grandfather."

"AW!" But Daniel and Joey's footsteps were already fading. "No fair."

"No, it isn't, but that's how things work out sometimes. If all of you had gone to town . . . it probably wouldn't have changed things." Joseph stopped himself from saying anything else. "Besides, your mother's right, we should get our rest."

"But—"

"Couldn't find any candles," Daniel said as he and Joey came in, bathed in a warm orange light, "but these lanterns are better anyway—safer, too, if you guys don't fool around with them. Now you can read until you're sleepy."

"Read?" Andrew wasn't about to be appeased that easily. "Couldn't Grandfather tell us a story instead?"

"Yeah!"

Joseph felt the warm glow of the kerosene from the lantern in Joey's hand as the boy walked over to him. His eyes were already shining in anticipation. Andrew's shadow flew across the wall like a raven when he began jumping up and down and shouting.

"Please? Please, please, pleeeeze."

Joseph looked from one boy to the other, then at Daniel and his wife, and finally at the swell of her belly.

"All right," he said, "but first I think we need a snack."

"Snack? But we ate only a little while ago. Are you hungry?"

"Only for some of that sweet-potato candy you made last week and have been hiding from us."

The lantern's glow caught the deepening color in Estralita's cheek.

"Oh," Daniel laughed, "is that what happened to it."

"I didn't hide it from you! I hid it from me . . ." And she laughed. "I'm already too fat—I didn't want to get any fatter."

Joseph hushed his son and grandsons. She would never get any fatter. None of them would.

"You don't have to worry about that, Little Star," he said as he took her hand and carefully led her into the dark kitchen. "Let's eat the candy until it's gone. Besides, this was supposed to be a night of celebration, wasn't it?"

There were more bodies in the hospital parking lot, some whole, others that were little more than piles of bloodstained bone, flesh, and clothing in tatters, fluttering in the constant wind. It looked as if those in charge had known something major was up and tried to evacuate the hospital just as all the supposedly shatterproof windows had blown out. Broken glass covered the parking lot like glittering transparent snow.

"Got us another update on this freaky wind"—the DJ's voice was struggling through the static—"and it doesn't look good, folks. A couple of tornadoes have apparently touched down, and early reports indicate that one of them may have done some considerable damage out along Highway 160 and thereabouts. So again, remember that hole and crawl inside. And remember, if you don't have to be out in this mess, don't be."

"Too late," Sam said as he pulled the truck into what had been the ambulance bay and shut off the engine.

Without the engine and radio to drown it out, he could hear the glass shards tumbling over each other—like a million wind chimes all jangling at the same time. The sound cut into Sam's head as he got out of the truck, and pressing the heels of his palms against his head didn't do a thing. He could still hear the wind chimes as he headed for the broken glass doors—slowly, one sliding step at a time, concentrating on where he put his running shoes, and all too aware that the top-quality leather uppers offered very little protection to the foot inside. If he hadn't been certain that one slip would have been fatal, Sam would have made a run for it.

But he wasn't about to add to the number of the dead—not when he was looking for one dead man in particular. He had no real idea where the morgue was, but if movies and television shows had taught him one thing, it was that hospitals always tucked the dead out of the way in basements. He had no reason to believe it would be any different in reality. He also didn't give a second thought to the possibility that those in charge of the ill-fated evacuation would have taken the dead.

Sam's stomach grumbled uneasily when he tiptoed over a frayed arm still wearing a gold charm bracelet around its denuded wrist just inside the emergency lobby.

The lights were still working, barely, but it was still bright enough for him to see her. The screaming woman.

She was curled into one of the dark-colored chairs bolted to the floor in what had been the hospital's main waiting room, clinging to the molded plastic of the seat next to her with bloodied fingers. The left side of her face had been peeled off the skull and hung, dangling, from her chin. Sam touched the tiny line of puckered flesh that ran from the corner of his eye to his scalp—he'd gotten off lucky.

He staggered against the reception desk when she saw him and reached for him. It was as if the wind had been waiting for her to make just this kind of mistake. The last thing Sam saw of her was her tongue, fat and pink and naked, sliding out the ragged hole that had once been her cheek.

The gust of wind knocked him flat as it swept the woman out of the chair and into the wall above the elevators. Her head popped like an overripe melon, adding a touch of crimson to the brass RICHLAND MEMORIAL HOSPITAL marque.

Satisfied, the wind died and left Sam to vomit in peace.

"Feelin' poorly, are yah, boy?"

Sam wiped his mouth off against the sleeve of his jacket and felt his belly lurch again when he looked up. Gideon Berlander was standing in the doorway of the demolished gift shop, ankle deep in flower petals and crushed candy bars. He was still wearing the tattered hospital gown Sam had seen him in earlier, the empty right sleeve hanging limp at his side.

"I knew it."

The old man smiled. "Knew what, boy?"

"That you were alive." Sam got to his feet and

started chuckling as he stumbled through the debris. The old man smiled back. "You know, she almost had me believing it . . . That look she gave me . . . Christ, she should think about going into acting. You should be proud of her—she's just like you."

"More'n you know, boy."

Sam stepped on a broken baby rattle and kicked the pieces out of the way.

"You know you're the one who blew it, old man. I was beginning to believe her, and then you answered the phone." The inside of his throat felt like he'd swallowed a few pounds of glass dust, but Sam forced himself to keep laughing.

"Suppose not, but it got yah here, didn't it?" The laughter stopped on its own when the old man began walking toward him. Sam's foot crushed the remains of a broken baby rattle as he backed up. "And that's what Ah wanted, company man. Ah needed me a good piece of transportation for the mornin'."

"What the hell are you talking about?" Sam asked—but he made the mistake of looking down at the old man's feet, hoping to see them being cut to ribbons on the glass and other debris that littered the floor.

He made the mistake of looking.

The old man didn't have any feet. A thick column of swirling dust rose from the floor where his feet should have been, encircling him to the waist. Gideon Berlander was riding a whirlwind and coming right at him.

"Don't worry, boy," the old man shouted above the howling wind, "it won't hurt much."

The last thing Sam Renyolds saw before the cyclone reached out and swallowed him were his lungs bursting out of his chest like pink balloons.

And the last thing he thought was that the Gideon Berlander was as big a liar as his granddaughter.

It hurt like hell.

Joseph stood outside his grandsons' room and listened

His son and daughter-in-law had fallen asleep almost immediately, but it had taken longer than usual for his grandsons to settle down. Even now, they were restless. Joseph could hear them tossing and turning as he fed bullets into the .22 rifle.

He knew it was because of the sweet-potato candy they ate, but there was still a small fear that tugged at the back of his mind. It was almost as if his grandsons knew what he was planning to do.

Outside, the wind toppled Estralita's washing tub and sent it crashing along the yard.

Joseph clutched the rifle tighter and pressed his ear to the door. Joey muttered softly but didn't wake.

"Thank you, Old One," he whispered, and fed another round into the breech.

Best not thank him yet, little brother.

The box of cartridges fell to the floor, scattering like frozen rain as Joseph spun around.

There was no one standing behind him in the dark. Nothing but the sound of wind and dry, hollow laughter.

Yer still a rabbit, little brother—jumpin' at sounds.

Joseph levered the first round into the chamber.

"No," Joseph whispered, "not this time. I'm ready to do what has to be done, if it comes to that."

Still lookin' for a way out, huh?

"You don't need to do this. They're innocent."

So was mah Glory, till that buck o'yers messed with her. Mah land . . . mah blood . . . man's got a right t'avenge what's his—yah can understand that, can't yah?

"No, I don't." Joseph ran his hand over the barrel of the gun he'd given Thomas on his tenth birthday. "If I come to you, on my own, will you let them live?"

The wind screamed its answer as it rammed the front of the house. Joseph could hear the hinges and dead bolt creak as the door began to buckle.

Lifting the rifle so that it crossed his chest, east to west, Joseph faced north and closed his eyes.

"Hear me, Old One. I have failed in my duty to you, but these who come before you now are strong— do not hold my weakness against them. Judge them fairly, Old One, and give them rest. Lead them into the land of the Sky People and make them welcome, as you have already welcomed my first son."

Joseph had only taken two steps down the hall when the front door splintered. He had to hurry before the noise woke Daniel up.

They were lying in each other's arms, their bodies molded into a single shape beneath the thick wool blankets. The sound of the wind seemed quieter here, but Joseph knew that wouldn't last.

Warming the muzzle of the rifle against his own cheek, Joseph walked to Daniel's side of the bed and took a deep breath before placing the muzzle into the hollow behind his son's ear. Daniel had to die first. He would have wakened at the sound of the first shot.

"They'll be right behind you, Daniel," Joseph whispered as he pulled the trigger. "Wait for them."

It was such a little sound, but Estralita stirred in her dead husband's arms.

"Daniel? Did you hear—?"

She was pushing the blankets off, preparing to get up to check on the boys, when the bullet entered her brain. A single sigh escaped her lips as her body fell back onto the bed.

Joseph let himself believe her sigh had been one of relief, that at the last moment she somehow knew he was doing this to save her and her family from unimaginable pain.

"You were the heart of this house," he told her as he pressed a hand to her swollen belly. He could feel the unborn child moving sluggishly against his palm: tiny, soft bumps of feet and hands, and finally, the curve of the head. Joseph pressed the muzzle against the spot and fired. The movements stopped. "Sleep well, little one."

The wind had gotten into the house; he could feel it tug at his robe as he crossed the hall and opened the door to the boys' room. There wasn't much time left—he had to hurry.

Yah ain't tryin' t'cheat me, are yah, little brother?

Joseph hunched his shoulders and pretended not to hear.

The boys were asleep, oblivious to the raging storm outside—safe and warm and dreaming beneath the soft yellow glow of lantern light. Andrew hadn't said anything about using one of the lanterns to replace his usual Pokemon night-light, and Joseph had been proud of him . . . but his mother knew how he really felt and set one in a bucket of sand at the foot of his bed so he wouldn't be frightened of the dark.

Joseph blinked hard and leveled a fourth round into the chamber.

"In the Land of the Sky People, nights are soft and bright with the light of a million stars." The wind was so loud, he didn't have to whisper. "You'll never have to be afraid again, my grandson."

Andrew was curled around his stuffed bear, his arm locked tight around the toy. Trying to move it or his arm would only wake him up—Joseph had learned that from his nightly visits. Moving slowly, Joseph wiggled the muzzle into the narrow opening between bear and boy, until it rested against the center of Andrew's pajama top. Joseph could almost feel the gentle thumping of his grandson's heart through the stock.

"Go quickly. Your mother is waiting for you."

Andrew's body convulsed once and something slipped from his hand. Joseph picked up the jackknife and pressed the motionless fingers back around it.

"You're right," he said, kissing the already cooling forehead, "a warrior needs a knife if he's to hunt in the world beyond. The Sky People will teach you all you need to know. Listen to them."

"And what about me, Grandfather?"

Joseph hid the rifle down at his side before he turned around. Joey was sitting up in his bed, staring at him with cold, black eyes.

"Will the Sky People teach me to be a warrior after you kill me?"

"Joey, you must understand."

"I understand, Grandfather. You're going to kill me like you killed Andy and Mom and Dad. Right?" Joey cocked his head to one side and chuckled. His voice deepened until it was no longer his. "What's the matter, little brother? Yah seem a mite overwrought."

Joseph swung the rifle up and cocked it, aiming it at his grandson's head. "No," he said, "I'm not going to let you hurt them."

Gideon shook Joey's head sadly. "Ah never intended to, little brother. That was always gonna be your job."

The rifle fired one last time as the wind crashed through the bedroom window.

". . . latest on the situation at Richland Memorial Hospital. Police and fire departments have been dispatched to aid in the cleanup operation, but from preliminary reports, it is being estimated that the fatalities may go as high as ninety-eight percent. To repeat, a tornado of Class Five or above apparently hit Richland Memorial Hospital at approximately eight forty-five this evening. The police and fire departments are on the scene but are still being hampered in their rescue efforts by high winds and blowing debris. It is requested that the public stay away. If you have a family member who was in the hospital as a patient or worked in the hospital, you may call the number on your screen for information. Again, to repeat: The worse disaster ever to hit Richland occurred this evening at approximately eight forty-five when a tornado struck and demolished Richland Memorial Hospital. Police and fire rescue are on the scene and request that the public stay away . . ."

Sky stared at the static snow covering the anchorman and pulled the afghan tighter around her shoulders. Reception had been lousy and growing worse as the evening and storm progressed, but she couldn't stop watching the ongoing disaster coverage.

And she wasn't the only one addicted.

Not one of her neighbors had stopped by with food and sympathy since nine-o'clock news broke the story. Mrs. Gonzales had been her last visitor, stopping by with a platter of warm sopaipillas and a haunted look in her eyes. Sky knew the woman worked days at Memorial, in the Prenatal Unit. She exchanged the casserole the Blackwells dropped off for the fried bread and told Mrs. Gonzales how sorry she was for her loss.

Just as Eugene, the young man from the crematory, and all her other neighbors had told her.

Sympathy and food exchanged for grief—not a bad custom, really.

Sky looked at the sopaipillas on the coffee table and felt her stomach turn. The pastries had gone cold, deflating into lumpy thick pancakes drizzled in congealed honey. None of the dishes she'd gotten that night had tempted her appetite more than a nibble or two. Of course, if that kept up she wouldn't have to go food shopping for at least a month.

A gentle knocking at the front door coincided with a commercial break.

"Or maybe even longer than a month," Sky said, and was startled by the sound of her own voice—it sounded much more hollow than she remembered it.

The knocking started again, a little louder this time. Whichever of her neighbors it was, they were anxious to get out of the wind and back in front of their sets.

"Coming." Sky tossed the afghan off her shoulders

and gingerly picked up one of the soggy sopaipillas, just in case her caller was Mrs. Gonzales come back to find what she thought was a kindred spirit.

Poor woman.

The knocking was much louder this time, hard enough to make the door tremble against its frame. It didn't sound like Mrs. Gonzales. Sky reached out and fastened the dead bolt.

"Who is it?"

The doorknob jiggled and a man answered, but she couldn't make out the words or recognize the voice over the howling wind.

"I can't hear you," Sky shouted back. "What do you want?"

The knocking started again.

"Look, tell me who you are or get out of here. I swear to God I'll call the police if you don't."

The knocking stopped.

Sky counted to five before inching forward to check the door's security peephole and exhaled loudly when the small fish-eye lens confirmed that her unknown visitor was gone. Sometimes being paranoid worked. Sometimes it didn't. If it turned out that it really was only one of her neighbors, she could apologize in the morning.

If not . . .

She rubbed her arms against a sudden chill as she walked back to the couch.

Knock. Knock.

Sky fell back across the coffee table when the door blew off its hinges.

The miniature cyclone swept into the apartment

and destroyed eight hours' worth of tidying up. One of her cheap, but pretty, framed Kmart prints flew off the wall and struck the back of her head. Sky felt the warm trickle of blood begin to ooze from the cut and dropped to the floor, covering her head with her arms.

Where were her wonderful neighbors who'd thought enough about her to bring food when they heard about her grandfather? Why weren't they there now? Couldn't they hear what was going on?

She had to get out of there.

Sky lifted her head just enough to squint through the whirling cloud of debris at the open front door and watched the wind suck up the platter of sopaipillas and the small yellow whistle that had been sitting next to it.

The whirlwind stopped, and Sky moaned from the sudden change in pressure.

"He give yah that . . . didn't he?"

Sky's head pounded and her vision was on the verge of shutting down completely, but she looked up and saw him standing there, glaring down at her. Him. He. Gideon. Her grandfather.

"Oh God, no."

The wind lashed her across the face. *"Don't lie t'me, gal, or Ah'll rip yah apart right now. And that ain't no easy way t'die—believe me. Now, answer yer granddaddy like the sweet child Ah raised and tell me what that damned red man told yah."*

When she didn't answer—couldn't make herself believe what she was seeing—the wind twisted itself into the hair on the top of her head and yanked hard enough to bring tears to her eyes.

He used to do that when she was little. Before she'd run away.

She'd forgotten that.

The wind jerked her head toward him.

"Ah said tell me, gal."

"What . . . what do you want me to say?"

"Tell me what he told yah 'bout this." He pointed to the whistle Joseph had given her—the silly little yellow toy.

"It's true."

"What's true, gal? What that ol' Injin tell yah . . . that yah had some kind o' power? Yah don't, and he didn't."

"Didn't? Joseph's dead?"

"Yup, he's a good Injin now. Just like yah'll be if yah try anything. Yah ain't got nothin', gal. That ol' man lied t'yah. It was just a story."

"A story."

"That's right . . . just one of them damned stories he was a'ways tellin'. That ain't nothin' but a whistle. And yah'll do best t'remember that. It won't do yah any good, 'cept get'cha killed if yah try t'come 'tween me and what's mine. Stay outta things yah don't understand."

Sky looked up at into her dead grandfather's face and then down at the whistle. The feathers were fluttering in the breeze, their motion rocking the whistle back and forth. It was just a whistle, just an ordinary willow whistle. He was right—her dead grandfather was right.

Sky had no idea what she was about to do until her hand closed around the whistle and brought it to her lips.

"NO!"

The note had barely sounded when the wind picked her up and hurled her into the bedroom.

When she woke up, it was morning and the world was different.

CHAPTER 21

Sam Reynolds adjusted the sunglasses against the early-morning glare and brushed a finger across the right side of his mustache. *Damn.* It had come loose again.

He kept his hand in front of his mouth, nodding when one of the guests noticed him as he walked to the office trailer. It was empty, and would remain so until the end of the groundbreaking ceremony and the last glass of champagne had been swallowed. Then, and only then, would Mackay's handpicked vultures swoop down on the unsuspecting cream of Richland society.

Sam Reynolds had seen it all before—the glad hands and wide smiles that offered prime locations and the choice of six different architectural styles along with a 4 percent prime interest rate that would balloon to 15 percent after three years—so that was the memory that kept playing over and over.

Stepping around the boxes of Sun Country Homes souvenirs and "Grand Opening" premiums, he picked up one of the bright blue SC Industries staplers and reattached the mustache to his lip. He put in two staples to make sure it held, then smoothed the bristly hair down to cover them.

As he left the trailer, Sam Reynolds took one of the giveaway plastic snow globes and slipped it into his pocket. The scene showed an isolated cabin in the woods. He liked it. It reminded him of what his home had once been and what it would look like again.

Soon.

He followed the sound of applause to the high ground.

Jennet Mackay—*the great and powerful . . . who, him?*—was standing where the front door of the cabin had been and waving the crowd into silence. He was dressed in a somber black business suit that clashed with the golden hard hat perched on his head.

Sam Reynolds wanted to laugh but couldn't. *Hush—big man's talkin'.*

". . . for braving the unpredictable weather," Mackay said into the handheld microphone. "I do appreciate it, but even spectacular views and fresh, clean air can't help us to forget the tragedy that befell our city last night."

Mackay placed the golden hard hat over his heart and closed his eyes. "So I'd like to have a moment of silence to remember those who were lost."

The moment of silence lasted all of twenty seconds. If that.

"Ah-men!" Mackay put the hard hat back where it belonged and smiled at the public officials and media reps assembled before him. "But, as my daddy always said, the best thing you can do for the dead is to remember you're alive. My daddy was a pioneer in his own way, always looking toward the horizon. Like the horizons the lucky homeowners will be able to see from Sun Country Homes' newest executive community."

Mackay exchanged the microphone for a golden shovel and relied on pure lung power as the tip of the shovel disappeared into the patch of ground that had been prepared for the event. The rest of the ground was as flat and hard and dead as concrete.

"Ladies and gentlemen of Richland . . . I give you Pioneer Ridge!"

Applause. Applause. Applause.

Since most of the usual groundbreaking participants, like the mayor and members of the City Council, were still busy dealing with the aftermath of the disaster, Mackay was the soul focus of the flash cameras and video monitors. He'd get his fifteen minutes on the local news.

Sam Reynolds had seen it all before.

"And now," Mackay was back on the mike, "if you'll all follow me into the refreshment pavilion, I'll try to show my gratitude for sharing this special day with me. Thank you, and please . . . remember to get your Sun Country Homes surprise goodie bags from any of our boys and girls in blue. Come on . . . drinks are on me!"

Applause. Applause. Hah-hah.

The pavilion was an old circus tent Mackay had bought cheap and still looked like it, right down to the sawdust covering the plywood flooring and blue banners fluttering in the breeze. Sam Reynolds smiled. He may have seen it before, but he'd always liked circuses.

"Well, imagine my surprise at seeing you here."

Jennet Mackay sipped from the plastic Sun Country Homes champagne glass in his hand. He'd taken off the hard hat and fixed his hair, but there was still a thin red line across his forehead where the plastic band had rested—like someone had started to scalp him. *Now, there's an idea.*

"Why?" The voice coming from him wasn't quite right, but Mackay didn't seem to notice. "I helped steal this land. Doesn't that rate a drink or two?"

Mackay's face got a little more color than one sip of cheap champagne would produce, but he chuckled gently when a man with a video camera moved toward them and took Reynolds's arm.

"Let's talk over here, Sam." He nodded at the man with the camera, mouthed *Be right back*, and walked them to a less crowded spot near the entrance. "What is this? Your girlfriend decide to try and shake a few more apples off the money tree, is that it? Well, you can tell Ms. Berlander that I paid more for this land than she even had a right to wish for."

A gust of wind blew the sawdust around their feet as Sam Reynolds shook his head.

"It wasn't her land."

Mackay finished his champagne and signaled one of the wandering waiters over.

"Here," he said, grabbing two plastic flutes, "you sound a little dry. So why don't you drink up and get off my land."

Sam Reynolds ignored the glass being held out to him.

The pavilion's northeast side suddenly billowed inward, knocking drinks and plates of cocktail weenies to the sawdust. The sound of people happily getting drunk stopped just as suddenly.

Mackay finished off both glasses when the less-than-happy sounds started up.

"Wow, is it *always* this windy up here?"

"God, you don't think it's another tornado, do you?"

"There's no shelter. What if it's another tornado?"

"Folks, folks," Mackay said, shouting over the sound of the flapping canvas, "it's only a little wind. Nothing to worry about. Really."

Sam Reynolds watched a woman in a blue blazer with a half-dozen or so blue plastic totes dangling from one arm weave her way through the crowd toward them.

"Excuse me, Mr. Mackay."

Mackay handed her the two empties. "What is it, Maureen?"

"There's a weather front coming in from the northwest." She kept glancing toward the man with the video camera. "Tony heard it on the radio in the bus."

"Shit, this would have to happen." The woman stepped back from Mackay's glare. "Goddamned weather. Okay, Maureen, you tell Tony to warm up the bus and I'll try to do a little damage control."

The woman scurried away, plastic goodie bags rustling.

"Havin' problems?"

The color in Mackay's cheeks deepened a tone.

"Look, Reynolds, this is not the time or place for whatever it is you and your half-breed girlfriend have cooked up. The transaction was legal and binding, and there's really nothing you two can do, short of extortion, to get any more money. But, of course, that's against the law. So, unless you want me to mention that to the deputy police commissioner right over there, I suggest you get into your truck and drive down to the office and tell security to follow you in while you clean out your desk." Mackay leaned in and patted Sam Reynolds on the chest. "I should have fired you the second you dropped the ball on this deal, and that was the first and only mistake I'm going to make with respect to you. Or with your half-breed girlfriend.

"And now, if you'll excuse me, I have a crowd to control. Get off my land."

"Ain't yer land."

Mackay ricocheted a glare off him before firing a beaming smile at his muttering guests.

"Ladies and gentlemen . . . Excuse me, may I have your attention for a moment?" He waved when the crowd finally noticed him, then rubbed his hands together. "Thank you. Well, what can I say? It looks like March isn't going to be a lady and give us one day of rest. Of course, once we start building up here and put in windbreaks and landscaping, she won't have much say in the matter—but that's going to take a few weeks at least."

There were some scattered chuckles at the comment, mostly from Sun Country employees. Everyone else still looked worried.

"But until then, and since I don't want anyone to come down with a cold, I think it would be best if we all load back onto the SUN-FUN bus and continue the festivities downtown at our very own Sun Country Sports Arena." Mackay raised his hands for silence as if the crowd had broken out into spontaneous cheering. Which they hadn't. The only sound in the tent, besides Mackay, was the rustle of heavy canvas. "And don't you worry—my representatives will still be on hand with survey maps and floor plans. Now, if you'll all start moving toward the exit in an orderly manner, please."

There were grumbles of agreement from the guests, but only a handful actually headed for the door. The majority of Mackay's free lunch crowd stood rooted to their spots, glancing uneasily at the bucking canvas that surrounded them.

"Doesn't appear that your sheep are listening to you, Mr. Company Man." The wind carried the comment deep into the tent and stopped the mini-migration in its tracks. "But Ah don't see why they should. It's only a little wind, and the wind can't hurt you . . . unless I tell it to."

A man in a plaid overcoat laughed. "So you're a weatherman?"

Sam Reynolds turned to the man and smiled. "Yah might say that. Yup, yah might at that."

Sam Reynolds's grin continued to grow until it ripped out the staple holding his mustache to his lip.

The staple bounced off the perfect square knot in Mackay's bright blue tie.

"Holy Christ."

Sam Reynolds followed Mackay as the smaller man stumbled back into the parting crowd.

"Guess that's what yah could call me, a'right." The dangling mustache muffled his words a bit, but he didn't mind as long as the message was clear. And it would be, shortly. "A man o'weather. Ah can call down the wind and make things clean again. Like they were up here 'fore yah showed up with all yer fancy plans. All Ah gotta do is snap mah fingers."

He did just that, and the east side of the tent surged inward, knocking over the porta-bar and bartender.

A few more guests headed for the exit. Sam Reynolds turned to watch them go.

"It's only the wind," he told those who hesitated and would soon be lost. Just like their host. "Wind's a'ways been bad up here. Real tricky."

Mackay's face had paled up nicely.

"What do you want?"

Sam Reynolds pulled the snow globe out of his pocket. "Ah want a house. Yah gonna give me one?"

"Yes, of—of course I can, Sam." The relief in the man's voice was absolutely pitiful. "Sure, easiest thing in the world to do. Let's just get on the bus and I'll be more than happy to show you the floor plans so you can pick out the model best suited to your . . ."

The man was two seconds away from dying and he still sounded like a salesman.

Sam Reynolds would finally be able to do the

world a favor. He shoved the globe straight through Jennet Mackay's chest.

"This is the only floor plan that belongs up here, company man." Sam Reynolds removed the sunglasses and winked a shredded eyelid over the empty socket. "Ah think yah can see that now, can't yah?"

The dying man's lips moved a little, like he was trying to say something—but everything that was going to be said that day, in that tent, on his land, had been said.

Sam Reynolds nodded his head and the wind descended on the tent like the breath of God. Red God or white, it didn't matter now—the wind wasn't discriminating.

It removed everything that didn't belong.

Only a handful of the hysterical stampede escaped the tent before it collapsed. Everyone else, most of Richland's high and mighty, struggled under the canvas, squirming like maggots in a corpse. He'd always hated maggots.

The office trailer was a flimsy thing—it split right in half when it landed on the tent—but the impact did stop most of the squirming. The one or two maggots that remained met the business ends of the shovels and pickaxes left by the construction crew.

If nothing else, it was quick, and they never saw it coming.

The ones on the bus weren't as lucky.

Without the trees and undergrowth and cabin to stop it, the wind had nothing to slow it down. He guessed it must have been traveling close to a hundred miles an hour when it hit the SUN-FUN bus. Maybe more, considering how far the blood-splattered glass flew when the windows exploded.

The driver had died at the wheel, literally, when the wind punched in the front end and driven the steering column up and through the man. His blood had spurted out of him like a geyser, but none of it hit the ground. The wind had lapped it up like soup and went on to finish its meal.

The steel frame twisted over on itself with the sound of a woman screaming in pain, gushing diesel fuel from the ragged hole in its gas tank as the wind pushed the bus and those few passengers still alive and kickin' toward the edge of the ridge.

And over.

Something else screamed when the bus struck the first outcropping of rock eighty feet down. Then all was silent except for the wind's soft whispering . . . just like it was supposed to be.

"Oh my God."

The wind fell silent as he turned.

She made a gagging sound deep in her throat when she saw his face, then stumbled back a dozen steps until she was standing almost exactly on top of where Glory's grave had been. It was just like her—*just like her father*—to disrespect her mama like that.

Gideon felt the back of Sam Reynolds's knuckles split open as he clenched the hands into fists. She was too much like her father . . . and his father before him. *Maybe just like him*, he thought, and smiled at the memory of Joseph's face right before the wind stripped it off. *She ran away from the power just like Joseph did. Hell . . . she is more him than me.*

He heard her scream—"NO! Sam run!"—when the whirlwind closed around him. The flying dust and glass and bone slivers did quick work of the cheap suit and rotting flesh underneath.

The only thing he regretted, while the ribbons of flesh writhed and snapped around his head like Medusa's snakes, was that he didn't have lips.

He would have liked the last thing she saw to be a smile on her dead lover's face. But a man—a god—can't have everything.

Sam disappeared an inch at a time.

First the tattered flesh around his eyes and mouth, next the skin on his cheeks and forehead. Nose. Chin. Everything that had been Sam Reynolds, that had been the man she thought she loved, was stripped away until only a bloodied skull smiled down at her. When the wind peeled off his scalp, it reminded Sky of someone pulling apart Velcro strips.

Sky stumbled backward when the dust devil released Sam's frayed corpse and started a weaving path toward her.

Last night, barricaded in her bedroom closet, she'd almost convinced herself that the stress of the past week, coupled with the unseasonable windy weather and whatever misplaced guilt she might have about Gideon's death—*or not*—had generated a momentary psychosis . . . a walking dream.

But that was last night.

Sky didn't remember falling asleep, but when she woke up that morning she was sitting behind the wheel of her car next to a large, blue and white bill-board at the foot of a newly paved road:

**WELCOME TO PIONEER RIDGE ESTATES
ANOTHER SUN COUNTRY
HOME COMMUNITY
PRIVATE PREVIEW PARTY**

She'd followed the blue and white banners and reached the top of the ridge just as the bus went over the side.

It wasn't a waking dream. It was a nightmare, a real one.

And it just kept getting worse.

"Yah never were much good at listenin' t'me, were yah, gal?"

Sky's heel caught on a loop of fallen cable and almost went out from under her.

He was little more than a shape within the swirling cloud of dust, no more than dust himself, but she recognized him.

"Oh Jesus, it's true."

He cocked his head to one side and half his face was swept away into the vortex. His half-smile was shattered like the rest of his face and it dissolved . . . only to re-form in the next whirl of air.

Sky choked on the bile that surged into the back of her throat as she turned and ran.

"That's right," his voice called after her, *"run! Yer just like him . . . that scared ol' man. Yah run once, gal . . . just keep goin' and Ah might let yah live."*

Something brushed against the back of Sky's right hand—soft and gentle, but unexpected.

She tripped and fell, gracelessly, onto a section of crumpled canvas and heard a faint squashing sound when she landed. The willow whistle's feathers brushed her hand again.

Sky moved off the squishy mound and stared at the whistle. The last place she'd seen it was in the bedroom closet, where she'd left it the night before.

She thought.

The two feathers, bound by a single tether, danced in the wind.

Two feathers, tied as one. Two becoming one. Joseph had said something like that . . . about two becoming one. One red-dirt man, one white. Two bloodlines finally becoming one.

CIELO. YOU ARE THE CHOSEN ONE. YAPONCHA CREATED YOU TO MEND WHAT HAD BEEN DIVIDED. CIELO, YOU ARE THE WIND CALLER.

"No," she whispered as a shadow settled over her.

"All run out, are yah, gal?"

Sky looked up to see Gideon rise from the center of the dust devil like a scrawny, naked phoenix. The outline of his body was indistinct as bits and pieces were added and subtracted from the basic form. If this is what Yaponcha looked like, Sky understood why his Kachina image never appeared at the dances.

The wind batted the whistle away when she reached for it.

"Damn, gal . . . what are yah doin'? Yah don't believe what that old red man had t'say, do yah?"

Sky turned and tried to grab the whistle again, but

this time, instead of just batting it away, the wind slashed her across the face.

"Damn, yah do believe it."

The wind came at her again, pressing her flat against the canvas. She could already feel the friction blisters forming on the exposed skin of her hands and face. In a moment, less, she'd look like Sam.

Or the red-dirt man who'd come to take her away all those years ago.

The man she killed.

Think a'this just like if yah was out huntin'.

Easy as shootin' fish in a barrel.

Yah got the power.

USE IT, CIELO.

The quarter-size blister on the back of Sky's hand burst when she turned over and reached for him.

"No . . . Gideon . . . I—I don't."

The wind stopped. Sky clenched her teeth against the pain as she pushed herself to her knees.

"Yah say somethin', gal?"

"Yes." A sudden coughing fit brought up the dust that had gotten down her throat. "I—I said . . . I don't believe it."

The animated dust face smiled at her as a hollow laugh rose above the hiss of the swirling column of air.

Sky let her own lips settle into a smile as she dropped her hand. "But you do."

The hollow laughter changed into a roar when a tiny gust of air picked up the whistle and spun it into her hand. The willow taste was still bitter against her tongue, but this time Sky didn't mind it.

"NO!"

YES, CIELO . . . CALL HER.

The note was sweeter than any sound Sky had ever heard.

And the wind answered.

She came from the four directions of the world in all her aspects—from zephyr to mistral, sirocco to cyclone—converging in a sudden flash of soft gray light.

Sky could feel her lungs burn, starved for the air she continued to feed through the whistle, but she couldn't stop. Not yet. Not yet.

NOT YET, CIELO.

The soft gray light brightened into an ice-white blade that pierced Gideon's image just below the belly button. Sky heard him scream above the rushing voice of the wind as the light spread outward, consuming the spirit hidden beneath the dust.

And scattering what remained softly back to the earth.

Sky collapsed to the canvas, panting as the whistle fell from her lips. When she looked up, all that remained was the devastation the sudden windstorm had caused. Another freak of nature. She had to find a phone and call it in.

Just as any other good citizen would do . . . even if they couldn't call the wind.

Sky took a deep breath and brushed the hair out of her eyes, wincing when her fingers touched the weeping blisters on her cheek.

"It really happened. Jesus." The twin feathers spun lazily at the end of their tether as she reached down and picked up the willow whistle. "I still don't believe this, you know."

A small breeze brushed against Sky's pants legs as she stood and looked past the crumpled canvas tent and flayed bodies to the mountains.

"But just in case, Old One, welcome the two who stand before you now . . . and let them rest in peace."

EPILOGUE

The first day of spring was warm and bright.

"Okay, are we all ready? Gene . . . where's yours? All right. Is everyone ready?"

Sky looked at the faces of her students and saw only smiles and eyes bright with anticipation. The last month had been hard, but that hadn't been restricted only to her classroom. Richland's entire school system had been inundated with government-sponsored grief counselors to help the children and their families cope with the aftermath of the disasters.

Unquote.

It had been a very expensive program, and one, if the local evening news was correct, that wasn't working as expected. There'd been a rise in the number of crimes committed by adolescents since the tornadoes, as well as an increase in teenage suicides and general disciplinary problems.

Outside the reservation.

Her people knew that something like that wouldn't happen again—as long as she was the Wind Caller.

Sky clapped her hands. "Okay, let's everyone spread out in a nice, straight line. Jeny, a *straight* line. Good. That's right—give yourself enough room to run. Great.

"Now everyone set your kite down so the wooden sticks are facing up and slowly start walking toward me as you feed out the string. Slowly! That's right."

Sky backed up until she was ten feet from the row of kites and stopped.

"Okay, looks like we're all here. Everyone ready?"

"Um, Ms. Berlander?"

Sky had been waiting for one of the children to notice. She looked down and smiled.

"Yes, James?"

"Ah, there's no wind, Ms. Berlander."

Sky blinked her eyes as if she hadn't noticed. "Oh. Hmm, let me think—what month is this?"

"April!" they all shouted, and Sky shook her head. "What month?"

The children looked at each other, muttering.

"Okay, try this—what *moon* is it?"

"Oh, I know this. Grandfather Joseph—"

Tears filled the little girl's eyes as she bit her lip. Sky walked over to the child and hugged her.

"It's okay, Mary. . . . We all miss him and Andy and Joey, but I think Grandfather Joseph would be pleased in the Land of the Sky People if he knew you still remembered some of the things he told us." Sky lifted the girl's chin and nodded. "Go on, Mary, tell us what moon this is."

"The Moon of the Windbreaks," she said proudly. "Kwuy—Kwyaa . . ."

"Kwuyamuyaw," Sky said. "And that's right, this is the month of the Windbreaks—so maybe the wind is taking a coffee break. You think maybe that's what happened?"

The children's shrill giggles sent a flock of crows into flight.

"Well, if that's the case, what do you think we should do?" Sky asked. "Do you think we should call her?"

"YEAH!"

"Okay, let's call her . . . let's call the wind. Here, wind! Come on, wind."

The children's voices echoed the call—"Here, windy, windy, windy!" "Come here, wind." "Wind, wind, wind, wind!"—and Sky let it go on for a few minutes before waving them into silence.

"Shh," she said, holding a finger to her lips, "listen. Do you hear her now?"

The wind sang a song of cottonwoods and pine as it rushed toward the playing field.

"Yeah!"

"Me, too!"

"YAY!"

Sky got behind the line of children and lifted her arms.

"Okay, then, hold on to those strings," she called out, "because here she comes. Kites up!"

Fourteen handmade construction-paper kites darted into the sky. Sky smiled as they danced in the wind's soft embrace and hoped the Old One was watching.

DEEP IN THE DARKNESS
MICHAEL LAIMO

Dr. Michael Cayle wants the best for his wife and young daughter. That's why he moves the family from Manhattan to accept a private practice in the small New England town of Ashborough. Everything there seems so quaint and peaceful—at first. But Ashborough is a town with secrets. Unimaginable secrets.

Many of the townspeople are strangely nervous, and some speak quietly of legends that no sane person could believe. But what Michael discovers in the woods, drenched in blood, makes him wonder. Soon he will be forced to believe, when he learns the terrifying identity of the golden eyes that peer at him balefully from deep in the darkness.

BRIAN KEENE

RISING
THE

Nothing stays dead for long. The dead return to life, intelligent, determined . . . and very hungry. Escape seems impossible for Jim Thurmond, one of the few left alive in this nightmare world. But Jim's young son is also alive and in grave danger hundreds of miles away. Despite astronomical odds, Jim vows to find him—or die trying.

DARK UNIVERSE
WILLIAM F. NOLAN

Welcome to William F. Nolan's *Dark Universe*, a universe of horror, suspense and mystery. For the past fifty years William F. Nolan has been writing in each of these worlds—and compiling a legendary body of work that is unsurpassed in quality, style . . . and the sheer ability to send chills down the spines of readers. At long last, this volume collects many of Nolan's finest stories, selected from his entire career. These are unforgettable tales guaranteed to frighten, surprise, delight and even shock readers who like to explore the shadows and who aren't afraid of the dark.

GRAHAM MASTERTON
THE DOORKEEPERS

Julia Winward has been missing in England for nearly a year. When her mutilated body is finally found floating in the Thames, her brother, Josh, is determined to find out what happened to his sister and exactly who—or what—killed her.

But nothing Josh discovers makes any sense. Julia had been working for a company that went out of business sixty years ago, and living at an address that hasn't existed since World War II. The only one who might help Josh is a strange woman with psychic abilities. But the doors she can open with her mind are far better left closed. For behind these doors lie secrets too horrible to imagine.

3 1221 06790 5385

ATTENTION
BOOK LOVERS!

Can't get enough
of your favorite **HORROR**?

Call **1-800-481-9191** to:

— order books —
— receive a **FREE** catalog —
— join our book clubs to **SAVE 20%**! —

Open Mon.-Fri. 10 AM-9 PM EST

Visit
www.dorchesterpub.com
for special offers and inside
information on the authors you love.